Turnaround Farm

Elaine Cantrell

A Wings ePress, Inc.
Contemporary Romance Novel

Wings ePress, Inc.

Edited by: Jeanne Smith
Copy Edited by: Christie Kraemer
Executive Editor: Jeanne Smith
Cover Artist: Richard Stroud

All rights reserved

Names, characters and incidents depicted in this book are products of the author's imagination or are used fictitiously. Any resemblance to actual events, locales, organizations, or persons, living or dead, is entirely coincidental and beyond the intent of the author or the publisher.

No part of this book may be reproduced or transmitted in any form or by any means, electronic or mechanical, including photocopying, recording, or by any information storage and retrieval system, without permission in writing from the publisher.

Wings ePress Books
www.wingsepress.com

Copyright © 2018 by Elaine Cantrell
ISBN-13: 978-1-61309-643-7
ISBN-10: 1-61309-643-7

Published In the United States Of America

Wings ePress Inc.
3000 N. Rock Road
Newton, KS 67114

What They Are Saying About Turnaround Farm

When one sits at mid-morning to read the first few chapters of the book you are reviewing, only to realize at sunset that you've missed lunch and read to the finish, has Elaine Cantrell's *Turnaround Farm* proven itself a model page-turner. I had been totally glued to it.

—Kev Richardson
Multi-published author of
Historical and Contemporary fiction including
The Soul of Australia trilogy.

The book is 349 pages in length and I've read every one of them. I didn't skim though it like some books I've read. More importantly, I couldn't stop reading. That's when you know you've found a good book. Turnaround Farm has a good plot, is well written and has well rounded characterisation.

—Andrew Williams
Author of *Arcadia's Children: Samantha's Revenge*
and *Arcadia's Children: The Tyfield Plantation*

Her scene setting shone through, as her mixture of wide open spaces and small country town meshed and melded together vividly.

There are twists and turns, broken dreams, and unfulfilled wishes, which the author weaves together with the finesse of the finest lace-maker.

Do not be fooled but the description of 'Sweet Romance.' Ms. Cantrell offers you a hard-edged family story with passion and romance, but for those who enjoy a story with the sex 'behind closed doors, Turnaround Farm is one well worth adding to your TBR list.

—Sherry Gloag
Author of *No Job For a Woman*

Dedication

For Wallace, my stalwart support.

* * *

One

"You've lost your mind," Loretta Patterson moaned as she doggedly trudged down the rough, graveled road behind Holly. "It's twenty degrees out here and getting colder by the minute. We have no business coming out in weather like this."

"The roads are icy, and our car slid into a ditch too," her employer Holly Grant said with a grin. She bent her head against the bitter driving wind that almost took her breath away. "It isn't like you to forget something like that, Loretta."

"As if I could," Loretta retorted, teeth chattering. "Why couldn't you have waited for the weather to improve to see the Wakefields?"

Holly glanced at the forbidding gray landscape. The clouds looked low enough to touch and thick enough to choke you. "Loretta, I've told you a million times. If you want to be a success in the real estate business, you have to work at it. Stop worrying so much. This is important to Grant Realty."

"The Wakefields refuse to even discuss selling their property. Why do you think they've changed their minds?"

Holly grinned. "I did a little research. They're broke, and Turnaround Farm is nothing but a white elephant. They work like dogs, but they never get ahead. I want them to think about what selling the farm would mean to them. And don't forget that my buyer upped his offer."

"Don't you ever think about anything but business?" Loretta asked, her voice almost snatched away by the wind. "There's a world of exciting things to think about besides business."

Holly rolled her eyes at her exasperating assistant. "No, I don't, and you should get your mind off Michael Stuart and think a little more about business yourself."

"I'm engaged to Michael! Why shouldn't I think about him? This time next year we'll be married, for goodness sake."

Holly scowled. "Marriage is a trap. Most men expect their wives to help them earn a living, but do they help out around the house in return? No, they don't. They're so egotistical they want to reproduce themselves, so their wives have to take care of the kids on top of everything else they do. Well, if you want to fall into that trap, go ahead. I'm not that dumb."

Loretta sighed and bent her head against the wind while Holly hid a smile. Her assistant had learned not to argue with her when she jumped on her soapbox. The leaden sky smelled of snow. How were they going to get their car out of that ditch? Call a wrecker maybe.

Presently, Loretta voiced the same concern. "Dan Wakefield is one of the most unpleasant men I've ever met. You're lucky you weren't in the office when he dropped by to ream us out about pestering his grandfather. I hope you don't think he'll be willing to get the car out of the ditch."

"Maybe not, but his grandfather Jeb is a true gentleman. At the very least, he'll let us take shelter from the weather until a tow truck comes."

Loretta sighed as she tucked her scarf more firmly around her throat. "Okay. I hope you can close this deal. You're sure working hard enough for it."

Another gust of wind buffeted the women who picked up their pace in an effort to reach Turnaround Farm before dark.

~ * ~

Several miles down the road, Jeb Wakefield took his biscuits out of the oven and brushed melted butter across the tops of the hot bread. The sweet scent made his stomach growl. What was keeping Dan? Dinner was ready, and he was sure to be hungry after working all day in the cold.

A sudden draft of bitter air announced Dan Wakefield's arrival. He pulled his gloves off and stuffed them in the pocket of his heavy coat, which he hung on a peg just inside the door. He sat down on a battered, old bench in the mudroom and removed his boots before padding into the kitchen to greet his grandfather. "What's for dinner?"

"Beef stew and biscuits." He ran a hand across his short gray hair and straightened his broad shoulders. "Hey, turn around. What's on the back of your shirt?"

Dan shrugged. "Blood, I guess."

"What happened?"

"Aw, I got careless, and one of the horses pushed me into a nail."

"Let me see." Jeb took his grandson's shoulder and turned his back around to the light. There was an awful lot of blood on his shirt. "Take your shirt off, and let me see what you've done. You don't want to get an infection."

"It's okay. Don't make such a fuss about it."

"I said, take off your shirt."

Dan scowled and unbuttoned his shirt. "Oh, all right. You won't let me eat in peace until I do."

Jeb studied the bloody hole in Dan's back as intently as any doctor would have done. "It isn't too bad. You've bled a good bit, so the wound has cleaned itself, and your tetanus shot is up to date." He removed a first aid kit from the cabinet over the refrigerator and doused a gauze pad with antiseptic. Then he cleaned Dan's back, applied an antibiotic ointment, and covered the puncture with a sterile bandage. "There you go. Good as new. Did you take care of the nail?"

"Yeah, I did." Dan pulled his flannel shirt back on and washed his hands before sitting down at the kitchen table with his grandfather.

"After dinner I'd like you to look at Mr. Ames' mare for me. She's still limping, and she's off her feed."

"Sure."

Dinner was a silent affair because Jeb's thoughts had turned to his grandson.

The Wakefield family had been one of the founding families in the town of Fairfield, prospering over the years through the raising and training of horses. A warm light briefly shone in his eyes. If he did say so, he had made quite a name for himself in the horse world.

His stomach knotted. If only Kyle…Well, Kyle was another matter altogether. As far as Jeb knew, his only son had done just one good thing during his entire life; he had married Millie Lane and produced Dan. His fingers tightened around his fork. Kyle had ruined the family financially and blackened their name in horse circles by using illegal drugs on the animals in his care.

To make matters worse, he had become addicted to drugs himself. At the time of his death in a high-speed auto chase with the police, he was high on cocaine and waiting to go to trial for illegal gambling and fixing the outcome of a sporting event. His wife had died with him.

In spite of the cold, Jeb broke into a sweat. He routinely gave thanks that Dan had been with him on that black day.

Dan was eighteen at the time of the accident. He had always planned to study architecture, but they didn't have the money for college. He had needed Dan's help to keep the farm anyway. His hands fisted. What a colossal waste. Dan had never complained though. The two of them had taken over the running of the almost penniless farm and begun the long, arduous task of repaying Kyle's debts and getting the farm on a sound financial footing. It had meant long hours of backbreaking toil in all types of weather.

Hiring help would have greatly simplified their lives, but they couldn't afford to pay a salary. Gradually though, they had found a few owners willing to trust them with their horses, but he knew the Wakefield name still had a nasty ring to it when horse people got together to talk.

His eyes swept around the beat up kitchen and family room. He remembered a time when everything was shiny and beautiful, but it didn't look that way now. The house had twelve rooms, and because of its age, it needed a lot of expensive repairs and maintenance, but they had neither time nor money to spend. In fact, they only heated the kitchen and family room. Consequently, the house became more dilapidated with each passing season. If they didn't find the money to fix the roof soon, the ceilings upstairs would fall down on them as they slept.

Oh, yes it bothered him to watch the house deteriorate, but worry about the house paled in comparison to his worry about Dan. Dan labored unceasingly to repair the damage done by his father, but he didn't have much to show for his efforts. Year by year his grandson's bitterness increased, a process he felt powerless to stop.

Dan nodded his head toward the plate of bread on the table. "Pass me another biscuit, please."

Jeb picked up the plate and held it out to Dan. As Dan reached for the biscuit, Jeb exclaimed, "Don't you have a better shirt than that to wear? It's paper thin, and the cuff is threadbare."

Dan laughed. "I didn't expect a commentary on my work attire. It's a work shirt. It's fine to wear in the barn. If you'll patch the hole in the back, it still has a lot of wear in it."

"It's too thin. If you have to work in the cold all day, you need a decent shirt. It's bad enough that you work like a dog. The least I can do is buy you a warm shirt."

Dan shrugged and shoveled another bite of beef stew into his mouth. "Fine. If you want me to have a shirt, buy me one. It's stupid to waste the money, though."

"You let me be the judge of that."

They finished their meal and got up to tidy the kitchen. As Dan threw a log into the fireplace, they heard someone hammering on the back door. "Are you expecting company?" he asked, surprise in his voice. Company very seldom darkened the door of Turnaround Farm. After working all day, neither of them felt much like socializing.

Jeb shook his head. "No, I'm not expecting anyone."

He hurried across the room to see who was out on such a bad night. Two shivering, snow-covered women stood on his doorstep.

"Why, Miss Grant and Miss Patterson!" he exclaimed. "Why are you out in weather like this?" He stood aside and gestured for them to hurry out of the cold. "Come in and get warm. You look frozen."

"We are frozen," Loretta wailed as she and Holly entered the warm kitchen. "Our car slid off the road into a ditch, and it's sleeting and snowing something awful." She paused to shake off her plaid scarf, scattering sleet and snow on the scuffed wooden floor. "I don't know how we're ever going to get home tonight."

"Loretta, please," Holly begged. "You're out of the cold now, and as far as getting home goes, use my phone to call a tow truck."

She fished in her bag for her phone and handed it to Loretta. "Mr. Wakefield, I know I should have called before I came out here, but I was so excited I couldn't wait to see you. The developer who wants to buy your farm just made another offer for your property. Unless I miss my guess, you'll be very pleased with it."

"I thought my grandfather had made it clear Turnaround Farm isn't for sale."

Jeb grinned as Holly's eyes went wide. Miss Grant had forgotten about Dan, but by the look on her face, she really liked what she saw. Well, why wouldn't she like his looks? Dan had dark blond hair, a handsome face, and expressive blue eyes. Hard work in the fresh air had filled out and sculpted his grandson's body. His shoulders tapered off to a waist that appeared narrow because of the width of those shoulders, and his body was layered in muscles so well defined strangers would assume he spent most of his time in a gym.

Yes, Holly liked what she saw, but Dan seemed almost dumbstruck. He cut his eyes toward Jeb and flushed, probably because his grandfather had caught him staring at Holly. It was no surprise that Dan was staring. With her height and golden-blonde beauty, Holly Grant belonged on the cover of a fashion magazine.

A daring idea struck Jeb. *She isn't the one I'd have picked for him, but the woman who wants Dan will have to be more than just fluff, and Holly Grant is definitely that.*

Loretta broke the spell that had fallen on the kitchen. "Holly, I can't get a tow truck to come out. They're all busy on other calls. They told me since we found shelter, we should stay put for the night."

"You're both welcome to stay with us," Jeb said.

The look of alarm on Dan's face tickled Jeb. "Gramps, I don't really think we have the proper accommodations for them. I'll take them home."

Jeb frowned. "I don't think so. If the weather is that bad, I don't want you out on the roads. I'm not willing to have anything happen to you just so these ladies can sleep in their own beds tonight. I'm sure we can make them comfortable."

Dan looked ready to argue, but Holly didn't give him a chance. "Thanks, Mr. Wakefield. We'd be happy to accept your hospitality. Maybe we can talk about my client's new offer."

Holly's ready acceptance amused Jeb as much as Loretta's feeble protestations. "We'll see, but right now, Dan and I have to check on one of the horses. There's plenty of stew and biscuits left. Why don't you and Miss Patterson sit down and have some dinner while Dan and I finish up outside?"

"We'd love to."

Dan didn't bother to excuse himself. He stalked into the mudroom and prepared to go outdoors. By the time Jeb reached the barn, he had already led the mare from her stall. Jeb watched him scratch the horse's ear and ruefully shook his head. Dan didn't approve of his hospitality.

Joining Dan, he ran a practiced hand down the horse's leg, feeling for heat or tenderness. "You liked her, didn't you?"

Dan made a noise that might have passed for a laugh. "Yeah, right. The woman wants to buy the place that's been in our family for generations. Sure, I liked her."

Jeb dropped the mare's leg and fastened his gaze on Dan. "You like her looks. She's a beautiful woman, and you're a young man. Why don't you ask her out?"

Dan grabbed a pitchfork and forked hay to the horse in the stall behind him, even though Jeb knew he'd already fed her. "Huh! What do I have to offer a woman like that? There's no reason why she'd have any interest in me."

"Nothing to offer? No, nothing except honor, kindness, and integrity wrapped up in one of the nicest packages anywhere."

The sharp lines that had begun to insinuate themselves around Dan's mouth in the last year or so deepened as a faint flush darkened his cheeks. "I don't think most people would use the words honor and integrity in the same sentence as the name Wakefield."

"In your case they'd be wrong, wouldn't they?"

"It doesn't matter. I'm too busy to take the time. Besides, a woman like that is too high maintenance for me to afford."

Jeb patted the mare's neck, and she bumped his chest with her nose. She'd always been an affectionate creature. "I have no idea why you'd think Miss Grant is high maintenance, but it doesn't matter if she is or not. I'm not asking you to make a life-long commitment to her. Just take her to dinner or a movie. You really need to get out more. Your social life is nonexistent."

"I don't think so, Gramps."

Jeb's lips marginally tightened. Dan was so stubborn. That was one thing he had inherited from Kyle, although he'd never said so to Dan. Any resemblance to his father horrified his grandson. "How do you ever expect to get married if you don't look around a little?"

"I don't want to get married."

Jeb's eyes widened. "Why not? Having a pretty woman to snuggle with would be a lot better than sleeping alone. I think you'd be a pretty good father too."

Dan looked at him as if he'd suddenly sprouted hooves and a tail. "You must be joking! Me, a father? I'd never have a kid who might turn out like my dad. Since most women seem to want kids, that rules out marriage. I can't afford to get married anyway. We can barely make it with two people in the house. We don't need three."

Jeb continued his work in silence, but his mind darted from one possibility to another. If Dan wouldn't help himself, his grandfather would have to do it for him. He had had to stand by and watch Kyle ruin his life, but if he had anything to say about it, Dan would get a happy ending.

Two

"Your grandmother wasn't too happy about us staying the night with the Wakefields," Loretta said as she finished washing the last of the dishes. She folded the dishcloth across the faucet to dry and sat near the fire with Holly.

Holly smiled at the mention of her grandmother. "You know Nana. She's a worrywart. I think it's the best thing that could have happened. Jeb'll listen to my offer because he's too polite to tell me to shut up."

"Dan may tell you to shut up."

Holly shot an exasperated stare Loretta's way. "While we're on that subject, why didn't you tell me he's so good looking? He may be rude, but he's awfully cute."

"When I saw him in the office, he was so verbally abusive I never thought about his looks," Loretta answered in an injured tone. Holly stifled a smile. Loretta never took criticism well.

"He sure wasn't pleasant tonight, was he?" Holly said. Thank goodness Loretta didn't know about her knees. When she first saw Dan, her knees had felt spongy, and she'd have given a sizeable commission just to see if his shoulders felt as muscular and hard as they looked. She'd always had a thing for nice shoulders.

Of course she had no intention of saying anything to Loretta. If Loretta thought she had any interest whatsoever in Dan, she'd go on and on about it and tell everybody in the whole dang real estate office.

"What do you think of this place?" Loretta asked as she extended her feet a little closer to the fire.

Holly looked around with a critical realtor's eye. The Wakefields appeared to live in this one big room that you entered through the mudroom. The living area was centered around the fireplace on one of the short walls. An old, faded sofa done in a plaid fabric and two beat up leather recliners clustered around the fire while a small TV sat just to the right of the hearth. An old fashioned kitchen with a farmhouse sink lay behind the living area.

The one thing Holly liked about the kitchen was the big window over the sink. The green appliances looked as if they had been manufactured somewhere around 1970 while the finish on the cabinets had been worn away near the hardware. A scarred maple dining table with four chairs stood in the part of the kitchen closest to the sofa.

"They could use new appliances and some furniture that didn't come off the ark," Holly said. "They also need to paint the walls and redo the floors. That vinyl is worn through in more than one place." Her nose twitched. "The room smells like a wood fire, which is nice while you're sitting beside it, but over time it does leave a smell in the house. Didn't you notice that this place smells like old fires and food?"

"That certainly isn't romantic," Loretta protested. "Michael and I often build a fire and have a little cuddle."

Holly just groaned.

With a blast of cold air that made the fire flicker, the Wakefields returned, stamping the snow and ice from their boots as they removed their coats and hats. Dan immediately zeroed in on the fact that someone had done the dishes and straightened up the kitchen. "You didn't have to do the dishes, Miss Grant. We'd have taken care of it."

"It's the least I could do to repay you for your hospitality," Holly answered.

Jeb smiled at her, which made Holly feel guilty for claiming credit for those dishes. But not too guilty. She wanted the Wakefields to think well of her.

"Would you ladies care for a game of cards?" Jeb asked. "Our television died a few weeks ago, and it's pretty early for bed."

"Let's do," Loretta enthused. "I love to play cards. How about Hearts?"

Everyone knew the rules, so that's what they did.

Holly enjoyed the game, but it was hard to concentrate on cards with Dan Wakefield at the table. Whether she wanted to admit it or not, the man was gorgeous. No wonder she was doing so badly. Hmm. Dan wasn't doing any better than she was. He was a terrible card player.

Holly waited until they finished their game to bring up business. She replaced the cards in the box and smiled at Jeb. "Mr. Wakefield, I really would like to show you the proposal I brought with me. My client's offer is incredibly generous."

Hostility returned to Dan's face in a rush. "Turnaround Farm isn't for sale."

Holly turned to Dan and calmly said, "Dan, I was talking to your grandfather."

Dan's jaw tightened. "I thought that..."

"Dan, hang on a minute," Jeb interrupted. "Are you still taking Tommy Price's horse to the show week after next?"

"Yes, but..."

Jeb raised a hand to silence Dan. "In a minute. Miss Grant, if you want me to look at your proposal I will, but only on one condition."

"And that is?"

"You accompany Dan to the horse show as his date. There'll be several social events he should attend, and I want you to go with him."

Dan's face turned several interesting shades of red. "No. I absolutely will not do it. If I want a date, I can get one myself. I don't need my grandfather to do it for me."

Holly's eyebrows shot straight up when Jeb refused to back off. "If you refuse, I'll look at her proposal right now, and after working in the cold all day, it might look pretty good."

Nobody spoke, but just as the tension in the room threatened to become unpleasant, Holly jumped in. "I'll go if you will." Good grief! What had she just done?

"Well, Dan?" Jeb asked.

Holly saw the half contrite expression on Jeb's face. Maybe his conscience had started to prick him. She imagined life had forced Dan to do many things he didn't want to do, and it wasn't fair. Everyone deserved the chance to follow his dream, and now his grandfather had made him to do something else against his will.

Dan shot his grandfather a hard look, which said they'd talk about this later, but he gave in quicker than Holly had expected. "Holly, it would be very nice if you would go with me to the horse show," he said.

Jeb beamed at him. "Good man. Miss Grant, have you ever ridden?"

"Please, call me Holly. No, sir, I've never ridden, but it looks like a lot of fun."

"I'm sure Dan would be delighted to give you some lessons."

"We'll see. I'm pretty busy with work," Holly demurred.

"You can let us know. Dan, do you think you can find these ladies something warm to sleep in?"

The shocked look on Dan's face almost made Holly laugh. No women lived at Turnaround Farm, so women's clothing was probably a mystery to him.

"How about sweat suits and athletic socks?" he asked. "That's all I can think of."

"Sweat suits are perfect," Holly declared with a big smile for him. No use to alienate Dan any more than necessary.

Dan went to find the sweat suits and soon returned with two sets of clothing and handed them to his grandfather who gave a set to her and Loretta. She didn't mind sleeping in Dan's clothes, but Loretta didn't look too happy about it. She probably wouldn't have minded if the clothes belonged to Michael.

"We only have one bedroom suitable for guests," Jeb said, "so I hope you two don't mind sharing a room."

"We don't mind at all," Loretta broke in. "Holly and I have some things to discuss."

"You may want to get ready for bed in the bathroom down here. It's freezing upstairs."

"Thanks, Mr. Wakefield. You don't know how much we appreciate this."

"Not at all, Holly. Dan and I are glad of the company."

~ * ~

"I never thought I'd live to see this day." Loretta chuckled as she and Holly struggled to get warm in the icy gloom of their dark bedroom.

Holly held up her hand to see if she could see it. She couldn't. Why didn't the Wakefields have a nightlight? This dense, suffocating darkness took her breath away. "What are you going on about, Loretta? I'm freezing to death up here, and now I've got to listen to you."

Holly couldn't see Loretta's face, but she could hear the smile in her voice. "Holly Grant, business woman, dedicated career girl, passes up the chance to make a sales pitch just so she can get a date with a man."

It galled Holly to admit that her annoying assistant was right. If she had kept quiet in the kitchen, Jeb would have looked at her proposal tonight. Going to the horse show just because Dan Wakefield was so drop dead gorgeous reminded her of something her mother, Rita, might have done, and she'd rather die than be like her mother. "You deserve to be fired for that," she groused.

"But you won't fire me, will you?" Loretta giggled. "Nobody else would put up with you. Oh, and Holly, I don't think it was my imagination that made me think you were sniffing his clothes. Were you hoping to find out how he smells?"

"No! For the love of goodness, let me go to sleep."

Loretta's tone turned serious as her cold feet met Holly's. "It's okay to be attracted to him, you know. He's a handsome man, and being a business woman doesn't mean you have to give up all interest in the opposite sex."

Holly refused to answer, so Loretta soon turned over, gave a little snort, and fell asleep.

How does she do that? My mind's going in circles thinking about Dan Wakefield because...because he's so...sexy, she admitted, alarmed at the direction her thoughts had taken. Her face burned in the dark as she imagined how it might feel to kiss him. His lips looked just right for kissing.

Uneasily, she flipped over in the bed. His shirt was awful, though. Loving clothes the way she did, she wouldn't be caught dead in a rag like that, but it did look good on Dan. He had a big bloodstain and a tear on the back of his shirt, so he probably hurt himself in the barn. Looks like he would have changed it before dinner.

She imagined herself unbuttoning Dan's flannel shirt and took firm rein on her libido. She hadn't built Grant Realty into a thriving enterprise by acting like a sex-starved old maid. *If you give your heart to another person, you deserve all the hurt you'll get. If it kills me, I'm going to sleep.* It took a while, but Holly finally dropped into an uneasy slumber.

~ * ~

Across the hall, Dan turned over yet again and stifled a groan when he thought of Holly Grant sleeping in the next room. Hard, physical labor usually made it easy for him to fall asleep, but tonight he imagined that even through two closed doors, he could still smell the faint, subtle floral fragrance of her perfume.

She was the most beautiful woman he'd ever seen. Tall too. He could kiss her by simply lowering his head. His breath quickened. Holly had enough curves to prove she was a woman, not a boy. Bet her skin felt as soft as a kitten's fur. He'd always had a thing for blondes.

A mental image of Holly, warm and submissive in his arms, presented itself. The image clarified, and he saw she was naked and ready to love him.

A heat wave swept him from head to toe in spite of the frigid room. *I'm a fool. She wants Turnaround Farm, not me, and even if she did want me, it wouldn't matter. I don't have a future to offer any woman.* He sighed. *I refuse to embarrass myself by losing my head and acting like a fool.*

He pounded his pillow into shape and forced his tight muscles to relax. Gradually he fell into a light, fitful sleep.

~ * ~

Holly awoke with both a raging thirst and a desperate need for a bathroom. The clock on the bedside table said two-thirty as she eased out from under the covers. *Oh, I hope Loretta won't wake up. She'll be as mad as a hornet if she does.*

Like the bedroom, the hallway outside her room had a lot in common with the North Pole. Besides that it was pitch dark. She'd probably fall and break every bone in her body. How could the Wakefields stand this horrible, cold house?

She tiptoed down the stairs and opened the door that led to the kitchen. The room looked gloomy, but at least the banked fire somewhat kept the cold at bay and provided a dim light to see by. She got her water, used the bathroom, and with no more reason to delay, she dashed back up the steps toward her icy room.

If they sell the farm, maybe they'll buy a warmer house with a night-light. I can't see a wink. Was my room on the right or left side of the hall? Wait. It was the right.

Holly hurried into the room and quickly slid under the bedcovers. Thank goodness for Loretta who had kept the bed warm. She stuck her cold feet on Loretta's side of the bed and gradually warmed up enough to sleep.

~ * ~

Holly snuggled closer to the hard, masculine form beside her. What a great dream! She sighed as she stroked a heavily muscled arm. Her hand curved around his shoulder, and she traced the outline of the muscles in his back.

She gasped as strong arms encircled her body. Her pulse raced as he nipped and nuzzled the sensitive spot below her ear. She turned her head so he could kiss her neck, and the movement brought her fully awake. This was no dream, and it wasn't Loretta either!

Puffing as if she'd just run a marathon, Holly struggled with the figure in the bed. He must not have expected her to resist his advances because he lost his hold on her almost immediately. Moments later the bedroom light came on to reveal Dan Wakefield who very obviously slept in the nude.

"You get away from me this minute, or I'm screaming for your grandfather!" Holly cried. She pulled the covers tightly around her for what little protection they offered. What a pervert!

Dan ran a hand through his short blond hair. "What the hell are you talking about? You're the one in my bed."

Eyes bulging, Holly gasped as she stared at the room. Uh oh. Dan probably hadn't switched out the rugs, drapes, and bedroom suite while she went to the bathroom. She didn't see Loretta hiding behind the drapes either.

Waves of heat swept across her face. With a strangled cry, she flung herself down in the bed, and pulled a pillow over her head.

Dan's voice reached her even through the pillow. "It's too cold in here for me to be out from under the covers. Whether you like it or not, we're sharing the blankets."

Holly waited until he covered himself before she removed her head from underneath the pillow. "This is...isn't what you think," she quavered. "I didn't come here to...to...well, you know. It was dark, and I couldn't find my room."

"I imagine you are in the wrong room," Dan replied, his voice almost as cold as his room. "You know very well that my grandfather owns Turnaround Farm, not me. If you planned on prostituting yourself for a sale, you'll need his room."

Fire to gunpowder might be a cliché, but it perfectly described Holly's reaction. "How dare you speak to me that way! Who do you think you are? I told you what happened. You're the most horrible person I've ever seen."

"You saw a lot of me too, didn't you?

Shaking with reaction and anger, Holly tried again. "You're wrong. I...I wouldn't do what you said."

Dan's eyebrows arched; his tone turned silky. "Oh? Are you in the right room after all? Did you think if you gave me sex I'd persuade my grandfather to sell you the farm?"

Anger raced through her veins. Too angry to consider the consequences, she slapped his face.

Dan touched his cheek. "I don't like that," he growled.

In spite of the cold and his nakedness, he flung the covers off, and before Holly could gather her wits and run, he grabbed her wrist in a steel grip. She kicked and hit at him, but she was no match for his work-conditioned body. Dan held her face down across rock hard, naked thighs and slapped her bottom twice before releasing her. The slaps stung.

"You're a brute, Dan Wakefield!" Holly spat as she retreated across the bed.

"At least I didn't plan on prostituting myself tonight. Wrong room my…"

Throwing caution to the wind, Holly slapped him again. She tried to run, but Dan grabbed her before she even made it off the bed. He jerked her across his lap again and popped her bottom twice.

She scrambled from his bed with her nose in the air and made her way to the door with as much dignity as possible. From that position of comparative safety, she taunted Dan. "You really are just an animal."

Scowling, Dan jumped out of bed. With a soft cry of alarm, Holly slammed the door and ran for her own room and Loretta. She hated Dan Wakefield! If she never saw him again it would be too soon.

Pauline Coffey surveyed the table with satisfaction. "Everything's ready, Sadie," she told the small, calico cat who brushed her legs demanding her attention. "As soon as Holly gets here, we'll have our tea, and you get a bowl of cream."

Sadie purred her approval as Pauline sat down in the living room to wait for her granddaughter's arrival. She was worried about Holly, who was acting as if something serious troubled her. For a week now she had avoided everyone's company and gone around with a distracted expression on her face. According to Loretta, she had even forgotten an appointment to show a house. Before this day ended, Pauline meant to get to the bottom of it.

At first she had thought Holly's odd behavior stemmed from her failure to close the Wakefield deal, but that seemed unlikely because, when faced with a business challenge, Holly usually worked twice as hard until she solved the problem.

No, she didn't think business played a role in Holly's unhappiness, but since her talk with Loretta, she had a feeling Dan Wakefield might.

Loretta said nothing out of the ordinary had passed between Dan and Holly, but that's what it had to be. Absently, she poked at a daffodil that refused to stay where it belonged in the arrangement on the coffee table. Oh, she did love daffodils! Their cheery, yellow color brought instant sunshine to a winter room. The local florist had a standing order for a weekly delivery of daffodils.

The sound of a car in the driveway brought Pauline to her feet. "Here she is, Sadie." Pauline set the cat down on the rug and met Holly at the door. "Hello, darling. How are you?" She gave Holly a hug and kiss. "I'm so glad you could have tea with me. I miss you something dreadful if I don't see you every day."

~ * ~

Holly returned her grandmother's kiss, feeling herself relax for the first time in a week. No surprise there; her nana's home always had that effect on her. She gazed appreciatively at the white sofa that stood in front of the fireplace. She and Nana had exchanged many secrets and confidences on that sofa.

A polished cherry table sat beside the window and gleamed with shining silver and sparkling crystal. Holly loved the table, a family piece dating back to the late seventeen hundreds, almost as much as her nana did. She liked the good prints on the walls and the rugs on the hardwood floors too, because she had helped to select them.

This small cottage shone and gleamed as brightly as any polished diamond ever could, but she didn't come here just to enjoy the sparkling little home. She came because her nana lived here. Nana had long been her bulwark against anything the world could throw at her.

"Everything looks wonderful," Holly said.

"Thank you, darling. I hope everything will taste all right. I tried some new recipes, and I want your opinion of them, especially my brownie pie."

"Everything you do is wonderful, Nana, and you know it." Holly giggled. "Are you fishing for a compliment?"

Pauline just laughed. "Sit down, Holly. Let's have our tea before everything gets cold."

The two women seated themselves at the table where Pauline poured Holly a cup of steaming tea and passed it to her. "Try this, dear. I got it in Greenville last week. It has just a hint of orange in it."

Holly sipped the hot tea and sighed. "It's heavenly. I believe tea tastes better in these nice cups than it does in a mug."

"Oh, it does, darling. You really should invest in some nice china."

Holly laughed. "I know. You've always taught me that details matter."

"I'm so glad you remembered. Are you still going to the horse show with Dan Wakefield?"

Holly clenched the handle on her cup so tightly she was afraid she'd break it. For a few moments there, she had forgotten her humiliation at Dan Wakefield's hands. "Yes, I guess I'll go to the stupid horse show with him. If I don't, Mr. Wakefield won't talk business with me, but Dan's nothing more than a disgusting, boorish, ill-mannered lout. No wonder his grandfather has to get dates for him."

Pauline frowned and stroked Sadie, who had decided to take a nap in her lap. "That sounds unethical to me. I'm surprised you're willing to do it even to close the sale. I'm also surprised you haven't told me what happened when you and Loretta spent the night at Turnaround Farm."

Holly blinked and refused to meet her grandmother's eyes. "Why, nothing happened."

"You won't look at me, so I know you just told me a fib." Pauline sighed. "I'm worried about you. You haven't been yourself this week. Loretta told me how attracted you are to Dan, so I thought he might be the cause of your unhappiness."

Annoyance flooded Holly's face. "Loretta should mind her own business. Doesn't she have anything better to do than gossip?"

Pauline dropped Sadie to the floor. The cat shot a reproachful look her way and wandered over to the sofa to finish her nap. "Did he try to kiss you, darling?"

"Nana, I told you, nothing happened."

"Yes, but we both know better."

"I really, really don't want to talk about this." Holly set down her exquisite cup and wandered over to the fireplace. Why did her nana have to be so perceptive? She could never hide things from Pauline. Even when she was a little girl, Nana could always figure her out.

Pauline held out her hand. "Come and sit back down, dear. Are you ashamed of your attraction to this young man? I know his father wasn't much account, but from what I hear, Dan is like his grandfather who's a fine man."

Holly sat back down and tried again. "Nothing happened. Really."

Pauline's cup clattered into her saucer; her face grew stern. "This is no time for stubbornness. I love you, darling. I have to know if Dan hurt you or not." Her tone turned severe. "If you don't tell me, I'll ask him."

"You wouldn't!"

Pauline's eyes narrowed. "Try me."

Holly's stomach rolled over because Nana usually did exactly what she said she would do. If Pauline talked to Dan, the real estate office would have to move to another town. Okay, that might be a little extreme. Telling Nana about it might make her feel better. Goodness knows she was tired of brooding over it. "It was the most embarrassing thing that ever happened to me," she mumbled.

As Holly finished her story, Pauline clapped her hands together as a spasm of laughter shook her. "What a perfectly delicious moment. Can't you see the humor in it?"

"How can you say such a thing! I can't imagine what you're thinking. What happened to me sounds like something my mother would get mixed up in. Do you want me to be as big a slut as she is?"

Pauline's smile faded. "I wish you wouldn't talk that way about your mother, Holly."

Holly reached for Pauline's hand. Why couldn't she learn to keep her big mouth shut? "I'm sorry. I just forget sometimes that she's your daughter, but my mother does have a weakness for men. You know she does."

Pauline nodded. "You're right, but your mother is to be pitied, not scorned. When your father died, something inside of her died too. She tries to recreate the magic she had with him by being with first one man, then another. Of course, that's impossible, but somehow she doesn't get it."

"Marriage is a trap," Holly muttered.

Pauline shook her head. "I've heard your *marriage is a trap* speech before, but we both know that isn't why you criticize Loretta and run away from any man who shows an interest in you. You're afraid you'll be like your mother, but I don't think that's likely to happen. You have too much of your father in you for that." She smiled at Holly as the twinkle in her eyes returned. "Too much of me in you also."

Holly managed a weak smile in return. "It doesn't matter. Once I go to the horse show, Jeb'll look over the proposal. After that I won't have to see Dan again."

"Then I guess there's nothing more to say, is there? Why don't you try these cream cheese and raisin sandwiches?"

~ * ~

Rita Grant picked up the phone to call her mother and Holly. Las Vegas excited her, but she hadn't communicated with her family since Christmas, and they'd be worried about her.

The phone had actually started ringing when Kevin Andrews, her current boyfriend, came out of the bathroom. "What are you doing?" he yelled. "Haven't I told you phone calls cost money? Put that thing down right now."

Rita obeyed. "I was calling my mother, Kevin. If you want me to pay for the call, I will."

"With what? You haven't got a penny to your name."

Rita started to cry because Kevin was right. She had spent her money weeks ago, and Kevin was too stingy to waste anything on her. He wanted his money to play at the casino.

"Shut up." He scowled at her. "I can't stand a blubbering woman."

"I want to talk to my mother and my daughter," Rita sobbed.

"I'm warning you."

She tried to stop crying, but she couldn't. Kevin hated her to cry, but sometimes she couldn't help it. It didn't surprise her when he sprang forward and hit her. She bit her lip to hold back the tears.

"I told you to shut up," he screamed. "If you know what's good for you, you'll shut your mouth."

Rita held it together long enough to get into the bathroom. By the time she finally came out Kevin had gone.

Four

"Would you say that the sky is azure blue?" demanded Jeb with a grin as he and Dan dismounted from their horses.

"I certainly would. I would also say the air is crisp and cold, and the horses are feeling their oats."

Jeb and Dan grinned at each other. They enjoyed the sunshiny afternoon as much as their horses obviously did.

Jeb stared at Dan. "Do your new shirts keep the wind off you better than the old ones?"

"They're fine."

Jeb allowed himself another brief grin, which Dan pretended not to see. His grandfather had purchased seven new shirts and several pairs of jeans for him. Not content to do the job halfway, Jeb had also bought briefs, undershirts, and socks.

"You never spend a penny on yourself," Jeb said. "When I looked in your closet to see what you needed, it shocked me to see how little you have to wear. Whether you want to admit it or not, I know the warmer clothes make life in the cold a whole lot easier to bear."

Dan's mount, a big chestnut gelding, snorted and bumped Dan's chest with his nose. "How's he coming along?" asked Jeb.

"He may take a ribbon for Tommy. He's a good horse."

They entered the barn where Dan tethered the animal to be unsaddled. He fetched a brush and comb and groomed the gelding while Jeb started to work on his own mount.

"Dan? When are you going to tell me what happened between you and Holly Grant? I've wanted to talk to you all week, but the time never seemed right. I figure since the sunshine put you in a good mood, I might as well bring it up now."

Dan jumped slightly at the mention of Holly's name, inadvertently pressing the comb too hard into the horse's coat. The big animal turned around and gave him a reproachful stare.

"We don't like each other, if that's what you mean."

"Son, I'm not blind," Jeb protested. "The two of you were fine when you went to bed the other night, but when you got up the next morning you were circling each other like wolves. So, what happened? Did you make love to her?"

"No!" The horse turned around and eyed Dan, disturbed by his vehement tone.

"Okay, did you kiss her?"

"Gramps, let it go. Everything's fine."

Jeb's jaw dropped as he stared at Dan. "That's exactly what your dad used to say if I questioned something he did. I learned the hard way what happens if you let it go, so this time I won't back off. What happened between you and Holly?"

"Aw, Gramps, don't look at me that way. I didn't have sex with her. You don't have to worry that I got her pregnant. There isn't going to be another family scandal."

Jeb shook his head. "I was worried about you, not her." The phone rang in the office. "Be thinking about how to tell me while I see who it is."

He returned in a moment. "Wrong number. Now tell me what happened."

"It's just so embarrassing," muttered Dan. If only his grandfather would butt out of his business. Sometimes Jeb forgot he had grown up and didn't want to be treated like a child.

Jeb sat down and started to clean his tack. "Keep working on the horse while you talk."

Dan drew a long, deep breath and blew out hard. He'd rather not remember what happened, but how could he forget parading around naked in front of a strange woman? He couldn't forget how he'd abused her either. Oh, he knew those slaps hadn't really hurt her, not through those thick sweatpants anyway, but his cutting, hurtful words had to bruise her pride, especially if she had told the truth about her presence in his room.

Behind him Jeb cleared his throat. His grandfather wouldn't be satisfied until he heard about the whole thing, so he might as well get it over with. People said women nagged, but they didn't know Jeb.

Relief shown from his grandfather's face by the time he finished his story. "Is that all? I expected much worse." His eyes found Dan's. "If you want to know, she never came to my room."

He'd rather have died than admit it, but he had wanted to know. Not that he'd ever share that with his grandfather. "I told you it was embarrassing."

Jeb slung the saddle he'd been cleaning over a pole and hung the bridle on a hook. "I think you should give her the benefit of the doubt. It was freezing cold, dark, and she'd never been in the house. It would be pretty easy to get turned around."

"Maybe, but..."

"Do you want her?"

"What kind of question is that?" Dan demanded. He led the horse into his stall and unclipped the rope from its halter.

"A personal question," Jeb admitted, "but if you want her, Dan, there's no reason why you can't have her. Call her and ask her to go out with you. I could see she liked your looks, so I'm pretty sure she'll say yes. You won't know if the two of you have a future until you spend some time with her."

Still ashamed, Dan refused to look at his grandfather. "After the way I treated her, I bet she'd rather die than go out with me, but even if she did, it wouldn't make any difference."

"Why not?"

"Isn't it obvious? I don't have anything to offer her, so there's no reason to waste her time."

His grandfather still wanted to argue the point, but Dan had finished grooming his horse, and he'd be blamed if he shared more confidences. He'd spilled his guts enough for one day.

~ * ~

"Turnaround Farm," Jeb answered when the kitchen phone rang that evening.

"Mr. Wakefield, my name is Pauline Coffey. Holly Grant is my granddaughter. We need to talk."

<h1 style="text-align:center">Five</h1>

The weather turned nasty overnight. Sleet and freezing rain coated power lines, trees, and roads and made driving a nightmare. Everyone who could stayed safely inside.

"I'm crazy to be going to town on a day like this," Jeb muttered as he carefully brought his car to a stop in Pauline Coffey's driveway. "But if it's good for Dan..."

He liked Pauline's house on sight. A picket fence whose gate stood invitingly ajar surrounded the small, white, clapboard cottage. Pauline had landscaped the front yard with berry-laden, evergreen shrubs. They probably attracted birds as did the bird feeders dotted around the yard. The entire house had a warm, friendly air about it in spite of the dreadful weather. If he ever had the misfortune to live in town, he hoped he could find a home just like this one.

Pauline answered his knock so quickly he knew she'd been watching for him. He immediately liked her, noting that her sweet smile and lively step contradicted her snowy white hair. "Mr. Wakefield, won't you come in? The weather is miserable."

Jeb handed his coat and hat to Pauline as he entered the house. "Please, call me Jeb. You look something like Holly, you know."

"So we've been told. I consider it a great compliment. Holly's a beautiful woman."

She led the way to the living room and seated Jeb by a roaring fire. A small calico cat strolled over to inspect the new arrival and then curled up by the hearth for a quick nap. "Would you care for tea or maybe something stronger to warm you up?"

"I guess I'll stick to tea since I have to drive in weather like this." Jeb looked around the pleasant room. "You have a lovely home."

Pauline beamed at him. "Thank you so much." She poured two fragrant cups of tea from a pot sitting on a table in the window and sat beside Jeb on the sofa. "Do you know what happened between them?"

"Dan and Holly? Yes, I do."

Pauline's eyes twinkled. "I think Holly is very much aware of Dan as a man. That's why she agreed to go with him to the horse show."

Jeb smiled back. "I'm sure he's aware of Holly as a woman. That's why he agreed to take her."

"She has some issues that may complicate their relationship," Pauline warned as she sipped her hot tea.

"Dan has issues as well."

"Well then, let's throw them together and see what happens."

Jeb nodded. "My thoughts exactly. Do you have any ideas?"

Pauline laughed, a sweet, musical sound that warmed Jeb's heart. "Oh, yes. Those two won't know what hit them."

~ * ~

Holly's eyes opened wide when she saw Jeb Wakefield standing on her doorstep. "Mr. Wakefield, what a nice surprise. Won't you come in?" She glanced over his shoulder, praying the entire time that Dan hadn't come with him. If she never saw that barbarian again, it would be too soon.

Jeb stepped inside out of the cold. "I'm sorry to drop by without calling first. I called your office, and they told me you'd gone home for lunch, so I took the chance of finding you here. It occurred to me that if you're going to the show with Dan, you should at least be able to say you've ridden a horse. The weather's supposed to be nice tomorrow, so I'd like you to come out and take a ride."

Holly barely managed to suppress a gasp. "I wouldn't dream of taking up so much of your time."

Jeb beamed at her as if she'd said something profound. "Oh, don't worry about that. Dan's the one who'll be riding with you, not me."

Exactly what she'd feared. She had no desire to spend an afternoon with Dan Wakefield, not after he'd smacked her bottom for her. Going to the horse show with him provided quite enough humiliation, thank you. "I'm sure he's busy too, Mr. Wakefield, and anyway, I don't have riding clothes."

"Now, Holly, surely you won't deny my grandson the chance to spend an afternoon with a pretty girl. Don't worry about riding clothes either. Just wear something warm."

I can't get out of it. This deal is getting harder to close by the minute. "If you're sure Dan won't mind, I'd be delighted."

"Dan won't mind. We'll see you tomorrow around two."

~ * ~

Dan threw a fit. "I'm too busy to waste an afternoon on a spoiled, money-hungry woman like Holly Grant." He set his cup of tea on the kitchen table and scowled at his grandfather.

"Wanting to buy Turnaround doesn't make her either spoiled or money hungry," Jeb objected. He passed a bowl of beans to Dan. "More beans? I cooked them with ham the way you like."

"No. I'm still not sure Holly wasn't hunting your room the other night. I don't want to spend time with a woman like her."

Jeb sighed and set the bowl on the table. "You know she never intended to sleep with either of us. It was an honest mistake."

In his heart Dan agreed with his grandfather, but still... "Even if that's true, I don't like her. She wants to buy Turnaround, and I don't want you to sell."

"As if I'd do a thing like that without your approval. If it weren't for you, I'd have had to sell Turnaround a long time ago, and when I pass on, the farm'll belong to you. How can you think your opinion wouldn't matter?"

Dan sighed. "I'm sorry, Gramps. I know you wouldn't do that. I just get a little crazy when I think of real estate agents throwing big money at you."

"Well, put your mind at rest." Jeb took a big bite of beans and washed them down with hot, fragrant tea. "Holly's never even been on a horse. I want her to go riding, so she'll know what she's asking us to give up."

"That makes sense, I guess. I don't want to waste my time, but if you want me to do it, I will. Maybe she'll love horses so much she decides to leave us alone."

~ * ~

The fat, placid mare ambled around the ring.

"Be careful, Kyle. Don't let him get hurt," Mama called from her place outside the ring.

"Millie, stop worrying. I know what I'm doing."

He turned his attention to Dan. "Sit up straight, son, and keep your heels down."

As Dan sat up straight, his father smiled at him. "Good boy. That's better."

"Daddy, why does this bridle have so many reins?"

"There's more than one type of bridle. You have to know how to use all of them."

"You're a born horseman, Dan," Mama cried, while Daddy smiled in agreement.

Dan's chest swelled with pride. His father and grandfather loved horses. He wanted to be just like them.

~ * ~

Dan awoke in the dark and smiled. It usually made him sad when he dreamed of his parents, but sometimes he'd dream of the good parts, and there had been some good parts. It warmed his heart to remember them.

Six

The weather man had promised good weather, and for once he delivered. The temperature still hovered close to freezing, but the sun shone in a cloudless blue sky, and much of yesterday's ice had melted away. Holly parked her car in the Wakefield driveway and inhaled the crisp, clean air. What a beautiful afternoon! If only she didn't have to waste her time at Turnaround Farm.

"You can do this," she said aloud. "Take a ride on the horse, and then you can go home. You don't have to stay more than an hour or so. How bad can it be?"

She had no more than knocked when Dan Wakefield jerked the door open. "Come in," he ordered, and by golly it was an order! His stony, set face told Holly he didn't want her here, but who cared? She didn't want to spend time with him either.

Jeb Wakefield beamed at her as she preceded Dan into the kitchen. "Hello, Holly. Are you ready for a riding lesson?"

"Yes, I've been looking forward to it." *Yeah, right, like going to the dentist for a root canal.* "Er, there is one thing that has me worried. The horse is gentle, isn't he?"

Dan and Jeb tried to smother their grins, but she saw them anyway. Jeb answered her. "Yes, the horse is gentle. It won't hurt you," he said, his tone kind and reassuring.

"Not that I'm afraid or anything, but it's all so new to me."

A smile still lingered on Dan's face. "You'll be fine with me. "You'll have to change your shoes, though. We've got a pair of riding boots that belonged to my mother. I think they'll fit you, so you can wear them."

"Why can't I use sneakers?"

"The boots have a heel on them. It keeps your foot from sliding through the stirrup. That would be dangerous."

"Oh."

Dan had guessed correctly; the boots did fit. Holly smiled as she strode around the kitchen. "I like these boots. They look great."

Dan snorted and looked bemused. "Women! Always worrying about their clothes. Did you bring any warm gloves?"

"I didn't think about that. All I have are these driving gloves." *How dare he criticize me?*

"That won't do. You can borrow a pair of mine. They're fur-lined, so your fingers won't go numb. I don't think you can beat fur for keeping out the cold."

He dashed upstairs for a pair of gloves, which he passed to her. She took a deep breath. "Are we ready now?"

"Yeah, I guess so. We'll see you later, Gramps."

"I'll have a little snack waiting for you when you get back."

~ * ~

Jeb stood at the window and watched as Dan and Holly made their way toward the barn. *They're being real careful not to touch each other, but they've both loosened up a little.*

Holly and Dan vanished into the barn, and Jeb left the window to continue his housekeeping chores. He hoped he and Pauline had done the right thing by throwing their grandchildren together.

~ * ~

"Let's go meet your horse," Dan said as they entered the barn.

Holly studied the barn, a big building that looked more spacious than the house. It had once been painted white, but most of the paint had long since worn off, leaving the boards a weathered, silvery gray.

They walked down the barn's center aisle, which had stalls on either side. As they passed one of the stalls on the left, they heard a loud snort and the sound of hooves thudding against the wall. A large black head with laid back ears and rolling white eyes thrust itself over the stall door.

Without taking her eyes off the horse, Holly pressed into Dan's side. "Is that a mean horse?"

Dan laughed outright. "No, he isn't mean. That's a stallion, a male horse. He probably smells the mare that was brought in yesterday."

"Does he want to hurt the mare?"

"No, he doesn't want to hurt her. She's coming in season, and he wants to mate with her."

"What if she didn't want to?" Holly demanded with a scowl. "That horse is entirely too aggressive to suit me."

Dan laughed again, but when she frowned, he brought himself under control. "He'd make her. That's what a stallion does. In the wild he'd sire her foal, baby horse, and then he'd take care of her and protect her."

Holly suddenly thought of how hard Dan had worked to protect his home and family. Like that horse, he had responsibilities he had lived up to.

Resentfully, she pushed those ridiculous thoughts away. What had caused her to think such a thing? Dan Wakefield wasn't a horse. He was a bully. *I still haven't forgiven him for smacking my bottom.*

Dan stopped in front of the last stall in the row and reached into his coat pocket. A pretty gray head poked over the top of the stall door. With a snort, the horse butted its nose against Dan's pocket. "You want your carrot, don't you?" Dan crooned. He gave the treat to the horse and stroked its face and neck affectionately. "Holly, come and meet Lady. She's yours for the afternoon."

"She won't bite me, will she?"

"No, Lady's very gentle."

Holly eased up to the stall and patted the mare's neck. "She's sure pretty."

"I think so. Lady's one of our own horses. My dad bought her for my mother right before he died. Mother was really afraid of horses, so Dad found Lady for her. Besides being as gentle as a kitten, she's a good horse. She'll give you a smooth ride."

He opened the stall door and fastened a rope to the mare's halter. "You can lead her."

With reluctance, Holly took the rope. *Why doesn't he lead the horse himself? What if she steps on me*? However, as Dan had promised, Lady had good manners. She followed Holly with no trouble, seemingly glad to have found a new friend. Some of Holly's fear vanished. *Dan may not like me, but he won't let me get hurt.*

Dan tethered the mare and bridled her, a process Holly watched with interest, but that saddle... "Is that the saddle? I thought they had horn things you could hold on to."

"Some saddles do, but we use flat or English saddles. They don't have horns."

Uh oh. Not what she'd expected at all.

Dan finished saddling Lady and turned to Holly. "I'll leave her tied here until I get my horse ready. Then we'll go out to the ring."

Dan's own mount, a bay gelding, greeted him with whickers of joy. Dan petted and caressed the animal, making little chirping noises to it. For some reason it pleased her to see that the animals liked him. She had always heard that animals could tell a bad person from a good person, and if so, the horses had just given Dan a good recommendation.

Dan tied his horse and began Holly's lesson. "You always get on a horse on its left side. Watch me. I walk up, take the reins and mane in my left hand, and put my left foot in the stirrup like this. Then I put my right hand here, give a little bounce in the stirrup, and swing my right leg over."

Holly laughed. "You made it look easy."

"It is easy, but I'll help you the first time. I'll put my hand on your bottom and give you a little boost."

Thanks for the warning.

She approached Lady in the way Dan had illustrated. When she felt his hand touch her bottom, she had a sudden urge to pull away, but how stupid would that be? She gritted her teeth and allowed him to help her onto Lady. "Hey, I made it," she cheered.

"Sure you did. Now, let me show you how to hold the reins." As Dan's hands covered hers, a strange tingle moved up her arm. It only took a moment for him to position the reins, so the tingle faded quickly.

Dan seemed at ease. He efficiently instructed her about the rudiments of horsemanship. "These horses are trained to move away from the pressure of your leg. If you want to go right, you press left and vice versa. They move toward the direction you pull the reins."

"That explains your thigh muscles." *Oh. My. Goodness! How could I have reminded him of that dreadful night?*

Dan's face turned a lovely shade of pink. "Uh, I...ah...need to apologize for...for..."

"Honestly, it's okay. Please, don't say anything else," she begged. "Let's just forget about it."

With a look of relief on his face, Dan changed the subject. "I need to shorten your stirrups. Slide your leg forward, and I'll take them up."

Anything as long he left the subject of thighs alone. As he shortened the stirrups, his hands brushed the back of her leg more than once, causing those little tingles to travel all the way from her legs to her chest.

A feeling of shame seared Holly and chased the sensation away. *Ridiculous. There's nothing personal about this, so get over it.* Very true, but it didn't matter. She *had* felt something when he touched her.

Dan repositioned her feet in the stirrups and stepped back. "Sit up straight, and look where you're going, not at the horse. Are you ready to go to the practice ring?"

"I guess so."

"Okay, to start the horse, squeeze both legs against her sides."

Holly squeezed Lady's sides, and Lady obediently moved forward. "She's moving!"

Dan smiled at her. Interesting. When he smiled, he had little crinkles in the corners of his eyes.

"I've been riding for so long I'd forgotten what a thrill it can be," he said. "Let's go to the ring."

Holly felt her confidence grow as she made her way around the ring without mishap. Dan rode beside her, giving instruction. She hadn't expected to enjoy riding so much.

After they completed three laps, Dan said, "You're doing great. Would you like to ride up the hill?"

"Yeah, let's do."

The fresh air and sunshine excited Dan's horse. Periodically, the animal danced around, snorting and prancing, but Dan easily brought him to a sedate walk beside Lady. "I don't see what you're doing to make him mind," Holly said. "You must be a pretty good rider."

Dan just shrugged, but he had a warm, gratified expression on his face after hearing her praise. "Constant practice," he explained.

The horses reached the crest of the hill and stopped of their own accord beside the lone oak tree on the hilltop. From this vantage point, Holly saw a miniature Jeb enter the barn. On the highway below a small toy car sped by. Overhead, white, fluffy clouds tossed by the wind fragmented and reformed into different shapes. The whole world smelled clean and fresh, much as if God or his angels had come along and given the world a good scouring. Holly took a deep breath. "It's beautiful up here."

Dan smiled, which made little crinkles around his eyes again. *How odd! Why do those little crinkles give me such a funny feeling in my stomach?*

"Yeah, I come up here a lot. You can see forever."

Holly hadn't expected he'd take pleasure in this beautiful place, probably because until this afternoon she had viewed him in the most unflattering light possible. "What do you see in forever, Dan?"

"Nothing much. It's just really peaceful. Up here you can forget about everything waiting for you down below and relax for a few minutes."

Without warning, a stab of guilt pierced Holly. If her deal went through, the developer planned to build a clubhouse for a golf community on this location.

Her face burned, and she hastily changed the subject. "How long has your family owned this farm?"

"Since the founding of Fairfield in 1799."

"That's a long time."

Dan absently patted his horse's neck and allowed the animal to snatch a bite of stray grass. "Yes, it is. That's the main reason I don't want the farm sold. I like feeling connected to my ancestors. Most of them were good, hard-working people."

He flushed and set his jaw. "I guess you're thinking about my dad. He wasn't such a good person, but most of the Wakefields were."

"Oh, I imagine most of the stories about your father are exaggerated. You know how it is in a small town."

He gave her a long look. "No, most of the stories are on the money. I've...I've always wondered why I wasn't good enough for him. He must have seen something in me he didn't like, or he wouldn't have done the bad things he did. He'd have wanted to take care of me and watch me grow up."

Holly's heart burned with empathy for Dan. She had wondered so many times why she wasn't enough for her mother. "I don't think he was disappointed in you personally. Once people start doing drugs, that's all they care about." She sighed. "I know what it's like to have a parent disappoint you."

His head cocked. "I wouldn't have thought you'd ever been disappointed in your parents. You operate an up and coming business, and people in the community respect you. I guess I assumed your parents had given you a wonderful life. Which one of them disappointed you?"

"My mother." *I don't like the direction this conversation has taken. I have no desire to exchange confidences with Dan Wakefield. Getting to know him on a personal level makes it hard to do my job. Besides that, whether I want to admit it or not, I like him.* She shivered. *I'd rather die than end up like Mother.*

Love for her father had sent her mother over the edge when he died. Since then the passion Rita felt for her never-ending parade of men had cut Holly to the bone and aged her grandmother before her time. So no, she didn't want to like Dan. Nevertheless, one confidence probably deserved another.

"My mother has a weakness for men," she said as she pushed her hair away from her eyes. It was windy on the hilltop. "After my father died, she had men one after the other." Her mouth turned down in a bitter grimace. "I never knew from one day to the next who she'd bring home. Right now, I don't know where she is. We haven't heard from her since she left right before Christmas. She'll be back once he dumps her, and they all do dump her eventually."

She peeked at Dan, expecting him to have a disgusted look on his face. He already suspected her of prostituting herself for a sale. Why wouldn't he think she was just like her mother? But instead of condemnation she saw compassion.

"Was she happy with your father? My parents loved each other, I guess, but my dad loved drugs and gambling more."

Holly nodded as she remembered all the happy times before her father's death. "My mother was fine as long as Daddy was alive, but after his death, she just went to pieces. I was only a child at the time so I spent a lot of time with Nana."

"That's rough."

"Yeah, it is, but it toughened me up and made me determined not to be like her. Your past must have affected you the same way. Somewhere along the line, you made a decision not to be like your father, and you aren't. You've made something of your life."

Dan laughed, a harsh sound that held little humor and caused his horse's ears to flick back and forth. "I don't know about that. I've done very little with my life except save the family farm, and lately that's beginning to look like a very big maybe."

Holly's ears felt hot, and so did her eyes. She cleared her throat. "How did Turnaround Farm get its name?"

This time when Dan laughed, Holly did too. "My ancestor, Thomas Wakefield, and his wife Drusilla took a drive one cold, snowy day back in 1799. When they reached the place where the house stands, she was ready to turn around. Thomas bought the property and named it Turnaround Farm."

"That's so neat." The sun went behind one of the fluffy white clouds as a gust of wind struck Holly. She shivered. "I know just what she meant. Are you ready to go back down? It's getting colder."

They rode companionably down the hill. This time Dan's horse seemed content to walk beside Lady with no shenanigans. Until then Holly had given no thought to the reason behind the Wakefields' refusal to sell their farm. She had simply seen obstacles she had to overcome, but Dan had given her something new to think about. He loved his home and wanted to keep it. Was that so bad? He seemed so competent, sincere, and hard working. How could she plan to take his land away when he loved it so much?

Whoa, I need an attitude adjustment! She had to remember what this deal would mean to Grant Realty. She'd become a big name in the local real estate world and secure the future of her business if she brokered this transaction. Anyway, with the money they got from the sale, Dan could buy another farm if he wanted to. Then he'd be the ancestor who started the farm.

They reached the barn where Dan showed Holly how to take care of her horse. For the first time, she appreciated the magnitude of work Dan and his grandfather handled each day. She had never dreamed keeping horses entailed so much hard labor.

Lady distracted her when she swatted Holly with her tail. "What manners," Holly chuckled. She stroked Lady's neck. "I like rubbing you down after we've been riding together."

Dan's face brightened. "You'll make a good horsewoman. There's more to being friends with a horse than just riding it."

They completed their work, and with a final pat to their horses' necks, they went in search of Jeb's promised snack. "I'm glad your grandfather is giving us a snack," she said. "All that riding made me hungry."

Dan laughed. "Seems like I'm always hungry."

They stopped in the mudroom to take off their boots and coats. Then they went into the kitchen where the fragrance of baking bread filled the room with a mouth-watering aroma.

Jeb rose from his big chair near the fire and beamed at them. "Here you are," he said. "Did you have a good time?"

Holly nodded. "Yes, I did. Dan let me ride Lady, and I think she liked me."

"Why, I bet she did. You two sit down, and I'll bring you a snack."

Wonder what Jeb will offer us. Store-bought cookies maybe. Those big loaves of bread on the cooling rack are probably for his and Dan's dinner.

Jeb had something much better to offer than store-bought cookies, though. He served them big slices of the fresh bread along with honey butter, apple slices, grapes, and big wedges of cheddar cheese. It almost looked like something her nana would have served, although she'd have had a better presentation for the food. The plates and cups Jeb used were thick and white with a red band around the rim.

Jeb sat a brown teapot filled with hot tea on the table. "I hope you like hot tea, Holly. Dan and I really like tea better than coffee."

Holly took a large bite of the fresh bread. Heavenly. "I love tea. Mr. Wakefield, you're as good a baker as my nana, and that's saying a lot."

"Thanks, but I bet she could out bake me any time," he said with a smile.

The afternoon had almost ended before Holly left Turnaround Farm. "Thank you very much," she said as she pulled on her shoes and took her coat from the peg where Dan had hung it. "I enjoyed the ride and the tea very much."

"You come back anytime," Jeb answered with a smile. "Dan, walk this young lady to her car."

Holly allowed Dan to help her with her coat, a thrilling experience because she felt those funny little tingles again. Then they went outside into the cold air. The temperature must have dropped ten degrees since they went inside for their snack.

Dan opened her car door for her. "I had a nice time today."

"I hope I didn't keep you from something you had to do."

"No, nothing."

The shadows were growing longer now. "It won't be long until dark, so I guess I'll let you go in now." *Even though I really hate to see the day end.* "I guess I'll see you at the end of the month when we go to the show."

Dan patted the side of her door. "Drive carefully."

~ * ~

He stood and watched the car for a moment before he went back inside. In spite of himself, his opinion of the lovely, ambitious realtor had changed for the better. Smiling, he thought of how she carried on over those boots. *She doesn't know a thing about riding safety; she just liked the way they looked on her.*

Come to think of it, Mother appreciated the way riding clothes looked on her. I'd seen her inspecting herself many times before riding with Dad.

He smiled. Obviously, this preoccupation with appearance must be a woman thing. When he went riding, he didn't care how he looked. He suddenly flushed. Maybe it made him sound like a pathetic loser, but he had enjoyed hearing Holly praise his riding skills.

Aw, what was he thinking? Nothing had changed; he still lived in a crumbling old farmhouse and didn't have a penny to his name. He was still his father's son too. What did he have to offer a woman like Holly Grant? Nothing. Just a big, fat nothing.

~ * ~

Rita Grant inhaled deeply and coughed as the smoke burned her lungs. She never had cared for smoking, but she had gained some weight, and she'd heard smoking would help keep her thin.

Goodness knows she needed to lose a few pounds. Kevin stayed whip-thin even though he ate all the time. She ate the heavy foods he liked, but they made her fat, so she had to do something.

Truthfully, Kevin had begun to worry her. They had gone to a club last night where he'd ogled the waitress something awful. The girl looked around eighteen, while Kevin must be at least fifty. Oh, yeah. She definitely needed to lose weight.

Wonder if Holly had had a good Christmas? She had promised to stay in Fairfield for the holidays, but when Kevin asked her to go with him to Las Vegas, she hadn't thought of refusing. The bright lights and shows excited her. Probably she'd like the casinos too, but she didn't have any money.

No doubt her family was angry about Christmas, but what did they expect her to do? At her age she couldn't afford to reject men the way Holly did. Just wait until her pretty daughter got old enough to have crow's feet around her eyes and sagging arms. She'd sing a new song then.

She paced restlessly around the small, tight, motel room. Actually, she could use some clothes too. Maybe she could call her mother. Pauline would surely send her some money if she asked.

She picked up the phone, but she changed her mind when she thought of the fit Kevin had thrown when she tried to call last week. He had arranged a poker game tonight. If he won, he'd probably give her some money. It would be better to wait before calling her mother.

Seven

Pauline arrived at Grant Realty early on Monday morning with a basket of freshly baked blueberry muffins on her arm. She found Holly and her entire staff, which consisted of Loretta and three other agents, having their morning coffee in the small reception area at the front of the office.

"Hello, everyone. I've brought you some muffins to go with your coffee," she called. As she placed the basket on the table, all of the agents crowded around; they had sampled Pauline's cooking before.

Pauline passed Holly a muffin and a napkin. "Did you have a nice time yesterday?"

"How did you...oh, never mind. Yes, I had a nice time."

Loretta peeled the paper off her muffin and took a big bite. "That is so good! What did you do yesterday, Holly?"

Pauline beamed at Loretta and answered for Holly. "Oh, she had a date yesterday."

All the agents perked up to listen. At one time or another, each of them had been privy to Holly's views on men.

Loretta glanced smugly at Holly who saw how much this news pleased her assistant. "Who'd she go out with?"

"Dan Wakefield."

"Oh, it was business," answered Loretta, her face falling.

"No, darling, it was pleasure. Holly's seeing Dan socially."

"Why don't you just take out an ad in the paper?" Holly snapped "I can just see the headline now...Holly Wakefield has a date..." She broke off as the entire staff burst into hysterical laughter. "What's wrong with all of you?"

"You called yourself Holly Wakefield," Loretta chortled. "Can I write Loretta Stuart on scrap paper now without you fussing at me?"

Holly felt hot all over.

Pauline passed another muffin to Loretta. "I think it's time I met your young man, Holly. I'll call and invite Dan to dinner tonight. You be there at six-fifteen."

Holly sputtered and protested, but Pauline paid no attention and left her granddaughter to deal with the fallout from her unfortunate blunder as best she could.

~ * ~

Should she go to her grandmother's dinner or not? Dan had shown her a good time when they went riding, but nothing had really changed. Buying Turnaround Farm for her client was still important to her. Anyway, Dan had behaved himself yesterday, but she knew his true nature first hand. Hadn't he smacked her bottom twice? She ignored the small voice in her head that insisted Dan was a sensitive, caring man who deserved her respect in spite of everything.

And whether she liked to admit it or not, she was mad at Nana. Nana knew she didn't want anything to do with Dan Wakefield. Why hadn't she minded her own business?

After fuming all day, Holly did what she had known all along she would do. She chose her outfit with care and arrived promptly at six-fifteen.

"Darling, you look lovely," Pauline said, as she hugged Holly and kissed her cheek. She set a vase of fresh daffodils on the center of the dining table. "Is your dress new?"

Holly refused to be distracted, even though she did like her new dress. It was red, and she loved red. "Nana, why have you done this?

You know what happened when I spent the night at Turnaround. Do you think I'm looking forward to sitting through a meal with a savage like Dan Wakefield?"

Pauline patted her hand. "I remember, darling, but you did slap him first. You're attracted to this young man, so I want to meet him."

"I'm not attracted to Dan Wakefield!" Okay, her blood pressure probably just shot up about a hundred points. "He may be handsome, but it's just business between us. When I see him, I see dollar signs."

"Then you certainly should be happy for a chance to get together with him and his grandfather."

Holly smiled. "Jeb's coming too?"

"Yes, of course."

Hmm. This dinner sounded like a good idea after all. If she could bring the conversation around to business, she'd have a golden opportunity to tell Mr. Wakefield what her client had offered for Turnaround Farm. Maybe then she wouldn't have to go to that darn horse show with Dan.

The sound of the doorbell sent Pauline to the door and stirred up about a million butterflies in Holly's stomach. *Get a grip, girl. A good businesswoman always takes advantage of any and every opportunity.*

Holly's heart took off in a mad gallop when Dan entered the room ahead of his grandfather. He wore a light blue oxford cloth shirt with a matching tie and a navy blue sport coat. The coat accented the width of his shoulders while his khaki pants showcased the muscles in his legs. She'd never seen him wearing anything except jeans and a flannel shirt. Who knew he'd clean up so nicely?

Shame flooded her. Why should it surprise her to see how well Dan presented himself in her grandmother's elegant establishment? He didn't live in a barn, did he?

Jeb seemed glad to see her; he was positively beaming when he said hello. "Hi, Holly. How are you? Were you saddle-sore after your riding lesson?"

"What's that?"

"It's when your muscles are sore from riding."

"Oh. No, I'm not. I guess I didn't stay on the horse that long."

"Dan said she's a born horsewoman," Jeb told Pauline, who held out a tray of shrimp rolls for his inspection.

Pauline smiled from ear to ear. "I'm not surprised. Holly told me what a good time she had yesterday."

She had done no such thing, but she declined to say so.

"We had Dan on a horse by the time he was a year old," Jeb boasted, as he selected a plump shrimp roll from Pauline's tray.

"Did he ride by himself at that age?" Holly asked, somewhat surprised they'd allow such a thing.

"No, we gave him a little help."

Good. The Wakefields might love horses, but she didn't think she'd trust a baby to ride alone.

Pauline soon called them to dinner where she seated Holly across from Dan. The minute she got an opening she planned on discussing real estate. Unfortunately for her plan, Pauline gave her no opportunity to mention work. Her grandmother conversed well on any subject, and tonight she made it her business to draw Dan out and put him at ease. And she never mentioned real estate. They were soon ready for dessert, so Holly accepted the inevitable. She wouldn't get that conversation with Jeb after all.

"I hope you like peaches and cream over pound cake," Pauline said with a smile for Dan. "It's Holly's favorite."

"Yes, ma'am, I do."

"I'll get dessert, Nana. You stay here," Holly said as Pauline rose to fetch the peaches and cake from the kitchen.

"Thank you, darling. Dan, if you would be so kind, maybe you can bring in the coffee."

"Yes, ma'am."

Dan followed Holly into the kitchen and watched as she assembled two trays. She fumbled as she placed a cup on a saucer. Ugh. Why wouldn't he stop watching her? "Do you really like peaches and cream, Dan?"

"Yes, I do. They're smooth and luscious together."

Holly heard something odd in his tone. Looking up from the tray, she saw the intense expression on his face, and her heart picked up speed.

"I like a juicy, ripe peach," Dan continued, his eyes trained on Holly's face. "One that's all golden and you can just about taste the sunshine. The juice mixes with the cream, and it's sweet and velvety soft."

Dan didn't look at the peaches even one time. He seemed totally focused on her. *I don't think he's talking about peaches at all.*

She thrust a tray at him. "Here. Take this coffee to the dining room."

When Dan reached for the tray, his fingers brushed Holly's. She dropped the tray, which bounced on the cabinet, rattling cups and saucers and spilling coffee onto the floor.

Dan ignored the spilled coffee. He took Holly's hand in his and gently brought it to his lips. "I had a good time riding with you yesterday," he whispered.

Holly's heart hammered in her chest so hard she heard the blood roaring in her ears. "I had a good time too." Why wouldn't he let go of her hand? She felt so...so funny, not like herself at all.

Instead of freeing her, Dan captured her other hand and pulled her toward him. "Holly Grant, when I'm with you, I forget things I ought to remember."

"Wh...Why?"

Dan laughed softly. "Because you make me forget."

Holly almost lost her breath. "I make you forget?"

"Yes, you do. I lose my focus when I'm around you. All I can think about is how pretty you are."

Holly had to clear her throat before she could speak. This wasn't supposed to be happening! "You think I'm pretty?" she breathed.

"Beautiful would be a better description. Just perfect in fact."

Holly totally forgot about real estate or Turnaround Farm. She took a step closer to him. When Dan released her hands and drew her against him, Holly closed her eyes and tilted her head. As Dan's lips brushed hers, fire seared her from head to toe.

"Holly, do you need any help?"

Pauline's voice broke the sensual spell in the kitchen. "No, Nana. We're coming." She refused to look at Dan. Her mother had never acted any sluttier! Yes, the man oozed sex appeal, but she barely knew him. Oh, she was her mother's daughter, all right. From now on she'd steer clear of Dan Wakefield. He brought out something bad in her.

Holly picked up her tray and hurried from the kitchen, leaving Dan to mop the spilled coffee off the floor. He had made her spill it; let him clean it up.

~ * ~

"Thank you for a lovely evening, Pauline. You and Holly will have to come out to Turnaround one night and let me cook dinner for you. My cooking can't compare to yours, but I promise it'll be edible."

"We'd be delighted to come. You just let us know when."

"Thank you, Pauline," Dan joined in. "I especially liked the peaches and cream."

"Oh, I'm so glad. You know, Dan, if you have the time, there's a favor I'd like to ask of you."

"Anything."

"Holly had such a good time riding yesterday, I wondered if you might have time to give her a few lessons."

Dan used every minute of his time and needed more. "Sure, I'll be happy to," he agreed.

Holly scowled at her grandmother. "Nana, he's too busy for that. Don't put him on the spot."

"No, it's okay," Dan said. "I have time."

Holly's stomach flip-flopped.

After they said their goodbyes, Jeb and Dan made their way to Dan's truck where Jeb at once turned up the heater. "Did you have a good time tonight?"

Dan took off his tie and tossed it into the back seat. "Yes."

"What happened in the kitchen?"

Dan gritted his teeth. "Nothing."

Jeb fastened his seat belt with a click that sounded like the closing of an inquisitor's door. "I'm not that old, Dan. She acted flustered and wouldn't look at you, but you couldn't take your eyes off her."

Dan sighed. Nobody in his family knew how to mind his own business. "Okay, I kissed her, but it won't happen again. I let down my guard for a minute, but I won't make that mistake a second time."

Jeb looked both ways as they pulled out of the driveway even though Dan was driving. He always did that, and it always irritated Dan. Once they were safely in the street, his grandfather settled back for a good talk. "Why don't you want to kiss her again? She's a beautiful woman, and I think she's very attracted to you. She let you kiss her, right?"

"All she wants from me is your signature on a sales contract. I need to remember that, and I need to remember who I am."

Jeb's head cocked. "What does that mean, who you are?"

"My last name is Wakefield. That means no money, no respect, and no future. I wouldn't do that to a woman I cared about."

Jeb's head wagged from side to side. "You're wrong. People may not respect your dad, but they respect you. Any woman would be lucky to make a life with you. It doesn't matter if you're wealthy or not."

Dan rolled his eyes even though Jeb couldn't see him in the dark. Had Pauline put something in his food? What else would account for his strange behavior? His toes curled. Gah, that peach nonsense! How could he have said something so stupid? He'd hate to know what Holly thought about him. Smooth and luscious? Juicy ripe? His face burned in the dark. "If Holly asks about riding lessons, I'm going to turn her down. I wouldn't have agreed if that kiss hadn't messed up my thinking."

"Well, you don't have to decide right now. You can sleep on it."

~ * ~

Jeb turned off the kitchen light, and used the dying fire to make his way to the door that led upstairs. Not that he really needed a light. He'd lived in this house since the day he was born and knew every square inch of it.

Pushing Dan about Holly Grant would only make him turn stubborn. His grandson needed a woman in his life, and Holly Grant seemed very interested. Maybe she'd be the one who could finally break through the wall of hurt, resentment, and anger Dan had erected around his heart.

Eight

"I don't know what's wrong with you this morning," scolded Loretta, who stood in the doorway of Holly's office impatiently tapping her foot. "I've asked you three times where the Johnson file is, and you won't answer me."

"I'm sorry," apologized Holly. "I guess I'm just tired. I stayed out late last night."

Loretta's eyes gleamed with interest. She strolled into the office and took the chair in front of Holly's desk. "Did you have a good time?"

"Yes, I did. Nana's a great cook, and her little dinner parties are fabulous."

"Yes, but you know what I mean." Loretta leaned forward, as if she could wring some juicy confidences out of her. "Did you and Dan hit it off?"

"Yeah, we talked some. It was okay."

"Holly Grant, what's the matter with you?" Loretta sighed loudly. "You know darn good and well you think he's gorgeous. Why are you refusing to admit it?"

Holly stacked some folders on her desk just to have something to do with her hands. "I'm not refusing to admit anything. He is good looking, but our relationship is business and nothing more."

"If you say so, but why don't you want to go out and have some fun for a change? Dan's cute. I bet you'd have a good time."

Holly jumped up so suddenly that her chair banged into the wall. "Oops." She rolled the chair forward and swiped at the black mark it had left behind. "Now that you've brought up the Wakefields, there is something I need to discuss with Jeb. I think I'll run out there and get it over with."

"You do that."

Holly wasted no time. She grabbed her purse and coat and flew out the door in thirty seconds flat.

As Loretta returned to her desk, Bonnie White, Holly's newest agent said, "Where's she going in such a hurry?"

"To see Dan Wakefield."

"You mean Jeb Wakefield," corrected Bonnie. "His name is on the deed to Turnaround Farm."

Loretta shook her head and smiled. "No, I mean Dan."

~ * ~

Holly turned onto River Road and began the fifteen-mile drive to Turnaround Farm. About half way there, she passed a new housing development called River Oaks. She had conspicuously displayed her own sign near the rock wall that framed the entrance. It was a nice little place, and once it was finished she'd make some money off it.

She arrived at Turnaround Farm and parked in front of the farmhouse. Too bad the Wakefields didn't have the money to pave the driveway. The path to the door was a minefield of mud and icy puddles left by last night's rain. Nobody answered her knock. *They're probably at the barn.*

Heedless of the beating her pumps were taking, Holly bent her head against the cold north wind and hurried toward the barn. The door opened with a creak of the hinges that announced her presence as well as any doorbell would have done. Dan stood about halfway down the center aisle forking hay into a stall.

He smiled when he saw her. "What are you doing out here this morning?" he called. He threw his pitchfork down and came to meet her.

It went against her principles to notice, but she did admire the way Dan moved. He lent an air of grace to even something as simple as walking. "Hi, Dan. I hope I'm not bothering you. We didn't set a date for my riding lessons, so I thought I'd do it before I forgot."

Dan's eyes twinkled so happily that Holly's breath caught in her throat. "Whenever is convenient for you is okay by me," he said. "Just let me know."

"Should I buy a pair of riding boots?"

"Yes, if you're serious about riding, you should."

The barn door creaked this time when it opened too. A small, dark-haired man wearing a plaid, wool jacket walked quietly into the barn. Holly didn't know him, but she thought he seemed nervous. He was biting at his lips, and his whole approach could only be called tentative. She didn't blame him. Dan didn't want to see this man and hadn't bothered to hide it.

"Hey, Dan." The man's voice was soft and low and held a note she couldn't quite identify.

"Hello, Uncle David. Holly, this is my uncle, David Lane. Uncle David, this is Holly Grant."

Holly held out her hand to Mr. Lane who hesitated but finally took it. "Hi, Mr. Lane." What was his problem? Why was he so unfriendly? He hadn't smiled at her once and didn't want to meet her eyes, much less shake her hand.

He cleared his throat. "It's funny you're here, Miss Grant, because you're the reason I came to see Dan."

"I'm sorry, but I don't understand. Do you want to buy or sell some real estate?"

Mr. Lane shook his head in the negative. "I don't believe in talking about people behind their backs, so I'll come right out and say what I came to say." He turned to Dan. "Did you know she approached your grandfather about buying Turnaround?"

"Yes."

Dan's cold, short answer didn't deter Mr. Lane. "It seems odd she never had any interest in you before, but all at once she's paying you a lot of attention."

Dan scowled at Mr. Lane. "What makes you think she's paying me a lot of attention?"

"People talk."

Dan stared at the floor and didn't answer, so David focused his attention on Holly. "Are you trying to use my nephew to get to Jeb Wakefield?"

"Uncle David, that's enough."

Dan's harsh voice startled Holly. Unwilling to be the cause of a family quarrel, she answered Mr. Lane before Dan could say anything else. Making her voice as sincere as possible, she said, "He has a right to wonder, Dan. Mr. Lane, it isn't what it might seem like. I'm not trying to get to Jeb through him."

Pure adrenalin flooded Holly. Didn't she plan on going with Dan to the horse show just so Jeb would look at her client's offer? Yes, and didn't that mean she was using Dan? Maybe, but she liked him; it didn't feel like she was using him.

David Lane stared at her a moment. It appeared to Holly that he wanted to look inside her heart, to see if she had told him the truth. "I hope you won't hold what I've said against me, Miss Grant. Dan's my nephew, and I want to look after him if I can."

His hand jerked, but stilled. She could have sworn he intended to give Dan's shoulder a hearty thump of masculine reassurance, but he checked himself. "I'm sorry to have bothered you, Dan. I'll see you later." He left the barn as suddenly as he'd arrived.

~ * ~

Well, that's just great. Holly gets to meet one of the notorious Lanes in person. Dan felt a rush of heat color his face. At least Uncle David was sober today. He usually wasn't. *Today…today he made a special trip just to see me, and I don't usually make him feel welcome. He couldn't really care about me, could he?*

His insides quivered as this revelation sank in. Tenderness and compassion weren't things he associated with his mother's family. Giving in to an impulse, he called, "Uncle David, wait and I'll walk out with you." He excused himself to Holly and went after his uncle.

As the two men reached David's rusty, old truck, Dan finally opened up. "You could have saved yourself a trip. I know why she's hanging around the farm. She may deny it, but Turnaround is the only reason she'd bother with me."

"That's not what she said."

Dan snorted. "There's a lot of money at stake. People say a lot of things when money is involved."

"There's a lot of man at stake too." The words seemed torn from his throat. "It looked to me like she meant what she said. I think she likes you."

Dan firmly tamped down the rush of pleasure that filled him. "Maybe."

"Maybe nothing," Mr. Lane insisted. "I saw the way she was looking at you when I came in. You take that woman out and have some fun for a change."

Dan tried and failed to stifle a silly grin. "How was she looking at me?"

"Like she was a cat, and you were a bowl of cream."

"I've got to think that one over."

"You do that."

Dan didn't know how to end this awkward conversation, and evidently Uncle David didn't either, but he finally climbed into his truck. "Well, I'd better let you get back to Miss Grant. Come over and see us sometime."

"Yes, sir. I will."

Mr. Lane looked down at his hands on the steering wheel. "I don't ever remember you calling me 'sir' before." He lifted his eyes. "I know how you feel about the Lanes, and I guess I don't blame you. Our reputation is a lot to live down. I want you to know that I've been going to AA meetings for two months now, and I haven't had a single drink the entire time. I intend to lick this alcoholism. Maybe when I do, I'll finally earn your respect."

"Uncle David..."

"You're my dead sister's only child, and I know how your parents neglected you. I also know that as an adult, you've worked like a dog to keep Turnaround. You haven't had much time for girls or fun, and I don't want to see you get your heart broken. I figured Holly Grant was just after the farm, but I'm not so sure now. Like I said, she looks at you like you're something special. Which you are." He gave a thump to Dan's shoulder, gunned his motor, and rattled down the driveway.

Dan watched until his uncle's car was out of sight, and then he went back inside the barn where he found Holly standing in front of Lady's stall stroking the mare's neck. "Look, Dan. I think she likes me."

"I think so too."

Holly arranged Lady's mane and gave her neck a final pat. "Your uncle seemed like a nice man."

"Yeah, well, he wasn't drunk today. He usually is."

"I guess he was worried about you."

Dan flushed. "I'm sorry about what he said. He had no right to upset you."

Holly gave Lady's neck one final pat and stepped away from the stall door. "I wasn't upset. Really. I think it's kind of nice to have somebody worry about you. Nana and a few distant cousins are all I have left unless you count my mother. I'd like to have some more relatives."

Dan's mouth turned downward in a bitter grimace. "Oh, there are a lot of Lanes still left. You can read all about them in the paper. Shoplifting, petty larceny, drunk and disorderly, you name it. The only one who ever amounted to anything is my cousin, Elizabeth. She left Fairfield with her mother after her dad died and went to Hollywood. She's a big star now."

"Wow, that Elizabeth Lane is your cousin? Everybody knows who she is. She makes the news and the tabloids almost every day. How many Oscars has she won?"

"Three."

"I love her movies," Holly enthused. "I think they're some of the best Hollywood ever made. Isn't she pregnant with her first child?"

Dan nodded. "Yeah, she is. She married a senator's son. Isn't it funny that a person like her is my cousin?"

Holly looked surprised. "I don't see a thing amusing about it. She may be the only famous Lane in your family, but I know of at least one more who turned out all right."

"Who's the other one?"

"You."

Dan's face burned. Wow, he hadn't expected that. Holly's face looked as red as his felt, and she refused to look at him.

Her flushed face put his discomfort to flight. He took her in his arms and kissed her just as he'd longed to do all morning. As he raised his lips from hers, Holly's eyes fluttered open. Dan's breath caught in his throat at the stirring of passion in those beautiful blue eyes. Could she really want someone like him? He had nothing to offer her.

This did not seem like the time for questions or doubt. With a sound low in his throat, Dan's mouth came down on hers. Boldly, he ran his hand down her side to her hip. When his fingers splayed across her buttocks, she started to tremble. And oh, glory be! She pressed herself against him and didn't seem to be in a hurry to go anywhere.

Dan almost didn't hear the groan of the hinges as the barn door swung open this time, but when Holly saw his grandfather, she jerked out of his arms so violently she would've tripped and fallen if he hadn't caught her arm.

Jeb said. "I'm sorry. I didn't mean to interrupt."

He turned around to make his escape, but he paused when Holly made a sound somewhere between a groan and a gasp.

"I apologize," she quavered. "I know how inappropriate my behavior has been. Please, please, forgive me."

She rushed toward the door as if wild horses pounded down the aisle behind her. "Holly, wait," Dan called, but she ignored him. She jumped into her car and roared down the driveway going way too fast.

Nine

"Let's go into the office," said Jeb, when Dan walked back into the barn, "or do you need a minute to cool off?"

Dan shook his head. Until he met Holly Grant he had never embarrassed himself this way. Imagine your grandfather asking you if you needed to cool off! Obediently, he followed Jeb into the office, a small room behind the tack area that contained a coffee maker, an old wooden desk, a chipped filing cabinet, and two chairs.

Jeb poured himself a cup of hot water from the pot behind the desk and dropped a tea bag into it. "Want one?"

"No."

Jeb seated himself in a battered old office chair with cracked leather upholstery. "What happened out there? Something sure spooked her. It's hard for me to believe a twenty-something-year-old woman would be so upset because she got caught kissing an attractive, unmarried man. Did you do something I didn't see?"

"No, I didn't!"

"Are you sure? You had a good hold on her when I opened the door."

Dan bit his lip to keep from saying what he wanted to. Did his grandfather really think he'd hurt Holly? "I didn't do anything to her!" he snapped.

"Okay, calm down. I believe you. Do you know what's wrong?"

"Yeah, maybe." He got up to make himself a cup of tea after all just so he wouldn't have to look at his grandfather. "I think it's because of Holly's mother. She likes men, all men, a little too much. I think Holly's afraid she'll be like her mom. That kiss was...heating up, and it scared the hell out of her because she liked it."

Jeb looked thoughtful. "Pauline told me Holly had some issues. I guess that's what she meant."

"I guess." Dan sat back down. "Gramps, you haven't changed your mind about selling, have you?"

Jeb shook his head and took a sip of his tea. "I'd never do that, especially not without your approval. Why do you ask?"

Because he needed some reassurance. Uncle David had been right about one thing. His experience with women was limited. He liked Holly, he liked her more than he should, but was Turnaround the only reason she seemed interested in him? How was a man supposed to know?

"I was just wondering if she'd still have any interest in seeing me once she finds out you won't sell," he finally said. "I guess it would be better for her if she didn't."

Jeb leaned over and patted his knee. "I think Holly likes you. I won't be surprised in the least if she wants to have a relationship with you."

Well, he hoped so. He hadn't intended to give Holly Grant the time of day, but he liked her. It would hurt if she refused to see him after the horse show.

"I'd better get back to work," he said. He got up and left the office, grateful for once that he had such a busy afternoon in front of him. Maybe he wouldn't have time to remember how Holly had felt in his arms.

~ * ~

Just like my mother. Just like my mother. Just like my mother. The refrain tormented Holly as she drove back toward town. She had proven herself as big a slut as her mother. Only a slut would let a man fondle her the way she'd let Dan touch her.

Her face burned when she thought of his lips against hers. That kiss had not faintly resembled the furtive, embarrassing kisses she had shared with other men. Dan's kiss had thrilled her so much it warmed her entire soul.

Instinctively, she turned her car toward Pauline's house, toward the one true, dependable source of comfort and wisdom in her life. Her nana always knew what to do. Maybe she could even help now.

Pauline stood in the front yard filling a bird feeder when Holly came to a stop in the drive. She turned around with a smile of welcome on her lips, but the smile faded as Holly hurled herself out of the car and into her grandmother's arms. "Oh, Nana, I've done something awful!"

Pauline patted her back. "Darling, I doubt it. Let's go in and talk it over. It can't be that bad."

Inside the kitchen Pauline stripped off her gloves and set about to make tea, her standard remedy for any emergency. She assembled the tray and guided Holly to the fire in the living room. "Now, Holly, tell me what the trouble is."

Holly told her story in fits and starts, refusing at any time to look into her grandmother's eyes. She couldn't. Nana was going to be so disappointed in her. Bitterly, she concluded her sad story. "I can still feel his hand on my butt."

She finally chanced a peek at Pauline. Why did her grandmother looked so relieved? Hadn't she been listening?

"My darling, is this all you did? From your expression I expected something along the lines of murder or grand larceny," Pauline said.

"Nana, you must not be getting the whole picture. Otherwise, you wouldn't make jokes. No decent woman would let a man she hardly knows put his hands on her the way I did. He just recognized the bad blood in me, and it made him think he could treat me any way he wanted to."

Pauline shook her head and snorted as her cup clattered into a delicate pansy-strewn saucer. "That isn't it. You're a beautiful woman, and he's a handsome young man. Of course he wanted to kiss you and touch you. It's perfectly natural for him to want to, and Holly, listen to me, it's perfectly natural for you to like it. If you let every man you meet touch you in that way, you would have a problem, but that isn't the case, is it? You shared a kiss with one particular man, and because of the attraction between you, the kiss became heated. That doesn't make you a bad person."

"I...I want to believe you more than you can imagine, but what if I like Dan's touch too much? What if I start wanting more than a kiss from him?"

Pauline thought for a moment. She set her tea down and took Holly's hands in hers. "Darling, making love is a beautiful thing between a man and a woman. I know you see a lot of things in the movies that aren't too pretty, but I think they pervert the truth. Love is so much more!"

She had caught Holly's interest with no problem. "What do you mean by that?"

"Real love is more than just the physical, darling. It involves the emotional and the spiritual too. When you've gotten to know a man emotionally and connected with him spiritually, then you'll probably want to consummate your relationship in a physical way."

"See?" interrupted Holly. Tears glazed her eyes. "I haven't known Dan for that long, and I still let him touch me."

"Sometimes it only takes a few moments for two souls to connect, darling. It was that way for your grandfather and me. Now, tell me the truth: Have you found yourself suddenly just knowing something about Dan's character without being told?"

Holly thought about her impression of Dan. It was all positive even though the two of them had been at odds almost since they met. "I do get the impression he's honest, hardworking, and decent, and I think he'd do anything for his family."

Pauline released her hands and sat back. "That's the kind of thing I mean. I'm not surprised at all to hear you say it. From what I've seen so far, you and Dan are fighting it, but you are connecting."

Holly bit her lip. "What about Mother?"

"She connected with your father, but I promise you she isn't making connections with those men of hers. That's the difference between you and your mother. You're connecting, and she isn't."

The knot in Holly's stomach eased. Nana had never given her bad advice. Maybe liking Dan's kisses didn't make her a bad person like her mother. *I hope so because I don't seem to have much control over my emotions. I like his kisses whether I want to or not.*

She drew a shaky breath. "Thank you, Nana. What would I do without you?"

"I have no idea," Pauline teased. "I'm always here for you, Holly. You know that. Now tell me. Do you feel better?"

"You know I do."

"Good." Pauline stood and started collecting the tea things. "I'm taking you to lunch at Marie's. This is perfect weather for grilled cheese sandwiches and vegetable soup."

"How do you know the diner has vegetable soup today?"

"It's Tuesday. They have the same thing every week."

Yes, come to think of it they did. It was always crowded on soup and sandwich day because everyone loved Marie's soup. Even in the summer time, soup and sandwich day was popular because Marie had a couple of cold soups on the menu in the summer. "Do we have time for me to stop by the office and check my messages?"

"Sure. They never run out of soup."

Ten

It didn't take long for Holly to check her messages. She and Pauline had just turned off the light in her office when Bonnie White detained them. "Holly, there's somebody asking for you out front."

"Be right there."

The young woman sitting on the sofa stood when she saw Holly coming down the hall. "You boys be quiet," she ordered the two children who wrestled in the floor at her feet. The boys obeyed long enough to give Holly the once over and then continued their scuffling.

Holly ignored the children and turned her attention to the young mother. In spite of the weather, she wore a short, tight black skirt and heels so high she almost teetered. Her blouse, which showed through her unbuttoned jacket, stretched across her breasts and dipped so low that even from across the room, Jim Edmond's eyeballs looked ready to fall out of his head. Her hair color could best be described as brassy blonde, and she had on enough makeup for three people. She didn't look like a good prospect, but Holly had learned not to judge clients by their appearance.

Offering her hand to the woman, she introduced herself. "Hi, I'm Holly Grant. How can I help you?"

The young woman appraised Holly in much the same way as her children had done. "I'm Nikki Lane. Word's out around town that you're dating Dan Wakefield. Is it true?"

Holly bristled. Her private life did not concern this woman, and even if it did, she would never discuss personal matters in front of her agents. "I'm afraid that's personal, Ms. Lane. If you have a question about real estate, I'll be glad to answer it. Otherwise, this conversation is over."

Ms. Lane grinned and looked amused rather than put in her place. "You don't think Dan's mine, and I've come to give you trouble, do you? He's my cousin, not my man."

Holly wildly searched for a reply, but none came to mind. What did the woman expect her to say, anyway? Was the whole town talking about her and Dan? There was no telling what terrible rumors were making the rounds. The knot in her stomach came back.

Pauline stepped in and effortlessly took charge. "Darling! How wonderful to meet Dan's cousin. My name is Pauline Coffey. I'm Holly's grandmother. You must call me Pauline. May I call you Nikki?"

When their visitor nodded, Pauline continued, "Holly and I are having lunch at Marie's. Why don't you and your beautiful children come with us? I'd love to treat you." She winked at Nikki. "We'll talk about Dan."

Ms. Lane twisted her lips to one side before saying, "I don't know. The boys can be pretty rowdy."

"We shall manage, I'm sure."

Pauline skillfully herded everyone toward the door, all the while keeping up a steady stream of conversation that hardly seemed necessary because Holly appeared to be stricken mute while Nikki had her hands full mediating a quarrel that had broken out between the two children.

The quarrel lasted all the way to the restaurant. Why would anyone want to be a mother and go through this exhausting spectacle every day? Nikki finally brought an end to the chaos by separating the children. The hostess seated them, and then Pauline helped Nikki take the coats and caps off the children. "How old are your boys, Nikki?"

"Well, Teddy's five, and Michael's ten months younger."

"It must be hard on you to have two children so close together in age."

"You don't know the half of it!" Nikki declared. She winced as Michael overturned his water glass, causing Teddy to roar his disapproval as the water soaked his legs.

The waitress heard the uproar and came running with a dishtowel. She mopped up the spill and brought another glass of water. "Don't worry," she said. "It happens all the time."

Holly felt sure everyone in the diner appreciated the relative quiet that followed as much as she did.

"Does your husband help you with the boys, Nikki?" Pauline asked with a smile.

"I'm not married. Their father is a no account bum, and I'm better off without him. Dan did get him to pay child support though."

"How did he do that?" Pauline gave a big smile to Teddy who still looked as if he hadn't forgiven Michael for the spilled water.

"You know that lawyer, Tommy Price? Dan trains his horse, and he had a talk with Tommy for me."

"It sounds to me like Dan's a favorite of yours," Pauline guessed. She patted Nikki's hand. "I like him too. He's such a gentleman."

Nikki nodded. "Dan's a good guy. His daddy was pretty bad, and his mama was a fool to put up with what she did, but Dan's okay. When Daddy went to jail in December, Dan saw to it the boys had Christmas."

"What did your father do, darling?"

Nikki's lack of concern over her father's whereabouts during Christmas made Holly wonder if it happened on a regular basis. "Oh, nothing bad," she said. "He got thirty days for being drunk and disorderly in a public place. Dan won't drink, you know. I think he's afraid he might be an alcoholic or something. A beer every now and then would probably relax him, but don't offer him one unless you want him to take your head off. I don't drink myself because of the boys. I want to set a good example for them."

Pauline sagely nodded and passed a pack of crackers to Michael, who'd been struggling to reach them. "Who keeps the boys while you work?"

Michael dropped his crackers, which Nikki caught in mid-air and returned to him. "I don't work. The jobs I could get don't pay enough to cover the baby sitter, but it'll be different after Michael's in school. I'd like to get on at Super Mart. They give you a discount if you work there, and they have really neat clothes. I got my blouse there." She stuck out her chest for them to admire her blouse. "Everybody just loves it."

Pauline gestured expansively. "But how do you make ends meet? It isn't cheap to raise children."

"Oh, I get child support and live with Mama, so it all works out."

"Holly met David Lane this morning when she went to the farm. Is he your father?"

"No, he's my uncle." Nikki turned her attention to Holly. "Was he drunk or sober? He's going to AA, so he's supposed to be sober."

"Sober," Holly whispered.

Nikki pretended to wipe her forehead in relief. "That's good. If he makes it, maybe my dad'll try too. Now, Holly, you haven't said a word, and I came to talk to you about Dan. Are you seeing him or not?"

Holly had a hard time speaking around the tension that had gathered in her chest, but she managed to croak, "We've seen each other a few times."

"Why?" Nikki's head tilted Holly's way. "People are saying you want to buy Turnaround, and that's why you're seeing Dan."

Pauline answered for Holly. "Holly met Dan because of business, but she's seeing him because she likes him."

Holly had imagined this awful conversation couldn't get any worse, but she soon found it could.

"People also say you're sleeping together," Nikki continued. "Did you really spend the night with him at Turnaround? I'm surprised his grandfather would allow it, but Dan is a grown man. I guess Mr. Wakefield can't tell him what to do."

Holly found her voice at last. "What! Who said that?"

"Are you? I said you weren't, because Dan doesn't know a thing about recreational sex. If he'd get laid occasionally, he wouldn't be so uptight all the time, but when I suggested it to him you'd have thought I propositioned him myself. He gave me a lecture that lasted for hours. Dan's so serious if he did sleep with you, he's probably in love. You do look like the kind of woman he'd like. He always notices tall blondes even though he pretends not to."

The bell over the door dinged to announce a new arrival, and since everyone's attention was riveted on Nikki, Teddy saw him first. "Hey, Dan," he shrieked. "We're having lunch with your girlfriend."

All eyes in the room traveled from Dan, who had just entered the diner, to the table where Holly sat. Everyone waited to see what would happen too. In this small town, most people knew each other, so naturally both Dan's father and Holly's mother had provided fodder for gossip for a great many years.

Dan strode over to the table, the frown lines on his face in harsh relief. "Teddy, don't ever yell at people in public. It's rude. Do you understand me?"

"Yeah."

"Don't say 'yeah' to him. Say *yes, sir* to him," Michael said.

Teddy scowled. "Mama doesn't say *yes, sir* to him."

"She's an adult. She doesn't have to."

"That's enough," Dan said. The boys fell silent. "What are you doing here, Nikki?"

Pauline beamed at him. "I invited Nikki and the boys to have lunch with me," she said. "Sit down beside Holly, and join us."

For the first time, Dan's eyes met Holly's. He was asking her permission before he sat down. *I can't embarrass him in front of his cousin.*

She swept her coat and purse from the vacant chair beside her and smiled at Dan. "Join us if you can."

Dan pulled the chair out and sat beside Holly whose hip had started to burn in the place where his hand had rested when they kissed. Besides that, the crowded table had caused another problem. Dan's shoulder pressed against hers, and his thigh touched her leg. No matter how Holly shifted in her chair, she couldn't move away from him. *Might as well ignore it. If I can.*

She stopped straining away from Dan and leaned against him. He twitched when her arm pressed into his. Did he feel as uncomfortable as she did? No, he wasn't blushing and he looked totally relaxed

The waitress returned with a tray laden with bowls of steaming vegetable soup. "I know you didn't order soup, hon," she said as she placed a bowl in front of Dan, "but everybody else is eating it, so you might as well."

"Soup's fine."

As everyone started to eat, the tension at the table lessened. They ate in silence for a moment before Teddy nudged Dan's elbow. "Hey, Dan, can I ask you something?"

"Yes, what is it?"

"Are you sleeping with Holly?"

The furor that broke out reminded Holly of the noise at a high school football game. Nikki's voice rose above the commotion as she tied to justify Teddy's little bombshell first to Dan and then to Holly. The noise made Michael cry, and when Teddy saw his brother crying, he started to roar himself. Without another word, Dan grabbed Teddy by the hand and carried him kicking and screaming to the restroom.

"Is he going to spank Teddy?" quavered Holly. The child was incorrigible, but she didn't want Dan to hurt him.

Nikki shrugged. "I don't know, but I doubt it."

"You don't seem too upset by it."

"No, he's mad at Teddy, but he won't hurt him. Dan's good with the kids. He'd be a great father, Holly, and his kids would probably be real cute."

"I'm su…su…sure he would…they would," Holly stammered.

"Yes, and one day he'll own Turnaround. That'll be a nice thing to hand down to his children, won't it?"

Thankfully, Dan and Teddy returned to cut this awful conversation short. Teddy had stopped crying and had a subdued look on his face, but Holly saw no evidence to indicate he feared Dan. She sighed with relief. Dan had looked pretty mad.

Teddy sat down and turned to Holly. "I'm sorry about what I said. I didn't know it was rude to ask that."

Her ears still felt hot, and her insides felt shaky, but she knew she couldn't refuse a child's apology. "It's okay, Teddy. I know you didn't."

The rest of the lunch went smoothly, even though the temperature in the diner seemed incredibly high for early February. And oddly enough, if Dan moved at all, a thrilling, almost painful sensation would seize her and jab her in the chest.

Teddy picked up his bowl and downed the last of his soup. "Hey, Dan, why'd you take your jacket off? When people open the door it's cold in here. I had to put my coat back on."

"He's warm because he's sitting so close to Holly," Michael answered. "His shoulder and leg are touching hers."

Everyone stared at Dan and Holly. "Can't you do something, Nikki?" Dan begged.

"No," Nikki replied with a huge grin, "and he's right. I guess sitting next to Holly did warm you up."

That seemed to be the signal for lunch to break up. "Dan, would you mind taking Holly back to her office for me?" Pauline asked. "I have to take Nikki and the boys home, and I have errands to run."

"Oh, Nana, don't bother him with that. I can walk back."

"No way. I'll be glad to give you a lift," Dan said, surprising Holly with his quick reply.

As they all put on their coats and got ready to brave the cold, Pauline picked up the check, but Dan held out his hand. "Lunch is on me, Mrs. Coffey."

"Thank you, Dan, and remember; I'm Pauline." She surrendered the check to Dan without any protest, because sometimes a man's pride took precedence over his bank account.

Eleven

Dan wished Holly needed to go anywhere in the world besides her office. The whole town would see him going in there and think they had decided to sell Turnaround. Somehow, though, it didn't sting as much as it would have several days ago. He'd willingly risk any gossip that might arise just for the chance to spend a few extra minutes with Holly. In fact, even though he hated to admit it to himself, it would suit him to spend the entire afternoon with her.

"So, you don't live with your grandmother," he said as he opened the door of his truck for Holly.

Holly gracefully got into the vehicle, distracting Dan who tried not to stare at her legs. "No, I have my own house," she said. "I bought it a year or so ago from Kurt Deveraux and his wife."

"I remember Kurt from high school. He was always crazy about football."

"I guess he still is. He got a coaching job at Tri State Tech, so they bought a bigger house."

Why had he bothered to ask? At one time his own future had looked every bit as bright as Kurt Deveraux's, maybe even brighter. Instead, he'd never gone to college, and he sure didn't have a good job at a university. He'd seen Kurt's name in the paper a couple of times too. The guy was active in several church and civic organizations. He drew a deep breath. Guess he knew who was the failure and who was the success.

He shrugged off his dark thoughts. He had done what he had to do and didn't regret it. If he had borrowed money to go to college, his grandfather would have had to sell the farm; no degree in the world compared to saving Turnaround.

Holly clicked her seat belt and snapped him out of his reverie. "Would you like to see where I live, Dan? It isn't anything like Turnaround, but I do love it. It's the first house I bought with my own money, and everything in it is done just the way I want it."

Warmth flooded Dan. He didn't have to take her back to her office yet. "I'd like to see it. I've been curious about your house ever since your nana bragged on it the night we had dinner with her."

Holly's house was located on Maple Street, a couple of blocks from her nana's house on Cherry Street. The house didn't look very big from the outside, but it was made of brick, which wouldn't have to be painted every time you turned around. They'd priced painting the house at Turnaround, but the estimate had nixed that idea.

A front porch with a white railing extended almost the entire length of the house. Holly had scattered rocking chairs and small, white tables along the porch. A swing hung from the porch's roof at the far end.

"The porch looks nice. I like this neighborhood too," Dan said. "It's convenient to everything."

She nodded. "That's one reason why I chose it. I can walk to the office if I want to. Come on in, and I'll give you a tour. We real estate types are big on house tours."

Dan followed Holly inside and immediately agreed with her assessment of her home; it was nothing like Turnaround. Everything at home looked old and worn out, but this place looked brand new from the paint to the nicely finished hardwood floors and the clean upholstery on the furniture.

"The house has an open, modern feel to it," Holly said, "but all my furniture is very traditional. I don't know if it works together or not, but I like it. I saw the house when the Deverauxs lived here, and they had a more streamlined, modern look."

"It looks great to me," Dan said. The small foyer led into a great room with a soaring ceiling and several big skylights that let in lots of light. An eating bar separated the kitchen from the living room. Holly had used blue and white to decorate the great room. To Dan, it gave the home a crisp, clean look. "It reminds me a little bit of your grandmother's house," he said. "Both places feel warm and welcoming."

"That's a nice compliment."

Holly led him through the house, but before she opened her bedroom door, she paused to make an excuse. "I didn't have time this morning to make up my bed, so you'll have to excuse the mess.

Dan grinned. "I didn't either."

They laughed together over this coincidence. When Holly pushed the door open, Dan saw this room too was very traditional. "I like your sleigh bed," he said.

Holly ran her hand across the headboard. "Lots of my stuff is old, but the bed is new. I got it for myself last Christmas."

"We've got a similar bed in one of the bedrooms at home."

Holly indicated a door on the far wall. "The bathroom is this way."

Dan stepped into the bathroom and looked around. "Nice. You've got plenty of mirrors, and I like the big shower."

"Two closets too." Holly opened one door and pointed to another.

"Are all those clothes yours?" he asked. It looked like she could start a shop with just the contents of her closet.

"Yes, isn't it dreadful?" Her eyes twinkled as she smiled at him. "I know how frivolous it is to have so many clothes, but I do love them."

Come to think of it, Nikki liked clothes too. Guess most women probably did. What a pity Nikki couldn't afford much of anything for herself. Michael and Teddy grew so fast Nikki spent most of her pitiful resources on them. He and Nikki needed to make a shopping trip to Super Mart very soon, but this time Nikki would get a new outfit, not the boys.

Holly shut the closet door and pointed at the bed. "My grandmother made the quilt on the bed, but you can't see it." She crossed the room and flipped the bedcovers so Dan could look at the quilt. "I love the design. It's called an Ohio Star. She did it in blues and golds to match the rest of the house. Isn't it pretty?"

"Yes, very pretty."

Holly turned around, and he saw her breath catch in her throat. She'd picked up on the fact that he didn't mean quilts when he said pretty. It struck him that the closed drapes and the turned down bed projected an air of intimacy Holly might wish to avoid. She cleared her throat and shifted nervously.

"You ran away from me this morning," he said.

Holly stared at the door behind him; her muscles tightened. For a minute, he thought she was going to run away again, but she didn't. "I was too embarrassed to stay after your grandfather saw us together."

"Gramps was sorry he interrupted us."

"It's probably for the best anyway."

He nodded. "Yeah, I know." The air swirled with tension that made his own breath catch in his throat. "I know you may not want to hear it, but I want to kiss you so much I'm having a hard time keeping my hands to myself."

"My hip is still burning where you touched me this morning," Holly muttered.

"What?"

Holly groaned and turned her back to him. "Nothing. Forget it."

A huge smile covered his face. She had liked his kiss and remembered his touch. He had no idea what had come over him, but he ignored the small voice in his head that told him to leave her alone and took a step closer to her. The aroma of her perfume teased his nose with its light, floral scent.

Holly gasped when his hands gently came to rest on her shoulders. Dan swept her hair to one side and brushed the side of her neck with his lips. He turned her around and pulled her close. "Put your arms around me, Holly."

He saw a pulse wildly beating in her throat, but she slid her arms around him.

Dan pulled her head onto his shoulder and stroked her hair, reveling in its silky, blonde beauty. "I love your hair," he whispered.

"We shouldn't be here."

Dan never knew how it happened. One minute the two of them were standing beside the bed; the next they were on the bed stretched out side by side with their arms around each other. Oh, the feel of her...soft and warm and yielding!

When their eyes met, he knew that if they didn't get out of bed immediately, he would make love to her. And he could think of nothing he wanted more.

Maybe Holly saw it too because she seemed to recover her senses. "We shouldn't do this," she gasped. "This is the kind of thing my mother does."

"I know." Dan sat up on the side of the bed and observed, "Your bed smells like you and the perfume you wear."

He stood up and had to extend his arms to keep from falling back onto the bed as Holly flung herself against him. She held him close and pressed her lips against his before jerking away and hurrying from the room.

Dan groaned aloud and trailed behind her Had he totally lost his mind? Holly wanted Turnaround Farm, not an uneducated, poor guy with no prospects. His fists clenched. Turnaround was slowly crumbling to dust due to their neglect, but without money he couldn't do a thing about it. He already worked twenty-five hours a day. What more could he do?

They had finally paid off most of his father's debts, but last year they'd had to put a new roof on the barn, and they owed the vet a fortune. The feed and seed store, too. Besides that, Jeb's truck had finally quit on them, so now they had a truck payment to make. It would take a long time to repay that much debt because they still had to pay for the day-to-day expenses of running the farm and the house.

If only more people would trust them with their horses! That's what they needed to put the farm on a sound financial footing; good horses. However, most people in the area knew of the Wakefield reputation and wouldn't think of letting him work with their horse.

The Wakefield reputation. If Holly got involved with him, her good name would be blackened by association with a Wakefield. Even her business might suffer. Thank goodness she'd come to her senses in time to stop him from doing something stupid. He liked her too much to hurt her.

He followed Holly into the living room. "We'd better go," she said, her tone so bright and cheerful it almost cut him. Since she wouldn't look at him, she probably regretted those kisses and caresses they'd shared.

He obediently picked up his jacket, but Holly made a sound of exasperation and took it from him. "We're not adolescents with raging hormones. We're adults. We can control ourselves. Yes, I know there seems to be some kind of...attraction between us, but we can still act like civilized human beings. Sit down, and I'll make some tea, and we'll talk."

Your hormones may not be raging, but mine sure are. Nevertheless, he sat down on the sofa. "Tea sounds great."

Neither one of them said anything as Holly prepared the tea, but strangely the silence didn't bother Dan, and that surprised him. In general, it was tough to talk to women unless they'd asked him something about horses. The occasional silences that had fallen during his infrequent dates were a source of embarrassment.

This silence felt very different; it almost seemed as if he belonged here. This silence reminded him of the stillness he and his grandfather sometimes shared. It spoke of an easy intimacy between two people.

Holly handed him his tea. "I liked Nikki. She doesn't mind what she says, does she?"

Dan almost cringed when he remembered Teddy's little question. "I'm sorry she showed up the way she did. Nikki doesn't know the meaning of the word tact. I don't know what she said to you, but I apologize anyway."

Holly touched his shoulder as if to reassure him. "Don't you know she's worried about you?"

He laughed. "Why? She knows I can look out for myself."

"Like your uncle, she's afraid I'm using you to get Turnaround Farm."

Dan sighed. He'd have to address this issue after all, and he wasn't looking forward to it because he was scared of what he might find out. "Holly, maybe we should get everything out in the open. My grandfather told me he wouldn't sell the farm without my approval, and if that's the case, Turnaround isn't for sale. If you're seeing me just for that reason, you're wasting your time."

Holly flushed, but she didn't let him throw her. "Things are pretty hard for you, or at least that's the way it looks to other people. Aren't you the least bit interested in knowing how much money my client is offering for Turnaround?"

"What would I do if I did sell?" He threw up his hands. "Have you thought about that? Training horses is all I know how to do. Anyway, if I quit now, it would look like I couldn't cut it in the horse world. Because of my dad, lots of people would never give me the chance to work with their horses, and I hate to fail in front of them. Besides, Turnaround has been in my family for generations. I don't want to lose it."

Holly thought for a moment, giving Dan the impression it hadn't occurred to her to wonder what would happen to him if they sold the farm. Maybe she thought everybody had the ability to do what she'd done and build a business from scratch. "Have you always wanted to train horses, Dan?" she asked.

"No, when I was in high school I planned on being an architect, but after Mother and Dad died, I gave up on the idea because I had to help Gramps. He wanted to keep the farm, and there was no way he could do it without my help."

Holly sat up straight and looked at him as if he'd made a wonderful point for her, which he hadn't. "If you sold the farm, you could go back to school and study architecture. You could still be an architect."

"I wish that were true, but I'm afraid it isn't." He set his cup down and laced his fingers together. "I'm almost thirty years old, and I don't want to sit in a classroom full of eighteen-year-old kids. I don't even know if I'm still capable of learning new stuff."

He hated the look of disappointment on her face, but it didn't change anything. "So, the bottom line is that Turnaround won't ever be for sale. Like I said, if you're seeing me just to get the farm, you're wasting your time."

Holly pushed her hair back. "I don't know what to say. I want to close the deal for Turnaround because I need the money. I need the recognition too. If I do this deal, my business will take off like a rocket."

"I'm sorry, but Turnaround Farm isn't for sale."

She shook her head as if he had taken an unreasonable position, one she couldn't understand. "If that's true, why did your grandfather tell me he'd look at my offer if I went to the horse show with you?"

"He knew I thought you were pretty and that I'd never ask you out myself."

"Because I was trying to buy Turnaround?" she guessed.

"No, because I don't date much," he replied, cursing his painful honesty. "I'm not much of a catch, you know. I'm broke, poorly educated, and my family consists of criminals, alcoholics, and unwed mothers. Not too many women are attracted by poverty and poor white trash."

"Nonsense," Holly retorted, her color high and her eyes snapping. "You're also handsome, kind, loyal, and sensitive. Don't forget about those qualities."

"I'm a paragon of virtue, I guess."

Holly laughed, just as he'd intended. "Well, don't let it go to your head."

"I wouldn't dream of it."

She kicked off her shoes and curled her legs beside her. "Do you still want me to go to the horse show with you?"

Was she even considering it? "I do, but if you don't want to, it's okay. Trust me, I'll understand."

The sun seemed to burst out from behind the clouds when she smiled at him. "No, I want to go. I like riding, and I want to see the show."

He smiled, almost dizzy with relief. "Good. I'd really like that. Who knows? You may want to buy a horse of your own."

"Would you give me lessons if I did?"

"Riding lessons?" Dan smiled as he remembered her initial fear of Lady.

She blinked. "Why, what other kind did you think I might mean?"

"There are all kinds of lessons."

"Hmm. What are you good at besides horseback riding?"

Dan shrugged. "I guess you'll just have to find that out for yourself."

"And how am I supposed to do that?"

In spite of the fact he had nothing to offer Holly, he indulged in a little wishful thinking. After all, unless he was greatly mistaken, she had just flirted with him in a big way. "You'll have to spend more time with me, I guess."

She nodded, which set her beautiful hair in motion and gave him a jab in his mid-section. "That would probably work," she said.

Dan set his mug down on the coffee table. "We've got to go."

"That's awfully sudden." Her eyes clouded. "Aren't you having a good time talking to me?"

"If we don't go now, I'm going to kiss you, and I don't know if you want me to or not."

A wave of color swept across her pretty face. Seconds later she laid her head against his shoulder. He almost lost his breath as he put his arms around her. "My hormones still seem to be raging," he muttered, and he kissed her.

~ * ~

Holly wanted to answer him, to tell him that her hormones too had gotten out of control, but Dan's kiss had literally made her so dizzy she couldn't think, much less speak, and her heart thudded so madly you could probably hear it all the way to Cherry Street.

In fact, the whole world seemed out of kilter somehow; Holly held onto Dan's shoulders and let him take care of her. He leaned back into the couch, and Holly let him pull her on top of him. Breathtaking! Absolutely breathtaking! Her soft curves melted into the hard, male body underneath her, and when Dan buried his hand in her hair and pulled her face down to his, she gasped and started to tremble.

Sanity returned with the ringing of the phone. With a moan of shame, Holly levered herself off of Dan and ran to answer the phone.

"Have you forgotten you have a business to run?" Loretta's sharp greeting could cut the phone line. "What are you doing at home in the middle of the day? You've got people waiting to see you."

"I...got held up, that's all."

"You got held up with Dan Wakefield."

"What are you talking about?" Holly floundered.

"I drove by your house on my way back from lunch, and I saw his truck parked in your driveway. Is he behaving himself?"

"Of course he is," answered Holly. Childishly, she crossed her fingers as the lie left her lips. "We're just talking business. I'll be there in a minute."

She hung up the phone to find that Dan had put his jacket on. "Loretta?" he asked.

"Yes, she keeps pretty close tabs on me."

Dan paused at the door. "I'm sorry about that kiss. I got a little carried away. Did I scare you?"

"I'd really rather not talk about it, if you don't mind." She couldn't because she didn't know what to say. He hadn't scared her in the way he meant, but the way she felt when they were together did scare her.

He jammed his hands into his pockets, and they left the house for the workday world with a discreet distance between them.

~ * ~

No matter how hard he tried, Dan couldn't get the scene in the bedroom out of his mind, and he had no business thinking about stuff like that.

After the horse show, Holly would find out Jeb really wouldn't sell the farm, and she probably wouldn't see him again. Sure, she had said some nice things today, but only because she felt sorry for him. Why was he asking for a broken heart? Did he truly want a whole new set of problems he didn't have any answers for?

Yeah, guess he did. He wasn't good enough for her, but he wanted her with every fiber of his being, and even someone like him had a right to dream.

~ * ~

"I thought I needed to send a search party out for you," Jeb commented as Dan entered the kitchen at Turnaround Farm. "Lucky thing Nikki called to tell me where you were."

"How did Nikki know where I was?"

Jeb turned around and stared at Dan, knocking a potato peel onto the floor. "Didn't she and the boys have lunch with you and Holly?"

"Oh, that."

"What did you think I meant?"

Dan shrugged as if it didn't matter. "I stayed awhile at Holly's house after I took her home. I thought Nikki was talking about that."

"No, she meant lunch," Jeb answered with a big smile.

"What's so funny?"

"Nikki told me you and Holly have the hots for each other real bad. I wonder what she'd say if she knew you were alone with Holly for several hours this afternoon?"

"Don't tell her," Dan pleaded, as he imagined the dreadful scenario coming to pass. "I'll never hear the end of it if you do."

Jeb laughed outright. "She also told me I should talk to you about birth control."

"Good grief!" Heat flooded his face. "Does she think I'm a child who doesn't know about the birds and bees?"

"She said she spoke from experience when she said it's better to have protection and not need it, than to need it and not have it."

Dan forgot his embarrassment and burst into laughter. "I guess she does know. What did you tell her?"

"I told her I'd take care of it." Jeb fell silent for a moment as Dan rummaged around the refrigerator. "Dan?"

"Do we have any apples?"

"No, have a banana. Dan?"

Dan found a stray apple and closed the refrigerator door. "What?"

"Take Nikki's advice. Don't put yourself in a position where you might lose your head and do something you'd regret later."

Dan opened his mouth to deliver a scathing reply, but without warning he remembered lying across Holly's bed with her beside him. The words died in his throat. If Holly hadn't stopped him, he would've made love to her, and he wouldn't have thought about the consequences. He nodded to Jeb. "Yes, sir."

~ * ~

Holly splashed some more water on her face and prayed she never did something so foolish again. Running home at lunch for a quick roll in the hay seemed exactly like the kind of thing her mother would do.

Of course she and Dan had stopped before things went too far, but Loretta's call had probably prevented her from making a huge mistake. Well, she had learned her lesson. She'd never be alone with Dan again.

~ * ~

The bedroom door stood slightly ajar, so Dan could hear what his mama and daddy said.

"Don't, Kyle."

"Why not? You're my wife, and I want you."

"Yeah? Then stop getting high. I'm not sleeping with you when you're like this."

Kyle laughed, but it wasn't a pretty sound. "Little Miss Goody-goody," he mocked.

"Say what you want. I don't care."

Dan heard the sound of the covers on the bed being flung to the side. "There are plenty of women in the world, Millie. If you don't want me, I'll find one who does."

"Kyle, wait. You aren't in any condition to drive," Mama cried.

"Too bad for you. You just lost your chance."

He stormed out of the bedroom and slammed the door behind him, and Dan heard his mother crying. He'd never be like his father! Never!

Dan jerked and wiped his face as his miserable dream woke him. Sometimes the stuff he dreamed had never really happened, but he remembered this time very well. His father didn't go out after all. He had gone downstairs and fallen asleep in front of the fire. The next morning his grandfather's anger had boiled over, and he had thrown a pitcher of cold water over his dad's head. Gramps knew all too well why Kyle had slept downstairs. His dad had been furious, but so had his grandfather. He vividly remembered the cutting, bitter exchange that had followed.

Shame seared Dan when he remembered his afternoon with Holly. He had no right to a woman like her. She didn't carry tainted blood the way he did. Why did he want to mess up her life?

Buck up, Wakefield, and do right by her. Holly didn't understand about his family. For her own protection, he shouldn't see her again.

He turned over and tried to sleep, but every time he closed his eyes, he saw Holly lying beside him on the bed, her perfume filling his head with its fragrance. Finally, he got up and went downstairs. Maybe he could read himself to sleep again.

Twelve

"Hey, Holly," called Loretta, who stood by the large plate-glass window in the front of the office. "Your boyfriend is coming this way."

"Dan isn't my boyfriend," Holly protested, as she gratefully shut down her computer. She'd had one long, tiring day and wanted to go home.

"Then how did you know who I was talking about? I never called any names." Several other agents glanced at each other and hid their smiles. Holly had sure walked into that one.

Holly moved to the window to stand beside Loretta and watched as Dan gracefully made his way across the street, his steps light, quick, and sure. "He's got real broad shoulders, doesn't he?" Loretta observed.

"Yes, he does. I noticed those shoulders the first time I saw him."

"He's got a nice butt too," Loretta leered, "and you can see his thigh muscles through his jeans."

From across the room, Jim Edmonds joined in. "Loretta, you're supposed to be engaged. Why are you ogling Holly's boyfriend?"

"I'm not," Loretta explained She stuck her nose into the air. "I'm just trying to call Holly's attention to his assets."

Gales of laughter swept across the room, laughter that broke out with renewed vigor when Dan opened the office door. "What's so funny?" he asked, his eyes darting from one person to another.

Holly smiled and moved across the room to join Dan. She didn't want him to suspect they'd been talking about him. "Loretta is," she answered. "Dan, do you know Jim Edmonds and Bonnie White?"

"No, I don't think so."

Holly made introductions and then turned to Dan. "Come on back to my office." As Dan followed her, Bonnie whispered to Loretta, "He does have a nice butt."

Holly wondered if she should close the door or not. She had promised herself not to be alone with him, but no matter what he'd come to say, it was private, so she shut the door. "Have a seat," she invited, indicating that he should take one of the chairs in front of her desk. "Can I get you some coffee or a soft drink?"

"Nothing, thanks."

Holly seated herself beside him. She supposed it would be more professional to sit behind her desk; he was a client after all, but darn it, she didn't want to think about business today. She'd rather think about...not business. "Thank you for lunch yesterday. I enjoyed it very much."

Dan smiled, a sweet little grin that stirred up the butterflies in her stomach. "So did I. I know it's late to ask, but I was so darn busy today I didn't think I'd get finished in time to...well, anyway, I was wondering if you'd like to ride to Chamberlain with me. I've got to pick up a saddle, and afterwards we could get some dinner."

"I'd love to go," Holly answered. It was imperative to spend time with such an important client.

They smiled at each other and stood up. "I'll get my coat," Holly said. She reached for the coat that hung on a peg behind her desk.

"Let me help you with that."

Holly passed her coat to him and broke out in goose bumps when his fingers brushed her shoulder. Honestly! Dan Wakefield had entirely too much of an effect on her. Seeing him as a client got harder every day. In fact, if she told the truth, she'd have to admit she already thought of him as more than just a client. Naturally, she refused to let anything come from this attraction, but still...

She didn't want to evaluate her relationship with Dan, so she resolutely pushed it from her mind. *I can think about it later.* Yes, that made sense. Once she didn't have so much to do, maybe after the horse show. That would be a better time.

Loretta still sat behind her desk when Holly and Dan went up front. Bet anything she had stayed behind on purpose just to be nosy and get the lowdown on what Dan wanted. "Are you two going out tonight?" she asked, as she switched off her desk lamp.

"Loretta!" Holly growled.

Dan answered for them both. "Yes, we're going out."

Loretta stood up and put on her jacket. "I hope you have a good time. Where are you going?"

"Loretta!" Holly cried. Would the woman ever shut up?

"I might need to reach you," Loretta declared, in an injured tone. "Anything could happen."

The corners of Dan's lips twitched. "We're going to Chamberlain," he said.

"What's in Chamberlain that isn't in Fairfield?"

"Loretta, that's enough. Mind your own business," Holly said.

Dan satisfied Loretta's curiosity. "A saddle shop," he answered with a grin. "I've got to pick up a saddle."

Loretta received this news with a frown. "I hope you aren't going to keep Holly out too late. She's got a business to run, you know."

Holly couldn't help laughing. She'd never imagined Loretta in the role of disapproving parent, but that's what she was seeing. The woman didn't have a subtle bone in her body. "Bye, Loretta. See you tomorrow," she said. She tossed Loretta a grin and took Dan's hand as they walked out the door to his car. Let her wonder about that tonight.

~ * ~

The ride to Chamberlain usually took about an hour, but today it seemed shorter to Holly because she had Dan to talk to. She'd never have dreamed he was such good company or that he had such a nice sense of humor. His dry, self-deprecating wit kept her amused during the entire drive.

They stopped by the tack shop before they went to dinner. "I still wish the saddles had horns on them," Holly muttered as they left the shop.

Dan laughed, a carefree, happy sound that gave her a warm feeling deep inside. "Is the saddle new?" she asked, running a hand across the shining surface.

"No, it needed a repair, and they do a good job here."

"It looks awfully good to be an old saddle. You must take pretty good care of it."

"I try to."

She stood aside so he could close the truck's tailgate. "Where did you get it?"

Dan's face assumed a pensive, half-embarrassed expression. "The saddle belonged to my father. I guess you think it's stupid of me to use it at all. I know he wasn't worth two cents, but he was my father."

Indignation suffused her. She had no reason to feel so protective of Dan, but she couldn't help it. "He was your father. There's nothing wrong with using his saddle. He may have done some bad things, but you're his son. You still love him, and that's okay."

"He was never mean," Dan explained. "He just never had any time for me. Most of his time was spent cooking up schemes, and at the end, he was high day and night."

"What about your mother?"

The corners of Dan's mouth turned down in a grimace. "She had her hands full with Dad. She pretty much let my grandfather raise me."

Holly's heart swelled with compassion for the boy Dan had been. This time when she reached for his hand, it had nothing to do with teasing Loretta. "Your grandfather did a good job. I'm sure your parents would be proud of how their son turned out."

Shame filled Dan's face, but he didn't have to feel embarrassed in front of her. She understood. It made him feel a connection to his father when he used that saddle, and she didn't blame him.

"I'd like to think both of them would be proud of me," he said as he opened the truck's door for her, "but I haven't done much with my life. They might think I'm just a big loser."

Holly laughed. "You're hardly a loser. I can think of a lot of things you are, but a loser? No, never that."

"Want me to cry you a handful?" he mocked. "Let's get out of here."

Men. So afraid of showing emotion. He had mocked his feelings, so she wouldn't think he felt sorry for himself. Oh, let him keep his pride if it made him feel better. "How did your parents meet?" she asked. "High school?"

Dan nodded. "Yes, they met when they were in high school. Dad was a year older than my mother, and to be honest, he came from a much better family than she did. Uncle David said my grandmother Wakefield threw a fit when Dad told her he was inviting Millie Lane to go with him to the prom."

"Has your grandmother been dead long?"

"Since I was sixteen."

Holly brushed her hair away from her face and wished she'd put on some fresh lipstick before she left the office. She might look pale and tired! "I just wondered. Go on."

Dan paused his commentary to make a turn onto a one-way street. "Well, Dad never was one to let the opinions of other people sway him from doing what he wanted, so he invited my mother to go with him to his prom. Mother told me it was a real big deal for her. My grandmother Lane bought her a pretty dress at a consignment shop, and her aunt who was a beautician came to her house and did her hair. I've seen the picture they had made at the prom, and she did look nice. No wonder Dad wanted to go out with her."

She'd never seen a picture of his parents, but Dan probably looked like his father. He wasn't short and dark like his Uncle David.

Dan stopped at a red light where she got a good look at his face. Uh oh. Judging by his dark expression, the next part must be bad.

"Dad picked her up, and they had a good time at the prom, but he had a bottle hidden in his car, and he got her drunk.

"I'm surprised he was honorable enough not to take advantage of her, but he didn't. He took her home, and the Lanes fell in love with him because of his noble nature."

"Wasn't he drunk himself?" Holly asked.

"By the time Dad was eighteen, he'd been drinking for two years. Anyway, in the Lane family, hard drinking was acceptable. They didn't think the less of him for it."

Holly's family had had their problems, but drinking had never been one of them. How horrible that must have been for Dan. "How long did they go out with each before they got married?"

"Almost two years. Dad graduated from high school by the skin of his teeth, and Gramps sent him to Tri State Tech. He almost flunked out his freshman year, but he managed to hang on, so Gramps gave him another year. The second year is when he started doing drugs."

He stopped at an intersection and turned to look at her. "You sure you want to hear this? It isn't pretty."

She reached for his hand and squeezed it. "If it's too hard, you don't have to say anything else."

Dan stared at her hand on his with a look of pleasure that both scared and thrilled her. *I'm getting in deep water here, but I can't seem to stop myself.*

His grip on her hand tightened. "You need to know who I am, Holly. You think you do, but you don't, so I need to finish the story. Dad smoked too much weed to do any studying, so at the end of the first semester, the school told him not to come back. Dad didn't care because he didn't like school. He went to work with Gramps full time, and even though Gramps didn't know it until later, he started selling drugs on the side.

"He married my mother the following May. The Lanes were glad of it. They thought my mother had moved up in the world, but Gramps and Grandma were really upset. They knew the Lane reputation as well as anyone, but when Mother got pregnant with me, they started being awfully nice to her."

"I bet they were crazy about you," Holly surmised, imagining how cute he'd probably looked as a baby with his blue eyes and blond hair.

Dan smiled as if this part of the story pleased him. "Oh, yeah, they were. My dad was their only child, and they loved children. They took to me like a duck to water."

"How come your grandparents didn't have a house full of kids?"

Dan shrugged. "Something went wrong when Dad was born, and Grandma couldn't have any more babies."

"Did you and your parents live at Turnaround with your grandparents?"

"Yes, we did." Dan laughed now. "Dad and Gramps had me on a horse almost by the time I could walk."

Holly shivered. "I can't imagine a child on a horse. Wasn't your mother scared you'd get hurt?"

"Probably, but Dad did whatever he wanted to. It didn't matter what she thought."

Until her father died, her childhood had seemed magical. She couldn't imagine a home like Dan described. "Were you happy as a boy?"

Dan thought for a moment. "I'm not sure what to say. I've never thought of my childhood in terms of happiness or unhappiness. It was what it was, but naturally it wasn't all bad. There were a lot of good times among the bad, so I guess I'd say it was up and down."

He made a right turn into the older, renovated part of Chamberlain where a lot of popular restaurants and boutiques had located. "I've never wanted to talk to anybody about my family. I always figured everyone in town knew the story, and I was too ashamed to talk about it, but I wish I had." He gave Holly a warm smile. "Talking to you makes me feel better."

Holly's heart jumped. "You can tell me anything, Dan."

The pleasure in his eyes humbled her. Had her opinion ever meant so much to anyone before?

"I imagine Dad would still be alive if he hadn't met Cam Simmons," Dan said. "Cam turned him on to hard drugs, and Dad was never the same after that. He dealt for Cam and got caught using drugs on the horses he trained. He was gambling and throwing classes at the horse shows too. Of course he finally got caught. In fact, he was out on bail when he died."

Should she stop him or let him continue? Well, he did say he that talking to her made him feel better. "What happened on the day they died?" she asked.

A faraway look came to rest on Dan's face. Holly knew he wasn't seeing her then. He was seeing another time, another place, and she didn't think he liked it very much.

"Dad had promised to take me and Mother to Tri State Tech to get me registered, but he got up in a bad mood. Hung over, I guess. Anyway, he and Mother had a huge fight. It was so bad Gramps got involved, and he never tried to interfere in their marriage. I remember he told Dad what a disgrace he was and how much he'd disappointed everyone. That made Dad even angrier. He jumped up from the table and screamed that he'd had enough of this sanctimonious bullshit.

"Gramps jumped up too. For a minute I thought they might fight, but they didn't. Dad picked up his coffee cup and hurled it into the fireplace. It broke and scattered coffee all over the hearth. He told my mother to get dressed, that they'd spent their last night under Gramps's roof."

Even though she'd never say so, this violent scene horrified Holly. How could people live that way?

"Mother didn't want to go anywhere with him," Dan continued, "but he grabbed her arm, so she got up and ran to get her clothes on. I'll never forget what Gramps said to my dad. He looked him straight in the eye and said, "Dan isn't going anywhere with you, Kyle. You'll get him into that car over my dead body."

Holly bit her lip as her arms broke out in goose bumps. He was so caught up in his story that he didn't seem to notice her distress.

"Dad couldn't believe what he'd heard, but Gramps meant it. I started to get up. I don't know what I intended to do, but Gramps grabbed my arm and squeezed so hard I had bruises in the shape of fingerprints for a week. 'Sit down, Dan,' he said. 'You aren't going anywhere.'

"By this time Mother was back, so Dad stormed out of the house with her right behind him. Two hours later we got a call that they were dead."

Holly broke the brief silence that had fallen inside the car. "Why did your dad try to run away from the police? Isn't that why he had the wreck?"

Dan nodded. "Yeah, it was. He tried to run because he had coke in the car. He was already out on bail waiting for trial. If the police had found drugs in his car, they would've put him in jail and thrown away the key, and he knew it. I guess he thought he could outrun them."

"I'm so sorry, Dan." Holly wished she had the words to heal what still had to be a gaping, raw wound, but she didn't. What could anyone say to take the sting out of this awful memory?

Dan managed a wintery smile, although she wondered how he could. "Yeah, well, it was all over and done with a long time ago. What do you say we end this trip down memory lane? Where would you like to eat? I'm hungry."

They eventually decided on a small, family owned, Italian restaurant that Holly insisted had the best food in the state. Since it was the middle of the week, the restaurant wasn't too crowded. Even though they took their time at dinner, they rolled back into Fairfield relatively early.

Should she invite him to come in or not? Even though they'd talked about a lot of things at dinner, it was hard to forget the horrible story he'd told her. How could a man not be affected forever by such an awful event?

No! The things that happened in his family had nothing to do with Dan. He was good through and through. She wasn't her mother, and he wasn't his father.

"If you have time, why don't you come in for a while?" she invited, as Dan escorted her to the door. "I'll make some coffee, and I have a cheesecake in the freezer. We'll have dessert and watch a movie or something."

"Are you sure it's no trouble?"

"No," answered Holly. "It's no trouble."

They removed their coats, and Dan followed her into the kitchen where she started the coffeemaker. "Oh, shoot, I forgot. You like tea better," she exclaimed.

"It doesn't matter. I can drink coffee."

"Of course it matters. Don't tell Nana I served a guest tea made from a tea bag, though. She'd die."

"Not a word," Dan promised. "Cross my heart."

Holly took the cheesecake from the freezer and tried to cut it, but she couldn't. "Let me try," Dan said.

When Holly relinquished the knife to him, Dan easily sliced the cheesecake. "Muscle does come in handy," Holly admitted with a laugh. She passed Dan a slice of the cheesecake and slid his tea across the cabinet. "Now that it's cut, the cheesecake will thaw in no time. Why don't we sit in front of the fire while we eat? It's a lot cozier that way."

They settled companionably together on the sofa. Holly used a remote to turn on her gas logs, which made Dan smile. "What's so funny, Wakefield?"

"I was just thinking how easy that was. At home I'd have to go outside, chop some wood, and bring it into the house. Then I'd have to get the fire going."

Holly wanted to take the opportunity to remind him that if he sold Turnaround, he could buy a newer, more modern home, but she refused to make him uncomfortable. Instead, she asked, "What will we be doing at the horse show?"

"Friday night there's a dinner for owners, trainers, and their dates, and Saturday night there's a party. It'll be formal on Saturday, but casual on Friday."

"I bet you always have a good time," she enthused. "I love parties."

"I don't usually go to parties or dinners."

"Well, I'm sure we'll have fun," she said.

Dan laughed at her. "Maybe."

Hmm. There were those cute crinkles in the corners of his eyes.

"I can just see you working a room," he said. "I don't like parties, but if you go with me, I bet things will be totally different." He reached for a small photo on the table beside the sofa. "Who are the people in the picture?"

"My parents."

"I told you about my father. Tell me about your mother."

Now she wished she hadn't asked him to come in. "Are you sure you want to hear something so sordid? My mother's a piece of work."

Dan grimaced "Yeah? It couldn't be any worse than what I told you."

"Let me get you some more tea first." Holly ran to the kitchen and brought him a new tea bag and a full cup of hot water. She curled up on the sofa beside him and started her story.

"My father's name was Charles Grant. He didn't grow up in Fairfield like Mother did. His dad, my grandfather, was transferred to Fairfield when my dad was eighteen. He and my mother had a lot of classes together at the high school. I've seen their pictures, and I think they were good looking people.

"Anyway, they fell head over heels in love with each other. Both of their parents wanted them to go to college, but they wouldn't hear of it. They wanted to get married. When their parents continued to oppose them, they eloped."

Holly sighed, remembering the happiness on her mother's face in those long-ago days. "Mother said it was the most romantic thing she'd ever done. She sneaked out of the house in the middle of the night, and so did Daddy. They drove to Chamberlain, and an acquaintance of Daddy's who was a justice of the peace married them. They spent the night in Chamberlain, and the next day they went home and confessed what they'd done."

"Did their parents throw a fit?" Dan asked.

Holly shook her head. "Strangely, no. The damage was done, so they accepted it and offered to send them to college anyway. Daddy did go, but Mother wanted to be a full time homemaker, and that's what she did."

"That's not a popular option these days," Dan said.

Holly shrugged. "I guess not. Anyway, Daddy graduated from Tech in electrical engineering and earned a good living for us." She paused for a sip of coffee. "My early childhood was so perfect it seemed almost magical. I don't ever remember a cross word being spoken, and my mother made even the most ordinary occasion seem festive and wonderful."

"How so?" Dan asked.

No wonder he was curious. After a childhood like he'd had, who wouldn't be? Bet his mother never went out of her way to do anything special for him. "When I was six, she gave me a birthday party that my friends talked about for years. She baked and decorated a tremendous cake in the shape of a castle. I remember it was almost as tall as I was and had pink flags flying from the top tower. She made me a pink princess costume to wear and even had outfits for the other little girls to wear."

Dan laughed. "I can just imagine it. Were there any little princes at the party?"

"Yes, a few. They didn't have costumes, but they had plastic swords and shields, so they were happy."

"No pony?" Dan teased. "What's a party without a pony?"

Holly rolled her eyes at him. "You're not the only person who keeps horses, Dan. We had a pony too. Mother hired a man who gave us turns riding on it, and while we ate our cake, some clowns entertained us."

"Wow, that's some party."

"Yes, it was. It may be silly, but I really did feel like a princess in a fairy tale. I remember thinking I was the luckiest little girl in the world to live with my mother and daddy."

The memory of the party faded, and Holly's heart filled with a familiar sadness. "I was nine when Daddy got a cough that wouldn't go away. Mother kept at him until he finally went to the doctor, but the doctor told him it was too late. He had inoperable lung cancer.

"They gave him six months, and he lived almost six months to the day." Her eyes dropped. "That's when my mother went crazy. If she hadn't been tranquilized, she'd never have made it through the funeral. Afterwards, everybody told us she was grieving and that she'd soon be her old self." Holly laughed, a bitter sound that expressed all of her frustration and anger with her mother. "They were wrong. She never got over it.

"She started dating almost immediately. Most of her dates weren't too nice because she wasn't fussy. Nana tried to reason with her, but it didn't do any good. It was like something inside of her was broken. Truly, she didn't seem to know what she was doing."

Dan awkwardly patted her shoulder. "She probably didn't."

"At first I didn't blame her, but as time went on and she started running off with all those losers, I got angry. Her voice hardened. "I'm still angry. She betrayed my father's memory and deserted me emotionally. I don't feel sorry for her anymore. If I feel sorry for anyone, it's Nana or the little girl I used to be."

She blessed Dan as he squeezed her hand in mute sympathy. He understood.

By mutual agreement, they changed the subject and carried their dessert dishes to the kitchen. "Let's find that movie," Holly suggested. If it killed her, she wouldn't think about her mother tonight. She and Dan had had a nice time, so it would be a shame to let her mother ruin it.

They picked a movie from Holly's DVD shelf and sat down to watch it, but she couldn't concentrate on the screen with Dan sitting so close to her. She could feel the heat radiating from his body, and it made her so tense she couldn't even breathe normally.

"Is it hot in here to you?" she asked. "I'm burning up." Waves of heat swept her from head to toe, but twenty-eight might be a little young for hot flashes.

Dan laughed. "Yeah, it's awfully hot. Would you mind if I took this sweater off? I've got on a shirt underneath."

"Go ahead," Holly replied. No power on earth could have made her stop watching as Dan pulled the sweater over his head. The man had a great body.

As the sweater cleared his face, Holly's breath caught in her throat. "D...Dan," she stammered.

His eyes dark with longing, Dan gently touched the side of her face. "I don't have any right to touch you," he muttered, "but you're so beautiful I can't help myself."

Holly groaned aloud, and Dan slid across the sofa and took her in his arms. The unique scent that belonged to Dan alone reached her nose. With a little sigh, she relaxed against him. "Dan Wakefield, you even smell good."

Dan nuzzled her neck. His warm breath dusted her skin as his lips brushed her throat. "It excites me to smell you," he whispered into Holly's ear. "You smell like a woman."

Holly shivered and tightened her arms around him. She never wanted to let him go. She liked the feel of all those hard muscles in her arms. Boldly, she caressed his shoulders. "I like that," Dan muttered. "It feels good when you touch me."

He closed his eyes and kissed her again, leaving Holly sure she had died and gone to heaven. She probably liked kissing Dan too much, but when his lips touched hers, she just melted. Yes, that was a good way to describe it. She was melting because of Dan Wakefield.

She made no protest as Dan's weight pushed her back into the soft cushions of the sofa. When his body partially covered hers, she held him close and placed frantic kisses on the side of his face and the top of his wonderful shoulder. Who knew it would feel so good to hold him? He moved with a slight aggressiveness that thrilled Holly all the way to her toes. She shifted on the sofa, allowing one of his knees to slip between hers.

"Holly? How far do you want this to go?" Dan's voice sounded ragged, his breathing shallow and fast.

His words cut through Holly like a knife. In an instant she realized that her skirt, which fell almost to her ankles, was pushed up around her thighs, and she lay flat on her back with a man on top of her. She was no better than her mother!

She covered her eyes with her hands, and her voice shook. "Please get up, Dan. I'm sorry, but please get up."

Dan immediately scrambled off of her and extended his hand. His face had turned neon red. "Are you okay?" he asked. "I shouldn't have done that. I'm sorry."

Holly wouldn't look at him because she didn't want him to see her cry. Dan wanted her, but her feelings came first with him. How could a man whom she'd only recently met be so attuned to her needs?

By turning her head away from Dan and biting down hard on her lip, Holly kept the tears from falling. "It's okay, Dan. I'm embarrassed about what...the kiss, but it's my fault. It won't happen again, so don't worry about it."

"No, it isn't okay," Dan declared. "I shouldn't..."

He turned Holly around to face him and uttered a mild oath. "I guess I was right all along."

"What are you talking about?" Was he angry that she'd stopped him before they made a major mistake?

"You *are* only seeing me because you want Turnaround," Dan growled. "You look sick to your stomach at the thought of almost making love to me, and you know what? I could just kick myself for letting you get under my skin. Yeah, Holly, do you want to hear me say it? Okay, here goes: yes, I do want you. I think about you all the time, and some of my thoughts aren't too platonic. Here's the kicker, though. I like you. You can want a woman and not like her, but I like you, and it makes you sick to think of the two of us together."

Dan spoke quietly enough, but his eyes looked dull, and his face held no hint of animation. She knew how he felt about his family; he probably thought she had rejected him because of them. "I like you too, Dan," she cried. "Don't you know that? Do you think I let every man I meet touch and kiss me? You're the only one in so long I can't remember when, if ever."

Dan searched her face. Something he saw there must have calmed him because some of the angry unhappiness faded from his eyes. "Then why did you have that expression on your face?"

"Because I hate myself when I lose control!" Holly exclaimed, her voice loud and strident. "Don't you get it yet? My mother's a whore, and I don't want to be like her!"

"Holly! Don't say things like that about your mother."

"Why not? You said your father wasn't worth two cents."

It looked as if he were trying to find some argument to defend his father, but he shrugged and gave up. "He wasn't."

"Then why shouldn't I tell the truth about my mother?"

Dan's cautious expression hurt her. He didn't know what to say. Dang it, why didn't she keep her mouth shut? He stretched his arm toward her, but she jerked away with a resounding, "No!"

"I wasn't going to start anything with you," he said. "I only thought you could use a little comfort."

"You still don't really get it, do you?" Holly marveled. "I can't let you touch me because I'll want more, and if I sleep with you, I'm no better than my mother!"

"What if we were married?" The words tore themselves from Dan's throat, shocking Holly to her core. Ha! He had shocked himself too. His mouth was hanging open, and his face had tensed to the point where it looked painful.

"I'm not marrying anybody," she gasped, "and you'd better watch what you say, or somebody will think you're proposing."

This discussion had gotten out of hand. Emotions ran high as old hurts and hangups put in an appearance.

"Before you say something you'll regret, you'd better go," Holly continued, her voice slightly firmer.

Looking almost panicked, Dan immediately leaped up to make his getaway, but he paused at the door. "Did I mess everything up? Will you see me again?"

Had she heard him correctly? She hadn't expected him to come back. He wanted her, and she had just told him he couldn't have her. Why would he come back? "I...don't...yes, I guess so," she answered. "You can...call me."

~ * ~

Holly dreamed of her mother that night.

"Mama, don't leave me tonight. It's Christmas Eve."

"Holly, you're a big girl now. You can stay with Nana until I get home. You know how much I've been looking forward to this party."

"You'd rather be with him than with me!"

"Don't be silly, Holly. Now, get your things. I'm taking you to Nana's house before Frank gets here."

Holly awoke with tears oozing from her eyes. She'd never forget the first time her mother took off with a strange man. They'd been frantic with worry, and of course neither she nor Nana could enjoy their Christmas. Rita had turned up two weeks later with a black eye and a couple of belated Christmas presents that nobody wanted.

Never, Holly silently vowed. *I'll never be like my mother. I'd rather die first.*

Thirteen

Dan thought about Holly all the way back to Turnaround. Nothing seemed clear anymore. Was she really using him just to get her hands on Turnaround? He hit the steering wheel with the palm of his hand. Hope really did spring eternal because deep down he had begun to believe she wanted him as much as he wanted her, but now he didn't know. She had explained the look of disgust and revulsion on her face, but if she wanted Turnaround bad enough, she'd lie if necessary.

He parked his car in the driveway and went inside. A fire still burned in the fireplace and warmed the room, so he threw himself down into one of the chairs beside the hearth. Thank goodness Gramps had already gone to bed. He didn't feel like seeing anyone because the more he thought about his near proposal, the sicker he felt.

What if Holly did want him? He craved her trust, acceptance, and...yes, he craved her love, but if he loved her, how could he plan to hurt her? If she married him, the town would paint her with the same brush it used on him, and it would ruin her reputation.

It would also ruin her chance to have a family. He couldn't risk having children who might turn out like his father. For Holly's sake, he should walk away and let her get on with her life, but how could a man turn his back on a woman like her?

Of course it might not be his choice to make. Holly might not feel the same way he did. When she realized they wouldn't sell Turnaround, she might walk out of his life in no time flat.

When the stairs creaked, he knew his privacy had come to an end. The sound of his car in the driveway must have wakened Jeb. He sighed as his grandfather padded into the keeping room to make sure he had gotten safely home.

Jeb took one look at him and blanched. "Right now you remind me of Kyle. Many a night he came home high or drunk and looking like the weight of the world sat on his shoulders. Maybe it's your posture. Yeah, that's it. Kyle used to throw his leg over the arm of the chair just like you've done."

Shame swept across Gramp's face. "I'm sorry, Dan. It was just that you looked so much like him for a minute...You look sick. Did you eat something that disagreed with you?"

Dan shook his head. "No, sir."

"Then what's wrong? Do you need something to settle your stomach?"

Dan attempted a smile even though he figured it came across more like a grimace. "It...isn't that kind of sick. It's just nerves. It's nothing really. Go back to bed. You need your beauty sleep."

Jeb took the chair beside him instead. "When you were a little boy, you'd get a sick stomach if you were worried about something. It's been a long time since that happened, so whatever upset you must be a doozy."

"Yeah."

"Come on, out with it. It might make you feel better." Jeb sat back and waited.

Dan's hands fisted as shame, guilt, and love fought for dominance. "I think I'm falling in love."

Jeb smiled and squeezed his knee. "Why does that upset you so much? You're old enough to fall in love, and it's time for you to think of marriage and a family of your own."

"I...I don't know if Holly feels the same way about me." He shrugged. "She probably doesn't."

Jeb laughed. "So talking about getting married made you think of Holly, did it? Why do you doubt that she returns your feelings? You've been spending a lot of time together."

"I asked Holly to ride to Chamberlain with me, and when I took her home, she invited me in for cake and coffee." He dropped his eyes. "We...we kissed, and we...both liked it, but Holly got real upset. I really don't think she feels the same way about me."

Dan rose and paced restlessly around the living room. "I think maybe she's only pretending to like me, so she can get the farm."

"Do you have any basis for that feeling?" Jeb asked. Laughter had been wiped from his face as if it had never been there at all.

Dan shrugged. "Just an expression on her face tonight."

"Did you talk to her about it?"

Dan threw himself back into his chair. "Yes, she explained it, but I still don't know."

Jeb laughed aloud. "Son, she's a woman, and there's no more complicated and hard to understand creature in the entire world. Beside a woman, a man is an open book. I don't understand 'em. No man does. My best advice is to keep going out with her and see what happens. After the horse show, you'll know for sure one way or the other. That's when she'll find out we won't sell the farm. If she keeps on seeing you, it'll be because she wants you, not Turnaround."

"I guess I can stand it for another week," Dan muttered. "It isn't like I have a choice about it."

"Good. Now let's go to bed. I'm an old man, and I do need my beauty sleep."

With a shared laugh and a slap on the back, they climbed the stairs to their frigid rooms.

~ * ~

Jeb turned over and burrowed even deeper into the quilts covering his bed. He was going to feel like a zombie tomorrow if he didn't go to sleep soon, but how could he sleep after seeing Dan in that chair? He had looked so much like Kyle. His thoughts turned to the first time Kyle came home drunk.

"Hey, Dad," Kyle said. He staggered over to the new armchair by the fire and fell into it. "Why are you still up?"

"I was worried about you. It's past your curfew."

Kyle giggled and tossed his leg over the arm of the chair. "Ish it?"

"You're drunk, son. Did you drive home in this condition?"

"Well, I didn't fly."

"Go to bed. We'll talk about this in the morning."

Kyle had been as sick as a dog the next morning and promised he'd never drink again. *And I believed him. I should have done something, but what? I couldn't follow him around twenty-four hours a day.*

With a sigh, he turned over again. He'd gone over this ground a million times before. Kyle's life was long over and done with, and all that remained was to seek Dan's happiness. Dan was the strong, good part of Kyle, and Jeb loved him as much as if he had been his own son. He prayed from the bottom of his heart that Holly Grant would fall in love with Dan. If Dan found happiness, maybe he could finally be free of the guilt he felt over Kyle's tempestuous life and untimely death.

~ * ~

"What if we were married?"

Holly made a sound of disgust and threw the Sullivan file down on her desk. Lord, but her head hurt. She drew her coffee cup forward and rubbed her eyes. She'd had precious little sleep after Dan left and was feeling the effects of her restless night.

"What if we were married?"

I can't stand any more of this. Why can't I get what he said out of my head? It's not like he meant it, and I don't want to marry anyone, so what's the problem?

"What if we were married?"

Well, what if we were married? Giving free rein to her imagination, she allowed her thoughts to wander where they would. She saw herself opening the door at Turnaround Farm where Dan waited in the kitchen to kiss her and ask about her day.

The scene changed as she imagined the two of them riding their horses up the hill. This time when they looked into forever, she saw they were together, living lives filled with love.

Holly's eyes widened. "No, oh no! It can't be! I can't have fallen in love with Dan Wakefield!"

Great day in the morning! She'd spoken out loud. Holly cringed, but thankfully she had shut the office door. *I'd die if anyone in the office heard me talking to myself about Dan.*

Frantically, she searched for a different explanation, but nothing she could think of would hold up under close scrutiny.

She blinked away tears. *No. No, it isn't true. It's just a physical attraction, that's all. I'm more like Mother than I thought, but there's no need to get so upset about all of this. I just won't see Dan anymore.*

If he called, she'd tell him she didn't think they should mix business with pleasure. He'd have to understand what she meant because her nerves couldn't take much more. She didn't want to get married; if Dan did, he should find some woman who'd appreciate all he had to offer.

Taking a deep breath, she picked up the Sullivan file for the sixth time that morning. Mind over matter, that's all it took.

~ * ~

Loretta tapped on Holly's door as the clock struck twelve. "Come and go with me to get some lunch," she said.

Holly nodded. "I think I will." Lunch with Loretta would certainly distract her. Loretta knew everything that happened in Fairfield and enjoyed sharing all the gossip with her friends. Holly had no idea how she found out so much, but listening to Loretta talk would keep her mind off a certain someone.

She put on her coat, but as she retrieved her purse from the file cabinet, the phone rang. "I'd better get it, Loretta. Just give me a minute."

She picked up the phone. "Grant Realty."

"Hi, Holly. You said I could call you."

Holly's heart raced as her hard won composure shattered. "Hi, Dan."

"Are you busy tomorrow night? It's Valentine's Day, and I'd like to take you to dinner."

Dan had provided her with the perfect time to tell him she couldn't see him again, but..."Yes," she said. "That would be nice."

"Good. I'll pick you up at six-thirty, if that's okay."

"Yes, that's fine. See you then."

Holly replaced the phone and gave her attention to Loretta. "Ready?"

Loretta pursed her lips. "That was Dan Wakefield, wasn't it?"

"Yes, it was," she agreed, even though it wasn't any of Loretta's business who called her.

Loretta gave her a beady-eyed stare. "Are you going out with him for Valentine's Day?"

"Yes. He wants to take me to dinner."

Loretta studied her so intently it made her uncomfortable. "Why are you staring at me that way?"

"You've fallen in love with him," Loretta accused.

Holly's heart leaped in her chest. "Don't be silly. I haven't known him long enough to fall in love. It doesn't matter how I feel anyway. You know I never want to marry."

"But you love him," Loretta insisted. "Does he return your feelings?"

Holly shrugged. "He likes me, if that's what you mean."

"In other words, he's in love with you too," Loretta said with a sigh.

She paused and Holly watched as her friend struggled to articulate her thoughts. It was amusing to watch because Loretta didn't have a tactful bone in her body.

"What's wrong with you?" Holly asked with a grin. "It's not like you to hold back if you want to say something."

Loretta refused to be baited. "I know I encouraged you to go out with Dan, but I didn't expect you to fall in love with him. I just wanted you to have a little fun with a cute guy. I feel so guilty."

Loretta often got on her nerves, but she was a capable employee and a good friend, and her concern proved it. "There's no reason for you to feel guilty, Loretta. I'm not a child."

Loretta rolled her eyes. "There's plenty of reason for me to feel guilty. I always imagined you'd get together with a professional man like Tommy Price. He's a lawyer, but Dan only has a high school diploma and trains horses for a living.

"Besides that, you said he's broke. I don't want you to spend your life pinching pennies and doing without. If you were Dan's wife and wanted to take time off work to have a baby, could he even support you and the child? And what about his family's reputation? Dan's father was bad by anyone's standards. What if Dan turned out like his father?"

Anger ran hot and swift through Holly's veins. Without a second thought, she sprang to Dan's defense. "Loretta! I can't believe you! There's nothing wrong with training horses for a living, and Dan isn't his father. He'd never do the things Kyle did."

Loretta frowned and shook her head. "You don't know that now, do you? I don't want you to make a mistake. You'd better think before you get involved with him."

Holly swallowed hard and attempted to take control of the situation. She'd heard enough of Loretta's judgmental opinions. "I appreciate your concern, but really, you don't have to worry. Dan asked me to dinner. That's all. One date or so is hardly reason for you to panic. Really, everything is fine."

Loretta sighed and gave up. "I don't believe you, but you've got that stubborn look on your face again. If you've made up your mind, nothing I can say will change it. Just promise me you won't do anything impulsive."

"I promise. Now, can we go? I'm starving."

~ * ~

"Why don't you marry Holly?" Jeb asked as Dan dried the dinner dishes for him that night.

Dan dropped a pot that clanged and bounced on the kitchen floor.

"Holly likes you," Jeb continued, "and you need a wife. You need the kind of comfort and support a woman gives a man."

"Aren't you forgetting something?" Dan asked as he picked up the pot and rinsed it off.

"What?"

"Holly would have to agree, and I don't think she would."

His grandfather laughed as if he knew something Dan didn't know. "I think she might."

Dan dried the pot and stuck in a cabinet. "Holly isn't interested in getting married right now."

Jeb shot him a look of surprise. "Did she say so?"

"Yes, she did."

Jeb ignored the dishes in the sink. "So, the subject of marriage did come up."

"Not exactly," Dan hedged. He put a stack of plates in the cabinet and wished he'd kept his mouth shut.

"It either did or it didn't, Dan."

"Well, I guess it did."

"Did you ask her to marry you?"

"No, not exactly."

Jeb slightly offended him by sighing as if he had an idiot for a grandson. "Why not? She can't accept until you ask her."

Dan's shoulders hunched. "She deserves better than me, that's why."

"They don't come any better than you."

Yeah, right. What did he have to show for all the work he'd done? He dried a cup and reached for the knife his grandfather had just laid down. "She does deserve someone better. Somebody like the guy she bought her house from, Kurt Deveraux. He's got a college degree and a good job coaching football at Tri State Tech. He bought his wife a big new house. I couldn't give anything like that to Holly."

Jeb shrugged and made light of Kurt Deveraux. "So what? Deveraux can do what he wants, and so can you."

"Let it go, Gramps. I'm not getting married."

"You think about it, Dan." Jeb passed him the last item, a cookie sheet. "Holly knows who and what you are, and if she's happy with you, that's all that matters."

Yeah, if only it were that simple. What did he have to offer besides a rundown farm and a suspect gene pool? Holly did deserve better. He'd already invited her to dinner on Valentine's Day, but after the horse show, he'd stop seeing her. Really, it was for the best. Really.

~ * ~

Jeb had gone to bed leaving Dan to lock up for the night. Could his grandfather read this situation better than he could? Would Holly really marry somebody like him? As he sat down at the table, his eyes fell on a picture of Michael and Teddy that he had posted on the front of the refrigerator with a magnet. They had both acted in a Christmas play, and Nikki had given him a picture of them in their costumes. The picture reminded him of the time he had participated in a Christmas play.

"Don't go out tonight, Kyle," his mother pleaded. "Dan wants you to go with me to the Christmas play at school. He's going to be a wise man, and he wants you to see him."

"Christmas plays are for children. He'll be happy enough if you go."

"But, Kyle…"

"Shut up, Millie. I said no. I've got important business to discuss with Cam."

"Every time you see Cam you come home high," Mille sharply retorted.

"Millie, you don't know what you're talking about."

"Oh yes I do! You aren't going out alone tonight. If you go out, I'm going with you."

"What about Dan's play?" his dad asked.

"Your dad can take him. Somebody has to keep you out of jail."

Dan made a sound of disgust and jumped up from the table. This bad memory pretty well summed up his entire relationship with his parents. Holly didn't need a man like him in her life. Only God knew what genes he carried that might suddenly go berserk and turn him into his father.

Fourteen

"What did you buy Holly for Valentine's Day?" Nikki demanded, not even bothering to say hello when Dan answered the phone the next day. "You're a man, so I know you don't think romantically, but you have to get her a nice gift. It's your first Valentine's Day together, you know."

"I'm fine, Nikki, and thanks for asking."

"Very funny."

Dan smiled. Nikki always tried to look after him. "I'm taking Holly to dinner tonight."

"I knew it," Nikki cried. "You do need help. Dinner is fine, but it isn't enough. Did you get a card yet?"

"No."

"How do you expect to keep a girlfriend if you act like this?" She sighed as if he had wearied her beyond belief. "Go and buy a nice card and a gift, but don't buy hair curlers or an umbrella."

"Hair curlers or an umbrella?" Dan asked. "That doesn't sound like a Valentine's gift."

"It isn't!" Nikki exclaimed. "The fool that I dated for so long gave me hair curlers and an umbrella, and I didn't appreciate it one bit."

Dan didn't think he would have either. Provided he used hair curlers of course, which he didn't. "I'd never have thought of hair curlers or an umbrella, Nikki, but I can't get out right now. I'm waiting for the vet. We've got a mare foaling, and she's in trouble."

"Hmm. Well, okay. I'll get something and drop it off."

Dan glanced out the window and saw a truck coming up the driveway. "The vet just got here. Are you sure you don't mind buying the gift?"

"I'll be glad to. You'd probably get the wrong thing anyway. You go tend to your horse. I'll get you a dynamite present."

~ * ~

The interminable day had finally ended. Holly slammed the door and gave thanks she had finally made it home. It was Valentine's Day, but in spite of her date with the sexiest men she had ever seen, she had seldom felt more depressed or confused.

She had spent an entire hour staring at Valentine cards and searching for one that seemed appropriate, but the ones she liked had sounded so sentimental and sugary sweet they had embarrassed her. She had finally picked a card that focused on friendship, but deep down she knew it too was inappropriate. Her feelings for Dan went way beyond friendship.

She'd also had trouble choosing an appropriate dress for the evening. The tailored business attire she usually wore to work didn't seem suitable for a Valentine's Day dinner, but dressing up would lend an importance and significance to the occasion she wished to avoid. She finally settled on a simple, red wool dress. If it showed her figure off to good advantage, so what?

Dan arrived promptly at six-thirty and gave her the impression he really, really was glad to be there. Thank goodness she had worn that red dress. He had a look of appreciation on his face that was hard to miss.

"Happy Valentine's Day, Holly. You look like a valentine yourself in that red dress."

Holly laughed as a little thrill chased up and down her spine. "Why, thank you, sir." She had made up her mind she'd never kiss or snuggle Dan again, but he looked so handsome her good intentions didn't mean a thing. Tonight, she'd initiate a kiss. Stepping closer to him, she brushed his lips with her own.

Dan's eyes darkened. He reached to take her into his arms, but the wrapped package he was carrying hit her in the stomach.

"Is that for me?" she asked with a smile. "It's beautiful." Did Dan wrap it himself? She loved the white paper and that fat, red bow.

"Yes, it's for you. I didn't mean to bruise you with it."

"Oh, I think I can forgive a man bearing gifts. May I open it now?"

"Please do."

Dan followed her into the living room and seated himself in a chair that stood opposite the sofa where she had taken a seat. There was a card stuck underneath the red ribbon, and she opened it first. It had a large, red rose and several fat cupids on the front. Her heart sank when she read the verse inside. It sounded every bit as sentimental as the ones she had rejected. Dan would probably be disappointed when he read his card.

"It's a lovely card, Dan," she said. Dan had willingly shared his feelings with her, a move she hadn't had the courage to make. She respected him for doing so and wished she had done the same.

It only took a moment to remove the paper from the box, but Holly didn't open it right away. It was too much fun to guess what was inside. "What can it be? It doesn't weigh much, so it probably isn't candy. No one puts jewelry in such a large box, and it can't be flowers."

Dan just laughed at her, but his open, happy smile made it seem as if he were enjoying all the suspense.

Holly eased the attached lid open and folded back a layer of pink tissue paper decorated with vivid red hearts. One glance and she quickly closed the lid. Dan had given her a fire engine red bra trimmed in heart shaped rhinestones and black lace. She had also spotted a matching thong snuggling underneath the bra.

She sneaked a peek at Dan whose face wore a hopeful, expectant expression. Apparently, he had no idea he had given her an inappropriate gift. Why, they'd only known each other for a few weeks.

Her nana would have a fit if she saw this stuff. *He said he hasn't dated much, and his mother probably never taught him any better.*

She smiled at him. "Thank you, Dan. That's a very thoughtful gift. Why don't you read your card now?"

Dan read his card and thanked Holly, but unless she was mistaken, he looked a little disappointed, although, he didn't say anything except *thanks*. He stuffed the card into the pocket of his jacket. "Our reservation is at seven. We really should go."

Good. Maybe a nice dinner would help her forget the red underwear. She sat the box on the coffee table. "Where are we going?"

"The Brass Heron."

"Dan, you shouldn't have. It's far too expensive."

The citizens of Fairfield loved The Brass Heron. It cost a great deal to dine there, but it stayed in business because of the delicious cuisine, impeccable service, and the elegant, understated décor. Dan couldn't afford to go there.

"It's Valentine's Day, and I want to take you somewhere nice. Go get your coat."

She had to go to the bedroom for her coat. When she returned, she caught Dan peeping inside the box that held the red underwear. "What are you doing with my present?" she asked.

"Holly, I...that is...Lord, how embarrassing."

"What is?"

Dan fumbled with the box and finally got the lid closed. "Nikki called me today to see what plans I'd made for Valentine's Day, and she didn't think dinner was enough. She said I had to buy a gift too, but I couldn't because I had a mare foaling, and she was having a hard time. Nikki said she'd pick up something for me to give you. I know how rotten it was to let her buy it, but it was either that or nothing, and I was afraid you'd be expecting a gift." Dan paused as if he didn't know what else to say.

"Did you like what she got for me?" Holly asked.

His eyes fell. "I'm ashamed to tell you, but she wrapped it, so I didn't know what it was. I looked while you were getting your coat. I can't tell you how sorry I am. I thought she'd get perfume or a scarf or something. I should have known better."

How sweet! He had tried so hard to please her. "It doesn't matter. I love it because you tried so hard to please me." She giggled. "We'll laugh about this later, you know."

"Yeah, right."

Holly reached for the box that Dan still held. "Give me the box, Wakefield. It's my present, and you can't have it back."

"Don't you want me to get rid of it for you?"

"Are you insane? It has heart-shaped rhinestones on it."

Dan groaned. "How well I know it."

"Oh, what the heck!" Holly exclaimed. "It's Valentine's Day, and I'm going to wear my present." With a thrill of horror, she realized what she had said. In her desire to reassure Dan, she had taken an action that was provocative at best, and she hated to think what the worst might be.

Refusing to meet his eyes, Holly took the box and hurried into her bedroom where she quickly changed her undergarments. Ha. Nikki had correctly guessed her size.

She blushed when she looked at herself in the mirror. *I look like a model in a cheap lingerie catalog.* The bra pushed her breasts up and somehow made it appear as if she might spill out over the top of the thing at any minute.

And that thong! The sheer, brief piece of fabric revealed more than it covered. She had *never* worn undergarments like these, but she'd bet her mother had.

Her spirits dropped. How could she face Dan after acting like a fool? Well, she had to do it sometime.

She rejoined Dan who, of course, couldn't take his eyes off her. It didn't take much of an imagination to know where his thoughts had strayed. Okay, she deserved it. Didn't she know better?

~ * ~

Holly had tried to make him feel better, but he didn't. His thoughts were definitely on the erotic side, and that was making him feel guilty. It took his breath away to think of her in his arms dressed only in red and black lingerie! *Forget it, Wakefield. You're acting like a gentleman whether you want to or not.*

~ * ~

The elegant restaurant quietly buzzed with well-dressed couples celebrating Valentine's Day, but not a single woman could hold a candle to Holly. Dan smiled. Going out with her had given his ego a big boost. Not many men had the chance to spend Valentine's Day with a beauty like Holly Grant.

He couldn't have told you what he and Holly ordered but if he'd had his way, the evening would never end. All too soon the waiter offered them dessert. He scanned the menu. "What would you like, Holly?"

"Nothing for me, thank you. I'm too full to eat another bite. If you'll excuse me for a minute, I'd like to go to the ladies' room."

Dan rose from his chair as Holly stood and smiled as he watched her walk away. Man, he'd had a good time tonight. He sat back down, and with no warning, two well-dressed men joined him at the table.

"Hello, Danny boy. How's it going?"

Dan remained calm only by a tremendous act of his will because the speaker, Cam Simmons, was the man for whom his father had once worked. His skin crawled with revulsion although, oddly enough, Simmons didn't look like a criminal. He looked like a successful businessman having a dinner meeting with an associate.

"It's going fine," he answered, with no expression whatsoever on his face or in his voice. He hated these goons, but he couldn't start anything in The Brass Heron. Maybe Holly would take a long time in the ladies' room. It was dangerous for this scum to even be in the same room with her.

Simmons sat back with a smirk. "That's a pretty woman you're with tonight. I bet she gives you real good loving." He jabbed his companion with his elbow. "What do you think, Joe? Do you think Danny's woman is hot?"

"Yeah, she's hot all right. I guess having those legs around you at night is a real turn on, right Dan?"

Simmons nodded. "Yeah, but a woman like that is expensive to maintain. Her dress doesn't look cheap to me, and this restaurant costs way too much. You making good money at the farm, Danny?"

"Is there a point to this conversation?" Dan asked.

Simmons nodded. "Yep, sure is. I've been watching you all evening. Your woman is drinking wine, but you're drinking water. You're not like your dad, are you?"

"No, I'm not."

"I could use a man like you, someone who keeps his head and could enjoy the benefit of a nice paying job."

Dan took a deep breath and tried to get his temper under control. If Simmons kept pushing this, he'd slug him. "I'm not interested."

"You don't have to tell me now. You think about it. The offer is always open."

The thugs finally stood up, and Simmons patted his shoulder. He swallowed hard against sudden nausea.

~ * ~

"Dan ain't much like his old man is he, Cam?"

"No, he doesn't seem to be, but he does have a weakness."

"I didn't see one." Joe shrugged. "We yanked his chain pretty good about the woman, but he kept his cool anyway."

"Yeah," Cam agreed, "but I saw a flicker in his eyes when I talked about women being expensive. He's afraid he can't afford her."

Joe grunted. "I still don't think you'll be hearing from him. I don't think he likes us much."

"Probably not, but we could grow on him. We'll see."

~ * ~

Pauline hung up the phone with a sigh. She had expected Rita's call any day now, and sure enough, her incorrigible daughter had called tonight. Her current...companion...had left her high and dry in Las Vegas.

Rita hadn't seemed too upset that he'd left her, but she seemed to take it as a personal affront that he had done it on Valentine's Day. Pauline's lips tightened. Surely Rita had enough sense to know the man had never felt anything for her.

Now she had to figure out how to tell Holly her mother was coming home. Holly had gotten to the point where she didn't want to ever see Rita. She had made her feelings very clear the last time Rita had taken off.

Of course, this time Dan Wakefield complicated things. Rita would certainly flirt with him if they met, and Holly might dump Dan because of it.

Of course that made no sense, but Holly had long since lost any objectivity regarding her mother. Should she tell Holly or not? It would take several weeks before Rita could save the money for a bus ticket. She had tried to get Pauline to pay for it, but for the first time Pauline had refused.

"It's time for you to stop this destructive behavior," she had sharply scolded. "Get your act together, Rita. I know you loved Charles, but Charles is dead and gone, and you've wasted your life and cheapened his memory by your behavior."

That had certainly made Rita angry. "How dare you say a thing like that to me?" she'd screamed.

"Because it's true. You've ruined your life, worried me to death in my old age, and you're about to ruin Holly's life too. For once try not to be so selfish. Everything isn't about you, and it never has been."

So, should she tell Holly or not? Yes, probably so. Holly would need plenty of time to get used to the idea. She could decide if she wanted her mother to know about Dan or not. Maybe, she'd call Jeb Wakefield too. A word of warning to Dan might avert some major blunders.

Fifteen

"Sheriff Kinkaid, your nine o'clock appointment is here."

Bill Kinkaid rose from his chair to greet his visitor. He extended his hand to the tall, well-built man in front of him and hoped that Lovinggood proved as impressive as the local FBI had promised.

"Mr. Lovinggood, come in," he invited.

"Thank you," Lovinggood said as he shook hands with the sheriff.

Kincaid indicated a chair in front of his desk. "Could I get you some coffee?"

"I'd break the law for a cup of coffee about now," Lovinggood replied with a flashing grin.

"Yeah, I know just what you mean." The sheriff poured two cups of coffee. "Cream or sugar?"

"Black."

Kinkaid passed one of the cups to his guest. "It's probably none of my business, but what's an FBI agent from California doing here in Fairfield? Our local guys said an agent with experience in our kind of problem would be in the Fairfield area, which is why they volunteered you to help me."

Lovinggood took a small sip of his coffee. "I had a few days off, so my wife wanted me to come with her to see about selling some property."

"Your wife owns property in Fairfield?

"Yes, she was born in Fairfield."

The sheriff reached for another sugar packet and stirred it into his coffee. "Who is your wife, if you don't mind my asking?"

"Elizabeth Lane."

"You're kidding! How about that? I remember now that Elizabeth married a Lovinggood, but I didn't connect you to her. Elizabeth Lane is Fairfield's most famous citizen. She really deserved the Oscar she won for *Paradise Bay*."

A look of pride crossed Lovinggood's face. "I think she's also the prettiest citizen Fairfield ever produced."

The sheriff laughed, a look of amusement on his face. "Well, I guess you do. They said on TV that she's expecting a baby."

"She is. He should be born in August."

"So it's a boy?"

"Yes, sir. We wanted to know." He grinned at the sheriff. "At least, my dad did, and we humored him."

"Senator Henry Lovinggood is your father, isn't he?" Kinkaid remembered.

"Yes sir, and he wants a boy real bad."

The sheriff gestured toward a picture on his desk that showed a boy in a little league uniform. "I guess I know why. Tell your wife I said hello."

Lovinggood nodded. "Yes, sir. I will."

The pleasantries completed, the sheriff got down to business. "Mr. Lovinggood, our problem is no different from that in many other communities around the country. We've got a large, well-organized drug ring operating in the area. We know they're using local sporting events as a cover for distribution, but we haven't had any luck proving it."

"Why don't you just put in an undercover guy?" Lovinggood took another sip of his coffee, frowned, and added some cream.

The sheriff sighed. "Fairfield's a small community. These guys know which side of the law people are on. We tried to bring in an outsider, but they saw through it quick enough."

Lovinggood sat up straight as if he'd had an idea. "Do you have any activity at horse events?"

"Yeah, that's one of the worst places. A lot of people in this area keep horses. Besides that, show entries come from all over."

Lovinggood smiled. "Then I've got an idea."

~ * ~

"That's not good enough, Dan. He can do better, and he'll have to if you want to win a ribbon for Tommy," Jeb said as Dan pulled his horse to a stop.

"I know it. I don't know what's wrong with him or me."

Jeb made no reply. He gestured toward the end of the driveway. "Who do you know that drives a black Mercedes?"

"Nobody."

The Mercedes came to a halt near the ring. A tall, blond man in jeans and a leather jacket got out of the car. He threw up his hand in greeting and walked around to open the passenger door. He looked familiar, but Dan couldn't quite place him. When he saw the brunette woman who got out of the car, he threw his reins to Jeb and jogged over to meet her. Now he remembered the man.

He threw his arms around her and kissed her cheek. "Elizabeth, what are you doing here? You look fantastic. Congratulations on your baby."

Elizabeth exuberantly returned Dan's hug. "Dan, I miss you so much. When are you coming to California to visit me? Better yet, talk your grandfather into moving out there. We'll take Nikki with us and have a grand time."

Dan laughed just because he was so glad to see her. Elizabeth Lane Lovinggood was his first cousin. Like many of the Lane men, Elizabeth's father had been an alcoholic. Her mother had had to work two jobs just to pay the rent and keep food on the table. When her husband drank himself to death, she had pulled up stakes and moved to California where Elizabeth became a Hollywood superstar.

She had fallen in love with Richard Lovinggood, the son of California's most powerful senator. Richard was an FBI agent, but Elizabeth had confided to Dan that one day he would be the President of the United States. After meeting Richard at Elizabeth's wedding, Dan guessed she would be the First Lady one day. The Lovinggoods looked like people who usually got things their way.

When the men shook hands, Dan noticed Elizabeth's husband admiring the horse. "Do you ride?" he asked.

"Yes, I do. Is that horse as good as he looks?"

Dan patted the horse's neck. "I think so. He goes to the show on Friday, and I expect to win."

Jeb handed the horse's reins back to Dan. "Elizabeth, why aren't you in Hollywood winning more Oscars?"

"Mother sent me and Richard to sell the last of her property here in Fairfield. When Grandma died, she left Mother half an acre of land adjoining Uncle David's place. He doesn't want it, so she decided to sell it."

Jeb beamed at her. "I know a good realtor."

"Great," Richard answered. "Maybe you could give the name to Elizabeth while I talk to Dan."

Jeb looked slightly alarmed, so Dan guessed he remembered that Richard was FBI. "I can tell when I'm not wanted," he said, "but is something going on that I should know about?"

Richard shrugged. "I don't know yet. I need to talk to Dan first."

"Want to go riding?" Dan asked.

"I thought you'd never ask." Richard took Elizabeth's hand. "Will you be okay with Mr. Wakefield for an hour or so?"

"Yes, you go on. I'm fine."

Richard kissed Elizabeth's cheek and followed Dan into the barn while Jeb and Elizabeth made their way into the house.

~ * ~

Dan liked Richard. He obviously knew horses, and judging by the look of love in his eyes when he had looked at Elizabeth, Dan felt sure he treated her like a queen. "When's your baby due, Richard?"

"End of August." Richard paused as the mare that he rode shied at the far away sound of a car backfiring.

"I don't know who jumped more, you or the mare," Dan said.

Lovinggood laughed. "Occupational hazard, I guess."

Dan didn't think he'd enjoy such work, but he didn't say so. "Is Elizabeth taking care of herself?"

Richard looked peeved for a moment. "She's giving me fits. She wants to ride and do all the things she always did, but she's pregnant! I don't think a pregnant woman should ride. Any horse could shy or fall. I had to threaten to fire any stableman who gave her a horse before she'd listen to me."

Dan laughed. "She always had a mind of her own, but this time I think you're right."

Richard's mare kicked up her heels, but he easily brought her under control. "I can't forget how she got kidnapped last year. I suppose it makes me overprotective, but I can't help it."

Dan shivered. If Holly got kidnapped as Elizabeth had, he didn't know if he could take it.

Richard brought his mare to a sedate walk beside Dan. "Say, Dan, I'd like to talk to you about something."

"Okay, what do you need?" It was almost funny to think he could do anything for a man like Richard.

"Do you have contact with anyone in the drug world?"

"What the hell do you mean by that? Did somebody tell you I do?" Dan demanded, the force of his anger causing his horse to dance and snort.

"Calm down," Richard soothed. "It's not what you're thinking. The local authorities need a favor, and they want me to ask you."

"Oh, yeah?"

Richard nodded. "Yeah, do you know the name of the man for whom your dad worked?"

"Yes."

"Would you like to see him punished?"

"Go on."

Richard's face lit up with enthusiasm. "Sheriff Kinkaid asked the FBI for help breaking up a local drug ring. The FBI knew I was going to be in the area, so they asked me to help the sheriff nail these guys.

I think we've come up with a good plan, but you're an essential part of the whole operation."

"Tell me about the plan."

Richard nodded. "It's pretty simple, really. We put out the word that you're involved with a high maintenance woman who wants a hell of a lot more than you can afford to give her. We'd suggest that maybe you might be willing to take a job if the price was right because you're crazy about this woman. Forgive me for saying so, but your father's reputation might be enough to make the bad guys fall for our story."

As much as Dan wanted Cam Simmons to pay for his crimes, he refused to have Holly come on that scum's radar. "I have started seeing someone, but I don't want her involved, so forget it."

"Well, let me finish," Richard said. "We have information that a major delivery is due within the next couple of weeks, and we think they're using the upcoming horse show in Fort Timothy as a cover. These men know they're all being closely watched, so we're hoping they'd recruit you to do the pickup. You'd be the logical choice. Your dad worked for them, and if you did get caught, you couldn't be tied to them. We'd be waiting at the delivery point, and when they took possession, we'd arrest them."

A sweet feeling of satisfaction filled Dan when he thought of Simmons in handcuffs. "Who's the man in charge?"

"Cam Simmons."

His father had worked for Cam, all right. "What if it didn't turn out the way you hope? I'm not working for them."

As Richard's horse danced sideways, he paused to bring the animal back in line. "One weekend is all I'd ask. If we didn't get them, we'd let it be known that because of your father you're under surveillance yourself. If we had to, we could stage a little demonstration for them, and after that I think they'd leave you alone. You would simply be too big a risk for them to take."

Richard's plan sounded simple, but..."Wouldn't it look funny if I didn't get arrested along with them when they take possession of the shipment?"

Richard laughed and looked amused. "Oh, you'd be arrested, but it wouldn't go on your record, and I could fix it so they wouldn't know you were working undercover for the FBI."

Dan thought for a minute. He couldn't do anything that might hurt Holly. "I've invited Holly Grant to go with me to the show."

"Good," Richard answered. "It would be a great cover."

"I don't want Holly in danger." In fact, the very thought of it raised his blood pressure at least twenty points.

"I really wouldn't ask you to put her in danger. I'm sure she'd be perfectly safe. She would need to share a room with you, though. It would lend even more credibility to the story."

The idea of sharing a room with Holly almost took Dan's breath away. She might be safe from Cam Simmons, but would she be safe from him? He wanted her with every fiber of his being. "Holly and I aren't sleeping together, so I don't think she'd want to share a room."

"You need to."

It struck Dan as funny despite the seriousness of the situation. "Need to what, share a room or sleep together?"

Richard grinned. "Share a room, but if you want to sleep with her..."

Dan only laughed.

"Well?" Richard continued, "Are you in?"

"Yes, I am. I know those...thugs didn't make my dad do anything he didn't want to, but I always wondered if maybe he wouldn't have made more of an effort to straighten out if they hadn't made things so easy for him. Your plan is even better than you know. Let me tell you what happened when I took Holly out on Valentine's Day."

"No operation is without some danger," Richard cautioned when Dan finished his story. "I think you'll be safe enough, but you do understand there are no guarantees."

"I know, and I still want to do it."

"Great." Richard held out his hand to Dan. "I think the time is right. This time they're going down."

Sixteen

"Hi, Mr. Wakefield," Holly called, as she parked her car in the driveway at Turnaround Farm. "Is Dan ready to go yet?"

"Just about. Where's your bag? I'll load it for you."

Holly unlocked the trunk of her car, and Jeb removed her bag and stowed it in Dan's vehicle. "Women always take plenty of clothes," he remarked with a smile as Holly removed a garment bag and makeup case also.

"I might need them," Holly protested with a laugh. "Clothes are one of my favorite weaknesses."

I hope she has some sensible pajamas with her. Since they're sharing a room, it'll be easier on Dan if she isn't wearing anything too revealing.

For about the millionth time since Dan had explained Richard's harebrained scheme to him, Jeb breathed a prayer that everything would go according to plan. He had tried to talk Dan into rescinding his offer of help, but he might as well have tried talking to the wall; Dan refused to budge. Now, all he could do was pray for a happy conclusion to a messy, hazardous business.

"I'm excited about the show," Holly continued as she folded her garment bag neatly over the top of her other luggage. "Do you think Dan will win anything?"

"He thinks he has a good chance, and he usually knows." Having Holly in the audience would motivate Dan to do the best possible job. Most men enjoyed showing off for the women in their lives, and so would Dan.

"I'm looking forward to the parties too. I always enjoy getting dressed up and going out. I bought a killer new dress to wear on Saturday. You should see it. If Dan doesn't like it, he's impossible to please."

Jeb reveled in the light, feminine conversation. Turnaround Farm suddenly seemed so exclusively male. *I wish Dan would marry her. She'd be good for him. She'd pull him out of his shell and make him enjoy living. Dan's the kind of man who needs a woman in his life, but I don't think he knows it.*

Jeb's ruminations came to a close as Dan led the Price horse out of the barn. The animal loaded quickly and quietly, and then Dan joined his grandfather and Holly. "Hey, Holly. Ready for the show?" he asked.

"Yes, I am, and I'm so excited. The sun is shining, and the sky is blue. The weather isn't too cold, and I'm doing something new with somebody I like."

Both men smiled as Holly's sparkling eyes and pink cheeks fired their own enthusiasm.

Jeb sent another prayer heavenward, but this time he tacked something onto the end. *Lord, let it work out with Holly. He needs her, and she needs him too.*

~ * ~

It was amazing how short the two-hour drive to Ft. Timothy seemed. Dan smiled slightly. He went to Fort Timothy several times a year to the big horse shows the city promoted, and the drive always bored him. Holly's presence made all the difference in the world. Talking to her made the time fly by.

They went directly to the show grounds where Dan stabled his horse and completed paperwork required by the officials. "What's next?" Holly asked as she and Dan made their way back to their vehicle.

Dan looked at his watch. "Let's go check into our own rooms. It's four o'clock now, and the dinner for owners and trainers starts at seven. You'll want time to get changed, won't you?"

Holly laughed and linked her arm through his. "I certainly will. I wouldn't dream of going to a dinner dressed in jeans. I need to do my hair too."

"Uh huh. That's what I thought. I saw your luggage."

"How many bags did you bring?" Holly teased. "One?"

"Yes, and it isn't full."

Holly snickered as if he'd said something hysterical. "Men! What's the schedule for tomorrow?"

Dan opened the door of his truck for her before he got in himself. "My event's being held at one, and the party starts at six and ends whenever."

"I'm looking forward to both of them," Holly said.

In the distance, Dan saw the upscale hotel where Richard had arranged for him and Holly to stay. As he turned his vehicle into the parking lot, Holly exclaimed, "Are we staying here? This place costs the earth."

"Yes, we are." No need to mention that Richard felt the expensive hotel would help with the cover story they had concocted.

They went inside, and Dan took a deep breath and started his part of the FBI plan. "I have a reservation for two rooms," he told the clerk behind the desk, a man whom Richard had assured him would be FBI. "The names are Wakefield and Grant."

The clerk searched his computer and frowned. "Mr. Wakefield, I'm sorry, but there's been a mistake. We only reserved one room for you, and we have absolutely nothing available. There's a convention and a horse show in town, and everyone is packed. I'd advise you to go ahead and take this room. It has two queen-sized beds. I'll call around for you and try to find something else, but really I doubt that I can, not if you want something safe and decent that is. Like I said, everybody is full."

"Holly?"

Holly's face had furrowed with disapproval. "We'll take it, but you do your best to find another room. Mr. Wakefield and I prefer not to share."

"Yes, ma'am. I'll do my very best."

The porter hurried to carry their luggage upstairs for them. Dan tipped the man, and when he left the room, he turned to Holly, his stomach churning. "Is it really so bad? We've got two beds, and we can take turns in the bathroom."

Holly looked around the nice space. "I'd rather have my own room, Dan, but if nothing else can be found, I'm not going to make a fuss about staying with you." She laughed. "This place is really fabulous. I mean, it's a room not a suite, but look at the furniture and bedding. It's great."

Dan studied the room, which had a sleek, contemporary feel. The beds were black, the bedding some sort of blue-gray that matched the carpet. An ornate silver lamp sat on a nice chest between the beds. Another sat on the black dresser across from the beds. Heavy blue-gray drapes puddled on the floor at the windows. It was elegant, but in spite of its classy, uptown air, he preferred his beat-up old recliner sitting beside the hearth at Turnaround.

"Thank you, Holly. I really appreciate it." Deceiving Holly made him feel guilty, even though he had to do it if it meant Cam Simmons' downfall. His father had seldom told the truth, and long ago he had vowed to be truthful even if he got into trouble for it.

Well, he couldn't help it this once. He'd have to continue the deception for Holly's safety as well as his own, but when this was over, he'd never lie to her again.

~ * ~

They didn't get a call from the desk clerk, so an hour later Holly sprang to her feet. "If I'm going to look good tonight, I've got to get ready. I can't wait any longer for that clerk to call."

Dan nodded. "Go ahead. Do whatever you need to do. I'll just watch television until you're finished. It won't take me long to dress."

What choice did she have? She gathered the things she needed and went into the bathroom. It certainly looked better than your typical, standard bathroom. She loved the nice bathroom in her own house, but this one put her bath to shame. Her bathroom didn't have a whirlpool tub or multiple showerheads in the shower, although her towels were every bit as nice as these. She ran her hand across the plush, satiny surface. Hmm. Maybe not.

Dan must have paid through the nose for these luxury accommodations. No, Tommy Price probably paid for the room. Dan could never afford a place like this on his own. Tommy must really think Dan was doing a good job with his horse.

In the other room, Dan made a noise and distracted her. How weird to know that he was waiting out there for his turn in the bathroom. With the attraction between them, this intimate situation wasn't a good idea.

Her bath concluded, she wrapped her hair in a towel and put on a plush, white, terrycloth robe provided by the hotel. Facing Dan was going to embarrass her, but she couldn't hog the bathroom forever. He had to shower and dress too. She opened the door, releasing a cloud of steam into the dressing area.

"Darn, it fogged the mirror," she exclaimed. She took a tissue to clear the glass. "There, that's better." Now to get the snarls and tangles out of her wet hair.

Her eyes met Dan's when she looked into the mirror. "It's been a while since I saw a woman comb her hair," he said. "When I was little, I'd watch my mother sometimes, but that was a long time ago."

Holly tossed her comb on the vanity. "My hair's real thick. I like it after I get it finished, but getting the tangles out and getting it dried is a pain."

She switched on her hair dryer and closed her eyes as the warm air swirled around her face, but they popped back open when Dan removed the appliance from her hand. "Dan, what…"

"Let me do it."

"Uh, no…"

He had already begun the job, and it felt wonderful. As his hand gently moved through her hair, Holly blissfully surrendered to the luxury of having someone else take care of her. Her eyes fluttered shut. "I feel like Nana's cat," she sighed. "When you pet her, she gets as boneless as I feel right now."

Dan chuckled, a sweet sound that stirred up some butterflies in her stomach. "Does boneless translate as very relaxed?" he asked.

"Mm."

When the dryer stopped, Dan ran his fingers through her hair. "I think it's dry now." He touched her hair again, leaving Holly in no doubt whatsoever; he had just caressed her. "Your hair is so pretty," he whispered.

Holly opened her eyes and studied him. "Dan, did you know that your eyes get darker when you're..."

"When I'm what, honey?"

Oh, that little endearment.

"Not...Nothing. I forgot what I was going to say." What was wrong with her? She'd been about to tell him that his eyes darkened when he was aroused.

Dan handed her the hair dryer. "I need a shower too. Excuse me and I'll do it while you finish here."

Lord, have mercy! Holly leaned against the wall for support. *This is* going *to be harder than I thought. It's all I can do to keep my hands off him.*

~ * ~

Inside the bathroom, Dan turned the shower to cold, gritted his teeth, and stepped under the icy water; it stung as if someone pricked him with sharp needles. After a second, he added some warm water to the mix and breathed a little easier.

Seventeen

A small stir broke out in the crowded room when Dan and Holly arrived at dinner that evening. Dan hid a grin. Most of these people thought he was surly at best because he avoided social events revolving around the horse show circuit. This was the first time he'd ever brought a date, and she just happened to be the most beautiful woman in the room.

He threw up his hand to Chief's owner, Tommy Price, who was in the corner talking to his friend, Bill Arnold. Tommy enjoyed the social events and usually attended the dinners and parties.

Tommy shook hands with Bill and made his way through the crowd to him and Holly. "Dan, it's good to see you. Did you have a nice trip?"

"Yes, everything was fine. Chief's a good traveler."

Holly cleared her throat, and Dan took the hint. "Holly, let me introduce Tommy Price, Chief's owner. Tommy, this is my date, Holly Grant."

Tommy shook hands with Holly. "It's very nice to meet you, Holly. I've heard lots of good things about Grant Realty. I think dinner's about ready to be served. Shall we find our seats?"

Nobody bragged about the food, but the knowledgeable horseman speaking that evening kept the interest of the crowd with no trouble at all, most of them anyway. Dan found that no matter how hard he tried, he couldn't get his mind off Holly.

Her presence had generated a lot of attention this evening. After all, she looked like a movie star or a model, and no one knew her. *They're probably wondering why she'd go out with me.* No matter. Spending time with Holly more than made up for any slights he might receive.

When the speaker concluded his address, Dan excused himself to go to the men's room. He had just finished washing his hands when the door opened. He turned around and saw Cam Simmons leaning against the restroom door watching him.

"Hello, Danny. Having a good time?"

Dan's heart picked up speed. If Richard's plan worked like they hoped, this meeting probably wasn't a coincidence. "Yes, I'm having a very good time," he said.

Simmons left the door and joined Dan at the paper towel dispenser. "That's the same woman I saw you with on Valentine's Day."

"That's right."

"Are you showing Price's horse?"

"Yes."

Simmons smiled at him, reminding Dan of a hungry coyote about to snap up his prey. "You're a man of few words, Danny. I like that. Where are you staying?"

"The Ballentine."

Simmons whistled. "That's an expensive place. I guess your woman is staying with you."

Dan cocked his head. "So?"

"So, I guess she does like the finer things in life."

"That's none of your business," Dan said, struggling to hold on to his temper.

"It might be," Cam disagreed. He reached into his pocket and took out a small, black case that he handed to Dan. "Open it."

Dan opened the lid of the small case to revel a diamond bracelet that even to his untrained eye looked valuable. "Are you trying to proposition me?" he sneered.

Cam smiled. "I wondered if you'd ever bite back. No, it isn't for you. I thought you might like to give it to your woman. I'll bet your loving tonight will be extra special after she has the bracelet on her wrist."

This is how you get sucked in! How could he even for one moment have visualized the bracelet on Holly's arm and thought of how much pleasure the gift would give her? A chill raced through him when he thought of his father. "I'm not interested," he coldly retorted.

"Yes, you are. I can see it in your eyes." Cam took the case and tucked it into Dan's pocket. "Give it to her, Danny. She'll like it."

Dan frowned, but he left the case in his pocket. "What do you want with me? This can't be a coincidence."

"You're right, it isn't. I heard you need money, Danny, and I want to offer you a job. All you'd be doing is taking delivery of a shipment of hay and then hauling it to my farm. That's all, and if you don't like the money, you don't have to do anything more for me. We'd be square."

Dan laughed. "A shipment of hay?"

"Yeah, hay. Are you interested?"

Dan fidgeted a bit and stared at the wall behind Simmons. "How much money?"

"A thousand dollars. Good money for just making a delivery. I expect you could really impress your woman with money like that for the taking most any time."

Dan hesitated. "Well, I could use the money, but I don't know. Getting involved with you is pretty risky."

"Life's risky, Danny. Live a little before you die."

"When would I have to pick it up?" Dan mumbled.

He saw that Cam almost smiled. "The truck should get in town around three tomorrow. You'd take possession from the driver and then bring the hay to my farm. I'd pay you, and you'd be on your way."

"Uh, how would I find the other driver?"

"He'd find you. Just hang around the barn after your event tomorrow, and he'll contact you."

Dan's fingers audibly tapped the jewelry case in his pocket. "All right." Without another word, he hurried from the men's room. He saw several of Cam's thugs guarding the door. Wonder how many people they'd turned away.

"I was about to send Tommy to look for you," chided Holly as Dan joined her at their table. "A lot of people have been asking after you."

"I'm sorry. I met somebody I know, and we started to talk."

The room had begun to clear now. "I'd better find my hotel," Tommy said. "Do you need a ride?"

"No, we're staying only a few blocks from here, so we'll walk," Holly answered. She smiled as she took Dan's arm. "It's a beautiful night."

Dan agreed. *Tomorrow will be awful, but tonight is magical. I'll worry about tomorrow when it comes.*

~ * ~

The weather had deteriorated since they had dinner. "Brrrr. I think it got lots colder." Holly shivered and bent her head against the wind. "My jacket was designed for looks, not warmth."

"Take my coat."

"No, absolutely not. You'd freeze."

"No, I won't." Dan settled the matter by shrugging out of his coat. "Here. Put this on." Holly allowed him to help her into his jacket. He put his arm across her shoulders and pulled her close against his side. She had to admit she felt warmer. Before she thought to stop herself, Holly's arm crept around his waist.

As they walked companionably down the street, Holly paused. "Look, Dan. There's a little hole in the wall shop that looks interesting. Let's go in."

A bell tinkled above the door, and the clerk, a pretty, fresh-faced teenager, greeted them with a smile. "Hi, folks. Welcome to The Rose. If you're looking for roses you're in the right place. Everything we sell is related to roses in some way."

"It smells like a rose in here too," Dan said.

"That's the rose soap and hand cream we carry. Try a sample."

Dan declined, but Holly tried the cream and rejected it. "Too greasy," she whispered.

They paused beside a vase filled with long-stemmed gold roses. "Those are real roses dipped in gold," the clerk called.

With a smile, Dan withdrew one of the roses from the vase and presented it to Holly. "For you. This is what I should have gotten you for Valentine's Day."

Holly's heart sped up. This was so romantic! The whole evening seemed like something from a romance novel. "Thank you, Dan. It's lovely."

At the checkout station, Dan picked up another rose wrapped in red and green foil. "That's chocolate," the clerk said.

"We need this, don't we, Holly? I love chocolate."

"Yes, definitely."

They completed their purchase and went out into the cold. Since it had been so pleasant walking with her arm around him, she tried it again. "It's beautiful here in the city with you." She sighed. "I feel like it's just the two of us, a million miles away from home."

He gave her shoulders a little hug. "It's one of the best nights of my life."

Somehow, possibly the influence of the rose, she forgot to speak to the clerk about her room when they got back to the Ballentine. The FBI agent behind the desk smiled as they walked by and drew a heart on the paper lying in front of him.

Eighteen

They had left their room lights on low, so when Dan shut the door behind them, he immediately created a pleasing air of intimacy. Outside, the dark and cold held sway, but inside everything seemed warm, cozy, and oh, so private.

Dan hung his coat in a palatial sized wardrobe and started to remove his tie, but it occurred to him that he might make Holly uncomfortable if he started removing clothes without her permission. "Do you mind if I take this tie off?"

"Of course not. In fact, if you don't mind, I'd like to change myself. This dress isn't made for lounging."

"I don't mind."

Holly dipped into her bag and vanished into the bathroom. She returned moments later wearing white satin lounging pajamas. Dan took one look, and his mouth went dry. The modest pajamas revealed nothing, but Dan felt the tension start to build anyway. The setting was tailor made for a seduction, and he could think of nothing he'd like more to do.

He made a Herculean effort not to stare at the vision in white, but as Holly chatted about dinner, he didn't hear a word she said. How was a man supposed to make light conversation or talk about horses when his insides were tied in knots? He had as much self-control as any man, more than many, but he wanted her so much he scared himself. He shifted uncomfortably, trying to find relief, when an idea occurred to him.

He interrupted Holly in mid-sentence. "I need something to drink. Do you want anything?"

Holly's eyes widened when he interrupted her. "Yes, I do," she replied. "Could we get some tea, do you think?"

"I'll order it." He had to move away from her; if he didn't he'd kiss her, and if he did...

He placed the call to room service and decided to hide out in the bathroom until the tea arrived. After locking the door behind him, he splashed his face with cold water, but it didn't do much good. Even thinking of his meeting with Cam Simmons paled in comparison to the vision of Holly in white satin pajamas. How much more of this could he take? He was a man, not a child, and he needed her with a gnawing, throbbing intensity that took his breath away.

~ * ~

Holly drew a deep breath and blew out hard. Thank goodness Dan had left her alone for a minute. Couldn't he feel the tension in the room? Whether she wanted to admit it or not, she was just as horrible as her mother. She wanted Dan. She had wanted him from the first moment she saw him, and nothing had changed.

Nothing had changed? What a joke! Everything had changed, and since she had decided to face the truth, she'd admit something else. She didn't just want Dan; she loved him. It had taken a long time to admit it, but she loved him to distraction, and what's more, she thought he loved her too.

How was she supposed to behave after such an epiphany? Her breath caught in her throat. The issue rested with Dan, not with her. He liked her kisses, but he'd never said anything about loving her. She frowned. There was no way she'd shame herself by declaring her feelings for a man who might not love her back. Maybe she could pretend this evening was nothing more than a trip she had taken with a good friend.

She was pouring the tea when Dan joined her. "Let's eat the chocolate rose," he said.

"Where is it?"

"In my coat pocket."

He got the rose and sat down on the loveseat with Holly who took the flower and unwrapped it. She broke off one of the chocolate leaves and held it to Dan's lips. "Try a bite."

Dan's eyes met hers. He took the chocolate from her fingers, but he also took her hand and kissed it. "Better than chocolate."

Desire, white-hot, raging, and unquenchable, hit her full force in the pit of her stomach. All he'd done was kiss her hand!

Dan extended a chocolate petal to Holly who had no interest in chocolate at the moment. Boldly, she took Dan's hand and placed it against the side of her face for one brief moment. She loved his capable, strong hands, but she loved their gentleness even more.

"I've never seen your eyes so dark," she marveled. Yeah, she was as big a slut as her mother, but right now she didn't care. For once she refused to worry if she acted like Rita or not. Tonight she intended to follow her heart, and her heart told her she belonged to Dan.

"I remember what you look like without your shirt," Holly whispered. Her finger trembled as she unbuttoned Dan's shirt and slid it off his shoulders.

Speaking above a whisper seemed impossible, but she and Dan needed no words. They needed something far more elemental than words. Why had she chosen to act on her feelings tonight? It was as trashy as anything that her mother had ever done, but at the moment she had no control at all over her emotions. She'd probably be sorry later, but right then she didn't care.

With a sound somewhere between a gasp and a moan, her hand came to rest, palm down, on the front of his chest.

Dan was beautiful. Maybe that word usually referred to women, but it was the correct term anyway. He was beautiful. She traced the outline of the muscles, examining a scar here and there and familiarizing herself with the texture of his skin.

When she slipped her arms around him, Dan hugged her close. He bent his head to kiss her, but Holly murmured, "No, Dan, please don't move. Just let me hold you."

She drew him close and rested her face against his for a moment before dropping little kisses on his neck and the front of his chest.

Dan groaned aloud and jerked, so Holly knew he couldn't wait any longer. He kissed her long and lovingly and thrilled her so much she hoped he'd never let her go, but he groaned and pushed her from him. "Why are you doing this? You know I won't sell you the farm."

She wanted him so much she couldn't think straight, so she told him the truth. "Because I lov...like you."

The fire in Dan's eyes intensified. "I like your first answer better. Do you really love me?"

Holly blushed from head to toe when she realized what she'd said. How stupid was she anyway? Was she trying to chase him away? He had never said he loved her. Her eyes filled with tears. "I'm sorry. I shouldn't have said it."

"Why not?" Dan asked as he reached for her hand. "I've been in love with you ever since the first time I saw you at the farm. That's why I was so angry when I thought you'd sleep with my grandfather just to make a sale."

"You don't have to say that," Holly mumbled, her eyes glued to the carpet.

"Even if it's true?"

She chanced a peek at his face. "You love me?" she breathed.

"Yes, I do. I'm just surprised that you love me back."

His humble, gentle tone upset Holly. Could he possibly think himself unworthy of her love? "Why would that surprise you?" she demanded as she tossed her hair from her face. "We've both known the truth for a long time now, even if we didn't want to admit it."

Dan grimaced. He looked at her as if she should know why he felt that way. "My father was a drug dealer, Holly, and my mother's family has been called white trash more times than I can count. You probably make more money than I do. Stuff like that is the reason you ought to think twice before you get involved with me, and dammit, I ought to care enough about you to walk away, but I can't."

"Oh please, don't walk away!"

"I'm not going anywhere." Dan wrapped his arms around Holly and kissed her, a passionate, deep kiss that sent waves of heat racing through her.

She had never felt this way. She hadn't known about the fire that made her heart pound and sensitized her skin until his slightest touch set her all atremble. She hadn't known that her knees would want to buckle, that an overwhelming desire to feel his bare skin against her own would torment her. She hadn't known about the hot, gut-wrenching desire to wrap herself around him, letting him touch her in a way no man had ever touched her.

She tore her mouth from his and hid her face on his chest. *Oh the scent of him- strong, male and primeval!* "Do you want to make love?" she whispered.

"You know I do." Dan eagerly bent his head to kiss her again but paused when she shook in his arms.

Holly turned her flushed face to his. "What's wrong, Dan? Don't you want me?"

"Yes, I want you." He gently stroked her cheek. "I want you so bad it literally hurts me not to have you, but I can't."

Some of Holly's euphoria ebbed away. "Why not? I want you too. It's okay."

Dan shook his head, frustration and regret emanating from him in almost palpable waves. "I can't do it because of the way you feel about your mother. If you sleep with me, you may hate yourself in the morning, and I can't, I won't, do a thing like that to you."

Holly's face burned as shame scorched her. "You don't want me," she cried.

"Marry me."

"Wha...What?"

"You heard me," Dan said. "Marry me. You couldn't hate yourself for making love with your husband."

"Dan, I... I..."

"Marry me, Holly." He grabbed her hands and held on tight. "I love you, and I want to spend my life with you."

Head spinning, she tried to settle down enough to think. Was he serious? Did she even want to get married? The words tore themselves from her throat without conscious thought on her part. "I wouldn't want a big wedding."

Dan drew a deep breath and snuggled her against him, which sent another bolt of lightning stabbing through her. "Why not? I thought women liked that sort of thing."

Holly shuddered. "No, not me. I don't think I could bear it."

"I don't want a big wedding either. Too many drunken relatives."

"We could have a party to announce our marriage."

Dan took a deep, shaky breath. "Are you saying yes?"

"Y...Yes," Holly quavered. *Marriage is a trap*, she thought, but it didn't matter. Nothing mattered except Dan.

She felt his lips against her hair. "When do you want to do it?"

"I don't know," Holly whispered. Who could think at a time like this?

Dan ran his hand through her hair. "Let's do it tomorrow. There's no waiting period in this state. We could get a license tomorrow morning and be married by lunchtime. I have some business I have to take care of tomorrow afternoon, but after that, we could have a short honeymoon."

Her mother would eventually come home. *If we wait, my mother will have to come to the wedding, and I couldn't stand it if she flirted with Dan before the ceremony. Yes, we should get married now.*

"Tomorrow," she agreed, with a weak smile while Dan echoed, "Tomorrow."

Nineteen

Holly tossed and turned all night long, tormented by nightmares that refused to let her rest. Dan didn't sleep well either. She heard him moving around in bed for a long time before he dropped off. It was still dark outside, and it felt early when she heard him get out of bed and tiptoe to the bathroom. The shower started to run, the sound of the pattering water lulling her into a fitful doze that ended when she felt Dan's weight on the bed beside her.

"Holly? Are you awake?" he asked as he smoothed her tumbled hair from her face.

"Yes, I'm awake. What time is it?"

"It's around six. I'm going to the stable to see to a few things. I'll be back around eight, and then if you want to, we'll get some breakfast."

"Okay. I'll be ready." She could have cried because she felt so odd and unlike herself. All the parameters of her life seemed to have been ripped away. She was left unable to respond in familiar, normal patterns, and it scared her to death.

Dan touched the side of her face and leaned over to kiss her forehead. "I'll be back soon. Sleep a little longer if you can."

He got up, and Holly heard him put his coat on and leave the room. She turned over and tried to go back to sleep, but her nerves hummed with tension. Might as well get up; she sure couldn't sleep.

Instead, she rolled over again and thumped her pillow into shape. Dan hadn't said anything at all about getting married. He'd probably changed his mind. Well, good. What could have possessed her last night? It was bad enough that she'd taken his shirt off and propositioned him, but to agree to marry him! Had she totally lost her mind?

Yeah, she had. Marriage was a trap she'd always intended to avoid. She liked her independence and being in charge of her own life. Her mother had shown her what loving a man could do to a woman, and she wanted no part of such nonsense.

Holly rolled over again. "Hormones, that's all it is, hormones," she said aloud. "He's so sexy, and I'm sharing a room with him. It's just hormones. Once we get home, everything will be fine. Thank goodness he came to his senses in time."

Holly hit her pillow again. *He kissed me and stroked my hair*. She sighed, the sound ragged and uneven in the still room.

Maybe she should call Nana. Nana could help her decide what to do. Holly threw back the covers and picked up the phone, but she replaced it almost immediately. This was not a decision Pauline could make for her; it was hers and hers alone.

~ * ~

When the door opened shortly before eight, Holly jumped and smeared mascara on top of her eye shadow.

"Steady girl," Dan called out. "It's just me. Did I scare you?"

"Yes, you startled me."

"I'm sorry." He crossed the room without removing his jacket and hugged Holly. "Could I get a good morning kiss?"

This didn't much sound like a man who had changed his mind overnight. Holly moved into his arms and gave him a chaste peck on the lips.

Dan frowned. "That was lukewarm at best. Aren't you a morning person, or have you changed your mind about marrying me?" He shrugged out of his coat and tossed it on the bed.

Holly hunched her shoulders. "I thought maybe you had changed your mind."

The smile on his face and the light in his eyes almost took her breath away. "Holly, don't you know how much I love you? I'd never change my mind. I need you so much it almost scares me, but if you aren't sure, I'd rather wait. We can take our time and get married this summer if that's what you want."

What a wonderful, wonderful man! In a split second, Holly threw years of conviction out the window. All those lectures about marriage and men. "I haven't changed my mind either. If you still want me, I'll marry you today."

"Then kiss me like you mean it."

This time Holly relaxed against him, and when his lips touched hers, she kissed him with all the love that was in her. "Is that better?" she gasped. Her heart was pounding so hard she could hear her own heartbeat, and her knees had turned to jelly. She didn't know how Dan had liked that kiss, but it sure had done things to her.

He didn't speak for a moment, but the smoldering look in his eyes gave Holly her answer. The fire had singed Dan too. A sense of feminine power she had never felt before filled her, and she'd have to admit she liked it.

~ * ~

"You aren't eating much," Dan said, as Holly pushed her eggs to the side of her plate.

"I'm not too hungry, I guess."

"It'll make you feel better to eat a little. Please try." He reached across the table to give her hand a squeeze.

He was so sweet, so thoughtful, and she loved him so much. "I love you, Dan," she blurted out, almost ashamed to have spoken the worlds aloud.

"And I love you. I hoped you'd tell me you love me before we get married. I needed to hear it."

Holly flushed and stared into his blue velvet eyes. "I told you last night that I love you."

"No, you said you like me," he corrected.

"Well, I do," Holly agreed with a smile, "but I love you too."

"Not as much as I love you."

Holly laughed. No doubt she loved him more. "You said you needed to hear me say I love you. What else do you need from me? I don't know anything about what a man needs. Tell me what you want from me."

Dan knew exactly what he wanted. "I want everything my parents should have had and didn't. I want you to live with me and share my life. I want you to sleep beside me every night. I want you to support me and encourage me. I want you to trust me and believe in me even though my last name is Wakefield. I want you to grow old with me."

Holly's eyes misted. Dan had described a common, shared life, the very thing she longed for. "There's one thing you left out."

"What's that, honey?"

"You didn't say you want me to be the mother of your children."

The look of tenderness on Dan's face changed, replaced by anxiety. "Is it absolutely necessary that we have babies?"

Holly blinked. He didn't want children? "Yes, it is necessary. I want at least two and maybe three babies. Why don't you want any kids?"

Dan put his fork down and gave up any pretense of eating. "I don't want babies because I'm afraid I have bad genes I might pass down to my children. What if they turned out like my father?"

"How could a man like you worry about something like that?" Holly gently scolded. "If anybody should be worrying about bad genes, it's me, but I don't think we have anything to concern us. I'm not trying to be difficult, but having children isn't negotiable. I want you to give me your word of honor that when I'm ready for babies, you'll cooperate with me."

Holly held her breath as she waited for his answer. What would she do if he said no? She didn't have the courage to let him go. Relief swamped her when he finally answered.

"Okay, I agree. Two kids, and I won't give you any trouble about it."

A little petting right about now wouldn't hurt anything. Nana always talked about the fragile male ego. "Thank you, darling. I promise you won't be sorry. With you as a father, our children can't help but be wonderful. Don't you know what a fine man you are?"

The look of tension melted from Dan's face, so he must feel better about being a father someday. He glanced at his watch. "Are you finished?" he asked.

Holly nodded, and Dan signaled for his check. "Let's get out of here. I want to find a jewelry store."

"Why?"

"Because I'm not marrying a woman without a ring."

Oh. She'd forgotten about rings. "Will you wear one?"

"Of course I will, but I don't want anything fancy. Just a plain gold band, please."

Holly nodded. "That's fine by me."

They found a jewelry store not far from the restaurant. Dan's ring was easy to buy; it was mainly a matter of getting the proper size, but when Holly asked for a matching band, Dan demurred.

"I'd like to see some diamonds," he said to the clerk.

"Would you excuse us for a moment?" Holly asked. The clerk smiled and moved away, looking faintly annoyed. "Don't buy a diamond," she whispered to Dan. "They're expensive, and it isn't necessary."

Dan sighed. "I don't know whether to be pleased that you want to let me off the hook because I don't have much money or insulted because you don't think I can give you a diamond like other women wear. It won't be as big as I'd like it to be, but you are getting one."

Holly got ready to argue, but Dan had made up his mind. "If it makes you uncomfortable, go and look at something else while I pick it out."

"You sure are being stubborn," Holly chided, with a laugh. She wandered over to a display of earrings, and Dan joined the clerk to look at diamonds. In spite of her best efforts, she watched as Dan looked over a tray of rings. Oh. He was handing one of them to the clerk who took both the ring and what looked like a credit card.

Dan signed a slip and handed it to the clerk. Surely, he didn't go overboard. He saw her looking at him and smiled, so she joined him. "Do you want to wear it out?" he asked.

"Yes."

Dan removed it from the box and slid it on her finger. It was beautiful. He had picked a small, marquise cut stones set in gold with small diamonds on either side of the stone.

"That's a pretty stone," observed the clerk. "It's small, but the color and clarity are excellent."

"I'm sorry it isn't bigger," Dan apologized, as they left the store. He twirled Holly's hand to let the sun catch the diamond's sparkle.

Holly bumped him with her shoulder. "You are so silly. Don't you know I love it because you gave it to me? I wouldn't trade this ring for anything in the world."

Dan's face flushed with what she thought was pleasure. "I'd like to give you the moon, Holly. You know how much I love you, right?"

Holly took his hand and laced her fingers through his. "Yes, I know how much you love me, but are you always so stubborn?"

"Probably. Think you can handle me?"

"I'll have to put a snaffle bit on you," she teased.

Dan laughed. "I like it when you use horse talk, but I think you mean a curb bit."

By this time they had reached the space where they had parked Dan's truck. They got in, and Dan gently kissed her hand. "Are you sure, Holly? I don't want you to do this just because you want sex with me. I want you to do it because you love me, and if you aren't sure, I'd rather wait. We could announce our engagement and take our time planning a wedding."

"How did I get so lucky?" Holly marveled. "You always think of me and my feelings first. You even bought me a diamond, and you didn't have to. Yes, Dan. I'm sure. I love you, and I don't want to wait."

Dan gave her a quick hug. "Let's go get married."

Twenty

They arrived at the courthouse in what seemed like the blink of an eye to Holly. Furtively, she wiped her cold, sweaty hands on her pants and tried to steady her heart. It had raced like a Thoroughbred's the minute Dan turned into the courthouse parking lot. Why wouldn't he stop talking about the horse show? Didn't he realize both of them were about to change the course of their entire lives?

It didn't get any better when they applied for their marriage license. "May I see your driver's license, ma'am?" the clerk asked.

"Yes, let me find it."

Her wallet had fallen to the very bottom of her bag. She jerked it out and dropped the entire thing on the floor. Gift cards, receipts, pictures, and change scattered all over the floor. "I'm sorry, I'm sorry. Give me a minute."

Dan had to help her pick up the mess.

Signing the required documentation was another little purgatory. No matter how hard she tried, her hand wouldn't stop shaking. Probably no one could read her name. She breathed a sigh of relief when the courthouse granted them a license and directed them to the second floor where they would find Judge Ross.

"So, you two want to get married?" the judge inquired, as they were shown into his chambers. He smiled and indicated that they should take a seat in front of his desk.

Dan answered for both of them. "Yes, sir. We do."

"Do you have a marriage license?"

"Yes, sir." Dan produced the marriage license, and Judge Ross looked it over to be sure that everything was in order.

He laid the document down on his desk. "Did you bring anyone with you to serve as witnesses?"

Dan shook his head. "No, we didn't. Do we need them?"

"Yes, the ceremony has to be witnessed, but don't worry. My secretary and I can do it."

Of its own volition, Holly's hand crept toward Dan's, seeking the comfort the touch would bring, but she jerked it back at the last second. Holding hands might not be appropriate in front of a judge.

Judge Ross saw and smiled at her. "You can hold his hand if you want to, Ms. Grant. I'll call Pamela, and we'll get started."

Holly blushed and Dan nodded, and moments later, the secretary entered the room and took her place beside the judge. "Dan, Holly, come and stand in front of me, please."

The judge waited until they had taken their places to begin. "Dan, are you ready to enter into this marriage with Holly?"

"Yes, sir."

"Holly, are you ready to enter into this marriage with Dan?"

"Yes, sir."

"Dan, do you take Holly to be your wedded wife, to live together after God's ordinance in holy matrimony? Do you promise to love her, honor her, and cherish her in joy and in sorrow, in sickness and in health, and to be a good and faithful husband as long as you both shall live?"

"I do." Dan's voice rang out strong and true.

"Holly, do you take Dan to be your wedded husband, to live together after God's ordinance in holy matrimony? Do you promise to love him, honor him, and cherish him in joy and in sorrow, in sickness and in health, and to be a good and faithful wife as long as you both shall live?”

“I do,” Holly whispered.

“Do you have rings for each other?” the judge asked. At Dan's nod, he continued. “Would you exchange them?”

Dan slipped Holly's ring on first, and it settled onto her finger with no problem at all. She had some trouble getting his ring onto his finger, but with a sigh of relief that she thought amused Judge Ross, it finally went on.

“Now,” continued the judge, who sometimes liked to wax poetic, “you will feel no rain, for each of you will be shelter for the other. Now you will feel no cold, for each of you will be warmth to the other. Now there will be no loneliness, for each of you will be companion to the other. Now you are two persons, but there is only one life before you. May beauty surround you both in the journey ahead and through all the years. May happiness be your companion and your days together be good and long upon the earth.

“Because they have so affirmed, so also do I declare that Dan Wakefield and Holly Grant are now husband and wife. Dan, you may kiss your bride.”

When Dan's lips met hers, Holly's heart took off in a mad gallop that would rival that of a Kentucky Derby winner. *Oh, Dan!*

They completed the necessary paperwork, and with the congratulations of the judge ringing in their ears, Dan took Holly's hand as they left the courthouse together.

~ * ~

“Your hand is freezing, and you haven't said one word,” Dan said, as they crossed the parking lot. “It's over, baby. You can relax now.”

Because he still held her hand, Holly could feel his wedding ring pressed against her hand, and she could see her own ring. The enormity of what she had just done had only just begun to sink in. If only she could throw herself down and cry her heart out. She had come to Fort Timothy for a horse show, not a wedding. Why had she lost her mind and done this thing?

Dan didn't help matters either. Once they reached his truck, he drew her into his arms and kissed her, a possessive, deep kiss that terrified her. She jerked away from him.

"What's wrong?" Dan asked as he touched her cheek. "Did I scare you?"

"A little. That kiss was ...possessive." How wonderful that she could speak after all. For a while there, she had feared her nerves had stricken her mute forever.

"Well, we do belong to each other now." He gave her shoulders a little squeeze. "I like that idea."

"I've belonged only to myself for twenty-eight years," Holly cried. "When I think of belonging to you, I get a funny, fluttery feeling in my stomach, and I get scared."

Dan smiled, and even in her fear, she recognized his gentle strength and good, tender character. "You don't have to be afraid of me, Holly. I love you, and I want you to be happy. I'd never do anything to hurt you."

"I know. It's just that everything is so new. Give me a little time to adjust," she begged. Gah, what kind of a spineless coward was she? People got married all the time. Why did she have to ruin things by acting like a child?

"It'll be fine, honey. Belonging to somebody you love is a good thing." Dan pulled her against him and rested his face against her hair. "I love you very much, and everything's going to be wonderful. Just you wait and see."

Twenty-one

"Do you want me to carry you over the threshold?" Dan teased as he used his key card to unlock the door of their room. Without waiting for her answer, he scooped Holly into his arms and carried her inside. He kicked the door shut with his foot, and as Holly's feet touched the floor, he pulled her against him.

"I love you, Mrs. Wakefield."

Holly Wakefield! "I didn't think about my name," Holly said. How had she let such a thing slip by her? "I forgot my name is Holly Wakefield now."

Dan was too busy nuzzling her neck to hear the note of regret in Holly's voice. "Mmm, I like that name. Holly Wakefield."

Sounded weird to her. She pushed against his chest to put a little distance between them. "If you're going to show that horse, you have to get dressed and leave very soon."

Dan grimaced. "I know it, and there's something I have to do for a few hours afterwards. Tell you what, after the class is over, you can drive back here, and I'll catch a ride home with somebody after I finish my business. Then, we can go to the party, or if you want to, we can start our honeymoon."

His voice fell on the last words becoming husky and oh, so suggestive. A ripple of desire laced with regret chilled Holly. What was wrong with her? Wasn't this what she'd wanted?

What was the difference between last night and the present? She drew a deep breath. If only she could figure out why she was so...so.... desperate and scared.

"We'll see how we feel about the party later." She hugged Dan briefly. "Go get dressed now."

Obediently, he began to take some clothes from one of the room's nice wardrobes and disappeared into the bathroom to change.

She wanted to change her own clothes, but she'd better wait because she had no idea what people wore to a horse show.

Dan came out of the bathroom wearing what looked awfully formal to ride a horse. He had on a white shirt and tie with a black jacket, well-fitted trousers, and knee boots. "You look really nice in your riding clothes, Dan. What do the spectators wear?"

"Anything is fine," Dan answered. "Some dress up, and some don't. You see a little bit of everything." He smiled at her. "You could wear a plastic bag and still be the prettiest woman there."

His compliment warmed Holly's heart. She took her taupe slacks and black sweater to the bathroom with her. While Dan was doing business this afternoon, she'd go shopping. The only nightwear she had with her were the white lounging pajamas and a flannel gown, neither of which seemed appropriate for a wedding night.

Holly's stomach lurched at the thought of lying in bed with Dan. *I'm lots more scared now than I was last night. I guess it's because last night I hadn't taken an irrevocable step like I did today.*

The more she thought about it, the plainer it became; being married scared her silly because once she consummated her marriage, it could only be undone by a divorce. She couldn't just pack her bags and go home. Last night she could have run away from a mistake, but today she couldn't.

"Holly? Are you okay in there?" Dan's voice sounded worried.

Holly wrenched open the door. "Yes, I'm fine."

"You look beautiful," Dan said, his voice warm and tender. He took her left hand and kissed her new rings. "I'm sorry I can't put off this business. I don't want to leave you on your own this afternoon, but there's no way to get out of it."

"I'd like to do a little shopping anyway. I'll do it while you're busy."

"Good idea." Dan took his wallet from his pants and handed Holly a hundred dollars. "Is that enough?"

Holly stared at the money in her hand. "I don't expect you to pay for my shopping trip."

"Take it, honey. You're my wife, and I want to do it."

Her eyes misted. Dan had no idea how much she actually spent on clothes. She'd have to take his money even though she probably had more in her purse than he did. She hugged him and cried, "Thank you, Dan. You won't be disappointed when you see what I buy."

"You have a good time." He paused to kiss her. "If you're ready, let's go. We can grab a bite to eat, and we'll just make it to the arena."

~ * ~

Thank goodness she wanted to go shopping. With Holly occupied at the mall, he could give his full attention to Cam Simmons. He'd waited almost his entire life for a chance to make Cam pay for all the lives he'd destroyed. It was nice to know that if things went like Richard planned, he'd have two reasons to rejoice each year when his anniversary rolled around.

~ * ~

Dan's appetite seemed to have returned. He cleaned up his lunch with no trouble at all, but Holly still found the thought of food unappealing and picked at her lunch as she had done her breakfast.

On the way to Chief's stall, they met Tommy Price. "Are we taking home a ribbon?" he cheerfully inquired. Tommy was almost always cheerful.

"We've got a good chance of it," Dan said. "He's been doing very well."

Tommy and Holly watched as Dan put the saddle and bridle on Chief. The horse's coat gleamed like new satin while his mane had several ribbons woven into it. Dan must have groomed the animal when he visited Chief earlier in the day.

"Where will the spectators sit?" Holly asked.

"You can sit with me," Tommy replied. "We'll watch Dan and Chief win a ribbon." He glanced at his watch. "I guess we should find our seats now."

"Good luck," Holly told Dan. Did he expect her to kiss him in front of Tommy Price? Maybe husbands expected good luck kisses.

Dan solved her dilemma by kissing her forehead. "See you in a minute," he said with a smile, and he guided Chief from his stall.

Tommy and Holly took their seats in the stands, and with little delay Tommy cleared his throat to get her attention. "Holly, if you don't mind my asking, how long have you and Dan been seeing each other?"

"Not too long. A few months."

"Dan's a good guy," Tommy said. "He's had some rough breaks in his life, though."

"You mean his dad?"

Oow, Tommy looked serious. Look at that little line between his eyes. "You know about Dan's father?"

Holly nodded. "Yes. He didn't try to keep it a secret from me, if that's what you're wondering."

"I don't really know what I'm wondering." Tommy shrugged. "I must be mistaken, but I thought I saw a wedding ring on Dan's finger, and it looks to me like you're wearing one too."

Holly struggled not to rub the new ring that was burning a circle into her finger. "You're not mistaken. I am wearing a wedding ring. Dan and I got married this morning. In fact, you're the first person to know."

Tommy looked relieved, probably because she knew about Dan's background. He smiled at Holly. "Congratulations to you both. I know you'll be very happy together."

"Thank you, Tommy." Her marriage wouldn't remain a secret once she and Dan returned to Fairfield, but Nana should hear about it from her, not somebody else.

She flipped her hair away from her face. "I haven't told my family yet, and neither has Dan. Please don't mention this to anybody. Dan and I want to tell them ourselves."

"Don't worry, Holly, or should I say Mrs. Wakefield? I won't spoil your surprise."

Holly thanked him, relieved that he understood.

"The horses are coming in now."

She looked in the direction of Tommy's nod and saw Dan almost immediately. "He looks so good on a horse," she sighed.

Tommy burst into laughter. "Spoken like a woman in love. Nobody gets all misty-eyed when I'm on a horse."

Holly had never attended a horse show, so all eight entrants looked good to her. The judge said something she couldn't hear, and the horses started to skim across the ring, their hooves slashing the air, manes and tails flying.

"Wow, that's pretty," she exclaimed. "What is it?"

"It's one of the five gaits these horses are trained to do. It's called a rack."

The horses lined up for the judges' review. Holly tensed and held her breath as they passed by Chief. The judges completed their work and conferred briefly before making their decision. She hadn't realized how tense she was until she heard them call the winning number; Dan had placed first. "That is so great!" she cried. "Can we go find Dan?"

"Sure, come on."

They made their way from their seats and found Dan who had dismounted outside the ring to give Chief a good petting and a carrot. His head turned at the sound of footsteps, and a big smile crossed his face when he saw her.

Holly still mourned the loss of her independence, but for the moment, love and pride conquered fear. Her eyes sparkled as she squeezed Dan's arm. "Dan Wakefield, do you know what a wonderful trainer you are? You made that animal do beautiful things. Let me see what you won."

He showed her Chief's ribbon, and then Tommy held out his hand to Dan. "Congratulations, Dan. Holly told me you two had gotten married."

"Thanks. I still don't know why she'd be willing to marry me."

"He doesn't have any idea how wonderful he is," Holly laughingly scolded. "I think that might be part of his charm."

Dan didn't say anything, but the hot light that danced in his eyes pleased her anyway.

Twenty-two

Dan took his time cleaning his horse and tack. He accepted congratulations on his win from several people who knew him and wondered who would soon approach him about a shipment of hay.

The voice came from behind him. "Dan Wakefield?"

Dan turned around and surveyed the speaker, a small, wiry man of indeterminate age. He had never seen the guy before. "Yeah, I'm Dan Wakefield. Who are you?"

The man didn't bother to give his name. "Your boss just bought a shipment of hay. I was supposed to give it to you to deliver."

"Okay."

"The truck's parked out front, the big red one. Here're the keys." The man handed Dan a set of keys and vanished as quickly as he had appeared.

Hoping the FBI was monitoring his every move, Dan put on his jacket and went to find the truck, which was exactly where the man had promised it would be. Nobody challenged his right to unlock the vehicle and drive away.

The farm where Cam Simmons lived lay twenty miles out of town. As Dan drove the truck off the show grounds, his heart picked up a little speed. So much could go wrong. Richard said the plan should work, but he also said every operation presented risks, which of course was true.

He took a deep breath and willed himself to be calm. *That scum is finally going to get what's coming to him.*

He passed the time by thinking of Holly. *She's scared. She wants me, but she's scared of me too. I do love her so much. I wonder what Gramps will say? He did tell me to marry her, but that was before he knew I'd really do it.*

What about her Nana? Pauline may not like Holly being married to me. She probably had somebody like Tommy picked out for Holly. Instead, she got a poor guy like me. Holly's friend Loretta doesn't like me or trust me. She'll be very upset when she finds out.

Dan paused his internal monologue long enough to be certain he had taken a correct turn. *I don't care what anyone thinks. Holly's my wife because she wants to be. I didn't kidnap her or force her to marry me. Whoever doesn't like it can just get over it.*

Dan sighed. He had to focus on the task at hand, but his thoughts strayed to his wedding night anyway. Had Holly ever had intimate relations with a man? His anxiety ratcheted up several notches. *If she's a virgin, I might hurt her, and I don't want to do that. It's great to think I'm the only one, but I don't want to be the one who hurts her.*

The thought of Holly underneath him, accepting him and hopefully deriving pleasure from their joining, sent such a jolt of need throughout him that he quivered from its force. *I want to get this mess with Cam finished, and I don't want to go to any party tonight either. I want to make love to my wife.*

Abruptly, he rounded a curve in the road and saw the entrance to Simmons' Farm. He passed through an impressive stone gate and turned down a long, tree-lined drive. In the distance he saw a big brick house sitting on a slight rise. Obviously, crime paid well.

He followed the drive to the place where it forked and found a small, discreet sign pointing the way to the stables. Dan turned as indicated, and moments later he switched off the motor in front of a large, well-maintained barn.

He didn't see anyone waiting to meet him, so he got out of the truck and made his way into the barn where a heavily muscled man with a neck as thick as any linebacker's greeted him. "Can I help you?"

"Yeah, the name's Wakefield. I've got a delivery of hay for Cam Simmons. Is he around?"

"Hey, Cam. Your hay just got here," bawled the goon. From the other side of the barn, Cam looked up and smiled at Dan.

"I hear you won today, Danny boy," he called, as he approached Dan.

"Yeah, I did."

Cam laughed as he dusted his hands on his pants. "Training horses must be in the blood. Your daddy was dynamite with a horse, and so is your grandpa. Looks like the apple didn't fall far from the tree."

"I guess not."

Cam gestured to the large man. "Call some of the boys to unload the hay."

Dan started to follow, but Cam detained him. "No, Danny, let them unload it. You come with me."

He led Dan into the barn's office and walked over to a refrigerator in the corner. "Want a beer?" He took one for himself and handed one to Dan who refused to take the bottle. "I don't drink. Not ever."

"Why not?"

"Because of my father."

"Yeah, I guess that makes sense," Cam replied. He replaced the beer in the refrigerator. "How about a ginger ale?"

"Sure."

Dan opened the ginger ale and remembered Richard's instructions. *"Don't talk too much, Dan. Let him do it. Don't agree to do anything more for him either. Just take your money, and if we don't interrupt you to arrest everyone, leave like everything is fine."*

Cam threw himself into a leather desk chair that was light years away from the beat up, rickety chair Dan used. "I heard a rumor that you're wearing a wedding ring, and you are. Did you marry the blonde?"

"Yes, I did."

"Bad move, Danny."

Dan bristled. "I don't see how that's any of your business. I think it was a great move."

"Nah. You were already having sex with her. You didn't have to marry her to get it." He shot Dan a shrewd look. "From what I've seen, you can't afford a wife like her."

Dan scowled and tried not to let Cam get to him. "Let me worry about that."

"I like you, Danny. I guess it's partly because of your father, but it's because of you too. You seem like a nice guy, but you don't get many breaks. How would you like to work for me full time? The pay would be good, and I think your wife would be a lot happier with her lifestyle."

Dan hesitated; he had to make this look good. "Look, I'm already feeling bad about this hay thing. I did need the money. That's why I agreed, but I never expected to work for you full time. I like what I'm doing right now, and I really don't want to make any changes in my occupation."

~ * ~

Cam smiled and made no further effort to convince him. Dan would come around. If he didn't have it in the back of his mind, he wouldn't have delivered the hay. It was funny how things worked out. He remembered the last time he'd seen Kyle, the day before the accident.

"So your boy's going to Tech, is he? There's a lot of business to be done on a college campus. Why don't you ask him if he'd be interested in working for us? He'd make good money. Probably, it'd be enough to pay for his education. That would save you a bundle, wouldn't it, Kyle?"

Kyle drained most of the beer in his bottle in one long swallow. "Leave Dan alone, Cam. He's different from me. He wants to be an architect, and I intend to see that he does."

"Hey, whatever you say. I was just offering."

"Don't. Dan's off limits to you. If I ever find out you've approached him, you and I are done."

"Kyle, you're getting all worked up over nothing," Cam placated.

Kyle shook his head; his eyes went cold. "I don't think so. My son is off limits, Cam. Remember what I said because if you ever bother him, I'll kill you."

Yes, Dan was a chip off the old block, all right. Kyle had thought he was different, but he was his daddy made over. They'd do good business together.

He took a key from his pocket and unlocked a drawer in his desk. "I hope you don't mind being paid in cash. This way, the IRS doesn't have to get involved."

"No, I don't mind at all."

"I won't press you for an answer today," Cam continued. "He took a slip of paper and wrote down a phone number. "This is my personal number. When you're ready to talk about working for me, give me a call. I could use a man like you, and I'd really make it worth your time."

Dan took the paper and the money and put them into his wallet. "I've got to go. Holly wants..."

What Holly wanted would forever remain a mystery to Cam because every entrance to the barn suddenly burst open, and dozens of armed men poured through the doors. "FBI! Hands in the air. Freeze!"

~ * ~

Dan whirled around. "Is there another way out of here?"

Cam shook his head in the negative. "I'm afraid not, Danny. Just stay cool. Remember, you don't know anything. You just delivered some hay, right?"

"Yeah, right."

From all over the property, the FBI rounded up Cam's men. Nobody as yet had approached the office, but Dan saw several weapons trained on him and Cam. He also saw Richard enter the barn. He approached the agents guarding the office and spoke briefly to them before entering the room. When he saw Dan, his face hardened, and his voice dripped icicles when he asked, "So, it's true after all, isn't it, Dan?"

"I don't know what you're talking about," Dan answered with a shrug.

"Kinkaid told me you'd met twice with this scum, but I just about called him a liar. After what happened to your father, I didn't expect you to be so stupid."

"I still have no idea what you're talking about," Dan answered, trying to make his voice as hard and abrasive as Richard's had been.

"Do you know this guy, Dan?" Simmons butted in.

"Yeah, he's married to my cousin. He's FBI."

The sick look on Cam's face almost amused Dan.

Sheriff Kinkaid appeared in the door beside Richard. The little smirk on his face annoyed Dan, even though he knew why Kinkaid did it. "It seems Dan might have made a small mistake in judgment," the sheriff observed to Richard.

Richard made no reply because an FBI agent escorted Joe Fisher, Cam's right-hand man, into the office. "Cuff Simmons and Fisher and take them out," Richard said to the agent at his elbow, "and somebody take Wakefield and question him. Sheriff Kinkaid and I are going through this office."

The agent made Cam and Joe sit down in two chairs that sat against the wall right outside the office. He didn't bother to close the door, so they could hear everything that was said in the office.

About a quarter of an hour went by before the agent who had questioned Dan returned to the office, ignoring Simmons and Fisher who still sat in those chairs.

"Richard, I don't really think Wakefield knows anything. He insists he was paid to deliver a load of hay, and that's what he did. He said it was a one-time thing he did just to get some extra money to spend on his girl, who by the way, is now his wife."

"His wife! When did that happen?"

"Just this morning."

"All right, hold him until I get there." Richard threw down the file in his hand. "Sheriff Kinkaid, I've got a favor to ask you."

"Yeah?"

"I want you to forget that Dan was ever here today. I know there's probably more going on than meets the eye, but he's my wife's cousin, and my wife is pregnant. I don't want her upset by any of this."

The sheriff practically exploded. "I've had Dan Wakefield under surveillance for years, and just when he makes a false move, you want me to forget it?"

"That's right. I want you to forget it," Richard said "Don't worry. I'll have a word of prayer with Dan, and I think I can guarantee that in future, he'll behave himself. If he doesn't, the next time I won't ask for any favors for him. Anyway, the case against him is weak at best."

"Weak? He delivered a load of hay and cocaine to this farm."

It seemed as if Richard could hardly contain his impatience. "He explained that. Now make up your mind. Will you do me this favor or not?"

Sheriff Kinkaid hesitated. "Do you give me your word that if he messes up again you won't stand in the way of his arrest?"

"You have my word of honor on it."

Kinkaid grimaced. "All right. Get him out of here."

"Thanks, I will." Richard hurried out of the office so fast he appeared not to notice the two men against the wall, but from their chairs, they could see him approach Dan who waited at the far end of the barn. The two burly agents who guarded him had handcuffed him with his hands behind his back.

Since Richard's back was turned to Cam and Joe, he smiled broadly at Dan. "We did it, Dan," he said. "We found the cocaine in one of the bales of hay. He's going to prison for a long time. We put the pressure on one of his men, and the man talked. We've got him."

Savage pleasure ripped through Dan. After ruining so many lives, Cam Simmons would finally get what he deserved. His mother at least would be proud of him. "That's great news, but how are you going to get me out of this mess?"

"That's already taken care of," Richard promised. "These thugs are all too willing to believe Sheriff Kinkaid agreed to let you go as a favor to me. They think you've been under surveillance for years. I don't think they'd touch you with a ten foot pole."

Dan felt the weight of a huge stone roll off his chest. "I never want to see Cam Simmons again."

"I don't blame you." Richard threw a big grin his way. "Hey, I heard you got married today."

Dan's expression softened. "I did. I still can't believe she'd have me, but she did."

"That makes what I've got to do even harder."

Uh oh. This didn't sound good. "What are you talking about?"

"I've got to hit you. Where do you want it?"

Dan tensed, and without warning the two agents behind him grabbed his arms.

"If you really were involved with these thugs, I'd be furious," Richard said, still keeping his voice low. "I told Sheriff Kinkaid I'd straighten you out, so this is the plan. I have to hit you once. When I do, you slump over, and before I can hit you again, these agents will let you go and grab me." He looked up at his men. "Do you understand what to do?"

"Yes, sir. We've got it. We've used this trick from time to time ourselves."

Richard tilted his head and thought for a minute. "If you just got married, you'd probably rather not have a sore face. Kissing and nuzzling are better if it doesn't hurt. Anyway, if you go home all beat up, it might scare your wife."

Dan flexed his arms. "I don't think this is necessary. I don't want you using me as a punching bag."

"I won't hurt you any more than I have to," Richard promised. He nodded at the FBI agents holding Dan. "Jerk him up straight."

Dan struggled to free himself, but the two large agents held him with no trouble. "Sorry, buddy," Richard said, and he swung hard at Dan's stomach.

Dan didn't have to pretend; he doubled over because he couldn't stand upright, and the agents had dropped his arms to grab Richard.

"Richard, that's enough!" Agent Tompkins ground out, his voice carrying throughout the barn. "You lose your head when you're angry, so I'm telling you, that's enough."

"Let go of me!" Richard jerked away from the men holding him, his face dark with rage. Both of the agents moved in front of Dan. "Richard, that's enough," Agent Tompkins repeated, more softly this time.

"Get him out of here," Richard snarled. "Take him wherever he wants to go." He stalked away as the agents hauled Dan to his feet.

Abruptly he swung around. "If you ever do anything like this again, I can't help you. Think about it." He strode outside where Dan heard him shouting orders to his men.

"Turn around," Agent Tompkins snapped.

Dan obeyed and Tompkins removed the handcuffs. The FBI man took his arm and led him outside the barn to an unmarked, black sedan. "Get in, Wakefield."

The agent's harsh demeanor changed once he got in the car. "You okay?"

"Yeah, I'm okay."

Tompkins smiled. "Good. Where do you want to go? To start your honeymoon, I guess."

The thought of Holly eased the pain in Dan's middle. "Yes. That's exactly what I'd like to do."

Tompkins fastened his seat belt and turned his car toward Fort Timothy. "Unless something happens and you have to, I wouldn't tell her if I were you. Your role in all of this has to remain a secret, and if more than one person knows a thing, it's hard to keep it quiet."

Tompkins had a good point. "You're right," Dan agreed. "I won't tell her." He didn't like keeping secrets from Holly, but this time he'd have to do it whether he liked it or not. Her safety was far too important to take chances.

Twenty-three

Dan opened his hotel room to the sound of water running in the bathroom. He waited a moment to see if Holly sang in the shower, but evidently she didn't. Warmth flooded his heart. He had a lifetime to learn new things about her.

He removed his coat and rummaged in the refrigerator for a bottle of water. His stomach felt achy, so maybe he'd take a couple of ibuprofen. He had a bottle in his coat pocket, and it might relieve the soreness.

He had just swallowed his ibuprofen when Holly charged into the bedroom. She had wrapped a huge towel around her, and he'd have sworn she jumped about ten feet when she saw him standing there.

"Hi. Did you miss me?"

Holly's face turned an enchanting shade of shell pink. "Yes, of course I missed you. When did you get back?" She fiddled with her towel and tucked it more firmly in place.

"Just now." Dan held out his hand. "You look good in a towel," he said, as his eyes boldly raked her, claiming her as his own. "Come here, Holly."

He made no move to close the distance between them; he waited for her to come to him, and she did. His arms closed around her. "You're trembling."

"I'm sorry."

Her nerves had betrayed her. Her voice was quivering as much as her body.

He touched her beautiful golden hair. "This is going to be all right. Now, forget that damn towel you're clutching and hold me back."

Holly put her arms around him, and the towel slid to the floor. Since he held her so tightly, she could probably feel his arousal, but he didn't mind if she knew how much he wanted her. She was his wife, and if she were willing, he'd take her here and now.

He stroked her back, moving leisurely across the curve of her hips to her buttocks. "Your skin feels like warm satin," he breathed.

He tilted Holly's head back and looked into her eyes. "Okay?"

"Uh huh."

He kissed her again, and she returned his kiss with eagerness, but when he touched her breast she backed away with eyes stretched wide. "Don't!"

"All right," he answered, keeping his voice nice and calm. He retrieved her towel from the floor and handed it to her. "I saw you had your dress out of the bag. Do you want to go to the party tonight?"

Holly tucked her towel around her as though it would be enough to protect her from him if he really wanted to have her. "You ought to go," she said. "People do a lot of business at parties. You did well today, and you should be available for people to talk to you."

"Okay, we'll go. Just let me shower and shave first."

~ * ~

When the bathroom door slammed behind Dan, she rushed over to the bed and dressed in record time. She took a deep breath and tried to relax. Lord, she was an idiot!

She hated to look when he came out of the bathroom for fear he'd be naked, but he wasn't. He had his robe on, and he wore it while he shaved in the dressing room. She watched him from the comparative safety of the bedroom, intrigued by the masculine ritual.

Dan noticed her attention as he glanced into the mirror. "What's so interesting about watching me shave?"

"Everything. I don't remember ever watching a man shave."

"Not even your dad?"

She shook her head. "Daddy was a real private person. He never let anyone in the bathroom with him, not even Mother."

"You can watch me anytime. I don't mind."

Holly did watch him for a few minutes more. "I'm sorry about what happened a while ago."

Dan looked at her through the mirror. "You mean when I touched you?"

"Yes. I'll try not to be...difficult. Just be patient with me."

Dan finished his shave, rinsed his razor, and joined her in the bedroom. "Honey, I know you're scared, but you aren't your mother, and we're married. You'll enjoy making love to me. You don't have to be afraid."

Holly rested her head on his chest. "I love you, Dan, and I don't want to disappoint you."

"I love you too, and you couldn't disappoint me if you tried. Now, get your party dress on." He ran his hand through her hair. "Let's not stay too long, okay?"

Holly's mouth went dry, and with a shiver of apprehension, she finished dressing. How could what you wanted change so drastically from one day to the next? Last night she had offered herself to Dan because she wanted him so much, but today she'd love to pack her bag and run away. Funny, huh?

~ * ~

"Who's that woman with Dan Wakefield?"

Everyone at the party wanted to know, and the news of Dan's marriage spread rapidly. Several people approached Dan about training their horses, and most folks offered what seemed like sincere congratulations on his marriage. Holly went out of her way to be charming and friendly to everyone she met. All in all, she thought she and Dan made a good impression.

She really did love parties, but she made no protest when Dan wanted to leave around seven-thirty. With a smile she passed her business card to the realtor whom she had discovered in the crowd. "If you need to get in touch with me, you'll have my fax and phone number handy."

Dan helped her with her coat, and they made their way to their car. "You got two horses," Holly exulted, "and my new friend in there may throw some business my way. I'd say it was a very profitable party for us both."

Dan laughed.

"What's so funny?" she demanded with a shove to his shoulder.

"I love that satisfied expression on your face. You enjoy doing business, and it shows. I hope you can help me think of new ways to make Turnaround pay. That would sure be nice." He gave her hand a little squeeze. "When it came to finding a wife, I did all right. Did my bride get enough to eat at the party, or does she want something else?"

"I'm not hungry."

"I'm not hungry either. Let's go back to the hotel."

Holly's heart raced like she'd just run the Boston Marathon. How could her mother sleep with men so easily? She felt numb with fear, but Dan was her husband, and she didn't intend to spoil her wedding night by acting like a frightened child. "Yes," she agreed as she reached for his hand. "Let's go back to the hotel."

They reached the Ballentine and went to their room. "That didn't take long," Dan said as he shut the room door behind them. "Holly, you do look beautiful tonight. I can't tell you how proud it made me to introduce you to everyone."

Holly's vision blurred. She had never known such a sweet, good-natured man, and he belonged to her. "Oh, Dan, I'm the one who felt proud. Don't you know every woman in the room envied me?"

Her heart swelled with emotion that had to find outlet. She moved into Dan's arms and gently traced the outline of his lips. They felt warm and firm beneath her finger. Taking this small liberty gave her courage, and she gently skimmed his face, familiarizing herself with his shape.

Dan kissed the top of her head. "Sweetheart, have you ever made love to a guy before?"

Holly's brow drew together in a frown. "Does it matter?"

"Yes, it matters. If you've never done this before, we'll need to take things slow and easy."

Holly's face burned. "You're the first." She couldn't meet Dan's eyes because she didn't know if he wanted a virgin or not. Maybe he would rather have an experienced woman.

To her relief, he didn't make a big deal out of it. "Okay, I just needed to know. Do you want to get ready for bed now?"

Holly's composure slipped, but she tried to pretend she looked forward to making love with him. "Yes, I'm ready," she croaked. "I got something new to wear too." She hoped her voice would stop misbehaving; she hated sounding like a frog.

"I can't wait to see it. Run in the bathroom and put it on."

Holly fumbled in her shopping bag for her new gown and entered the bathroom, making sure to lock the door behind her. She tried to unzip her dress, but the darn thing got stuck, and it took forever to free it. *Finally. I guess I should have called Dan to do it.* Now there was a thought. Dan would now be available to help with stuck zippers and pull things down from high shelves. *Not the major benefits of a husband, but nice anyway.*

She glanced at herself in the mirror. Her eyes looked enormous and scared in her pale face. *I wonder how many brides go to their husbands looking like I do? I look like the dentist told me I need a root canal. It would have been easier to get this over with last night when I was so hot for him.*

She pulled on her new semi-sheer gown, switched off the bathroom light, and reluctantly left this final sanctuary. Dan had turned the bedroom lights on low and got into bed. He had taken his shirt off, and Holly would have taken odds he had removed his briefs too. Her heart pounded and roared in her ears; the unthinkable was rapidly becoming the reality!

"You're beautiful," Dan breathed. "Take off your gown and come to bed, sweetheart."

Almost frozen with fear, she forced herself to obey him. What else could she do? He was her husband after all. Anyway, this was what she'd wanted, right? She slipped out of the gown she had just put on, and Dan turned the covers back invitingly. "Come on, honey," he gently urged. "Come to bed with me."

As she pulled the covers over her legs, she felt the warmth from Dan's body reach out to touch her. "I guess that's another benefit of marriage."

"What?"

"You've got the bed warm. That's a benefit of marriage."

Dan laughed. "Yes, it is, and if you live at Turnaround Farm, it's a very important benefit."

Remembering the cold bedroom she and Loretta had shared, Holly had to agree.

"Lie down, Holly," Dan coaxed. "Let me hold you."

Holly lay down and shivered as his arms closed around her. With his arms around her, she couldn't run away if she wanted to! "Hold me," Dan whispered.

Her fear receded when she hugged him. He felt warm and masculine against her, and he didn't rush her at all. He took plenty of time for kisses and caresses, and if she faltered or drew back, he patiently coaxed her until her fears melted away.

Her heart swelled with love, and the name Holly Wakefield had a beautiful ring to it. She forgot about her mother and all of those men. She wasn't her mother. Her name was Holly Wakefield, and she loved Dan Wakefield to distraction.

"I love you, Dan," she cried at the end of a passionate kiss that sent chills racing up and down her spine.

"I love you too, baby," he said, and he made her his own.

~ * ~

It took what seemed like a long time for the sensory daze in which Holly floated to subside. She snuggled closer to Dan and rested her head on his shoulder. She had acted so silly. Dan had told her not to be afraid, and he'd been right.

He roused and kissed Holly's forehead. "How do you feel, Mrs. Wakefield?"

Holly smiled and gave his ribs a squeeze. "I feel married, and I like it very much. I feel like I really do belong to you, and it gives me the warmest, most wonderful feeling I've ever experienced. My mother probably felt this way about my father. What a pity she let grief mar the memory of their love."

"I love you, Mrs. Wakefield."

"Oh, Dan, I love you too!"

Dan's arm briefly tightened around her. "Your nana won't be angry with me for marrying you, will she?"

Holly laughed. "You're joking, right? Nana'll be thrilled. She may fuss because we didn't have a big wedding, but we'll let her help plan our party. What about your grandfather? Will he be happy or not?"

"He told me several days ago that I should marry you."

"He did! Isn't he afraid I'm only using you to get his farm?"

"I guess not." Dan paused a moment. "Turnaround still isn't for sale, you know."

Holly hid her face against his shoulder. "I'm embarrassed that you even thought you should mention it. I know you won't sell. I married you because I love you, not because I hoped to get your property."

Dan kissed her, the look of relief on his face telling her that she had laid a fear to rest.

"What are we going to do when we go home tomorrow?" he asked.

"What are you talking about?"

"Well, for starters, where do we sleep tomorrow night?"

Holly stared blankly at him. "I really didn't think about it. I just pictured me going to my house, and you going back to Turnaround."

"Holly, you're my wife, and I expect to live in the same house with you."

"I know that, and I guessed you'd want to live at Turnaround. I somehow just didn't picture it happening tomorrow."

"Do you mind living at Turnaround?"

Oh, she minded all right. She thought of her own small, beautifully decorated home located so close to her office. Who'd want to give it up for an old, drafty, inconvenient farmhouse?

Dan tensed beside her. "There isn't a problem, is there?

"No," Holly said. "It'll be an adjustment, but I'll get used to it."

"I don't want to make you unhappy. I want you to like being my wife."

She smiled and cupped his cheek in her hand. "I already like being your wife. Don't worry. I'll adjust to life at Turnaround." She shifted against him. "It is going to be a little embarrassing for your grandfather to know we're sleeping together a few rooms away from him."

Dan smiled. "He's been married, honey. He knows about the birds and the bees."

Holly thought about the huge, cold house heated in only two rooms. *If I were selling it, I'd call the room they live in a keeping room,* she mused, remembering the kitchen, dining, and living area all rolled into one. *I don't like it, but I'll get used to it.* Marrying Dan had come with a price, but what a good deal she had made. Exchanging a house for Dan Wakefield had to be the best transaction of her entire life.

Dan reached for her hand and kissed it. "I think Loretta's going to be ticked off at you. She doesn't like me much."

"But I do," Holly said with a scowl. "Loretta will have to grin and bear it, and she'd better not be rude to you. I won't tolerate it."

"Don't make a fuss over it. She'll come around faster if you don't."

"What about Nikki?" She pushed the blanket away from her shoulder. Dan gave off so much heat she didn't need it.

"She'll be over the moon," Dan promised. "Did you ever buy any riding boots?"

"No, I didn't have time."

"We'll have to get you some right away. I want you to ride with me."

Holly yawned and snuggled her face against Dan's neck. "I'm sleepy."

"We could take a nap," Dan offered. "Then when we wake up, if you want to..."

Warmth flooded Holly's face. "Well, if you want to."

Dan laughed as he rolled over and turned off the bedside lamp. Snuggled against him, the large, elegant room felt warm and cozy to her. Lulled by the gentle sound of his breathing, she soon drifted off to sleep.

Twenty-four

Several miles away at the local FBI office, Richard Lovinggood accepted the congratulations of his peers.

"I've got to hand it to you, Lovinggood. Getting your wife's cousin involved really did the trick," said Chris Barnes, one of the local agents.

"I'm just glad it worked out. I think we should bring Dan in and thank him."

"Oh, we'll definitely bring Wakefield in. Maybe tomorrow morning. If the bad guys hear about it, they'll think we're trying to bully some information out of him."

Agent Harry Thomas arrived just in time to hear Barnes' last comment. Thomas was the new kid on the block, and he needed to make a name for himself. *I think I'll run out and get Wakefield tonight,* he thought, totally forgetting that he had been reprimanded once before for acting without authority. *Maybe I'll score a few points with the boss.*

He pulled on his coat and left the office.

~ * ~

The pounding on the door awakened Holly, leaving her disoriented and confused. The bedside light came on, and Dan muttered, "Who the hell is beating on the door like that?"

He jumped up and jerked on his pants. The pounding continued, and he yelled, "Hold on, I'm coming."

Holly didn't recognize the man at the door.

"Dan Wakefield?"

"Yeah, what do you want? It's the middle of the night."

"Get dressed and come with me," the man answered. He flashed a badge at Dan. "The FBI would like to question you about your role in a drug deal that went down this afternoon."

"Now? This isn't a good time. I just got married."

"Sir, if you won't get dressed and come voluntarily, I'll have to use force."

"All right, all right."

The FBI man started to step into the room, but Dan thrust out his arm to block the way. "My wife isn't dressed either. Wait outside."

"Very well."

Dan slammed the door, his face tight with anger. "The man's an idiot. Didn't he stop to think I might have a gun in here?"

"You have a gun!"

"Hey, don't look so scared. I don't have a gun. It's just that if I were a criminal, he should watch me, not give me a chance to find a weapon."

Holly's breath came in short gasps. What should she do? Nothing like this had ever happened to her before. Inspiration struck. "I'll call Tommy Price for you."

"Honey, don't do that. I haven't done anything. I don't need a lawyer."

"He said they wanted to question you about a drug deal. Of course you need a lawyer!"

"Holly, do what I tell you. Don't call Tommy. I don't need a lawyer. I didn't do anything."

Holly pulled the covers across her breasts and refused to meet Dan's eyes. "If you didn't do anything, why are they here?"

"I can explain, but not now. Let me get this straightened out first."

She watched him as he dressed, her fear rapidly mingling with humiliation. What would her nana say if she found out that the FBI dragged Dan away from his own honeymoon? In Nana's world, law enforcement officers did not knock on your door to talk to you about drug deals.

Dan tied his shoes and kissed her forehead. "Honey, just go to sleep. I'll be back before you know it."

She still couldn't look at him, but he put a gentle hand under her chin and raised her face to his. "You don't believe me, do you?" he asked.

"I...I don't know what to believe. Why would the FBI arrest you if you didn't do anything?"

"Holly..."

The pounding on the door interrupted Dan. With a soft oath, he wrenched the door open.

"Put your hands behind your back," the man commanded. Dan did, and the man handcuffed him.

"Go to sleep, Holly," Dan soothed. "Everything's fine. Trust me."

As quickly as he had come, the FBI man vanished, taking Dan with him. For several minutes Holly just sat there. There had to be some mistake. Dan would never deal drugs.

Unable to sit still any longer, she sprang out of bed and wrapped her robe around her. *I wonder where he went this afternoon? He didn't say what kind of business he had to do.*

Shivering with cold and nerves, she hurried to the dressing room to find the thicker terrycloth robe. Her hands trembled so much as she took the robe from its hanger that she knocked Dan's jacket to the floor. *That's the one he was wearing last night when we went to the dinner. He disappeared for a while then too. Dan has a lot of explaining to do.*

She picked up his jacket, and a small leather case fell out of the pocket. Where did this come from?

It didn't belong to her, so she probably shouldn't open it, but under the circumstances, she was going to anyway. "My goodness!" she exclaimed as the diamond bracelet blazed under the light.

Her heart pounded so hard she felt light-headed and had to sit down on the edge of the bed she had just shared with Dan. *How did he get the money for a bracelet like this? I recognize the name of the jewelry store, so I know Dan doesn't have enough money to shop there.*

She jumped up and flung the bracelet down on the bed. It might be an invasion of Dan's privacy, but she was going through his things anyway.

She started with the pants he wore at the party. When she found nothing, she moved to the pair he had worn to the horse show. His wallet was in the back pocket, and with no hesitation, she pulled it out and started her search.

A picture of Dan and his parents was the first thing she saw. She stared for a moment at the picture. Dan looked so much like his father. Kyle had those same blue eyes, blond hair, and muscled body.

She moved past the picture and found Dan's money. Oh, sweet goodness! Where did he get such a lot of cash? There was a phone number behind the money, but she had no idea who it belonged to.

She burst into tears. Where did Dan get such a lot of money? How could he afford to take her to The Brass Heron for Valentine's Day? How could he afford this hotel? Surely, Tommy Price wouldn't pay for luxury accommodations for his trainer.

Gray mist swirled in front of her eyes, and she dropped her head between her knees to keep from passing out. In spite of his reputation as a good guy, Dan was very much his father's son. Terror shot through Holly. Dan was her husband, so she couldn't just pack her bag and go home. He had completely fooled her. She'd thought she was a good judge of character, but he was just like his father after all.

She stuffed the wallet back into the pants and flung herself down on the bed where she cried as if her heart was broken, which of course it was. Lost in her grief, she almost didn't hear the phone ringing. She wiped her eyes and steadied her voice. It might be Dan! "Hello?"

"Holly, it's Tommy Price. Could I speak to Dan?"

She almost asked him to go and help Dan, but Dan didn't want him involved. "Tommy, he's in the bathroom. Can I take a message?"

"If you don't mind. Tell him I've decided to go back to Fairfield tonight. I'll see him in a couple of days."

Holly saw her chance and took it. "Actually, Tommy, if you wouldn't mind, you could do Dan and me a big favor."

"Sure, if I can."

"I got a call from my assistant, Loretta Patterson. Something's come up that I need to see about immediately. Do you think I could catch a ride with you? That way Dan can bring the horse home tomorrow at his leisure."

"I'd be glad of the company. Can you be ready in thirty minutes?"

"No problem. I'll meet you in the lobby."

Holly hung up the phone and dressed quickly. She stuffed her clothes into her bag, careless of wrinkles or delicate fabric. After a quick look at herself in the mirror, she splashed cold water on her face, combed her hair, and put on some lipstick. In the dark she could probably pass muster.

Without a backward glance, she fled from the room, and when Tommy arrived, she sat serenely in the lobby reading a magazine, or at least pretending to.

~ * ~

Jeb dreamed of Kyle that night. For a long time after Kyle's death, he'd had nightmares, but as time went by, the bad dreams had gone away. They had returned with a vengeance. In this dream, he and Kyle stood in Dan's bedroom.

"How could you do this, Kyle? How could you hide drugs in your son's room? If the police searched the house, they'd assume Dan was the dealer, not you. How low can you get?"

"Stop worrying so much. It's easy money, and the vet's dunning us to death. Pay him and be done with it."

"If you ever stash anything in Dan's room, again, I'll turn you in myself."

Jeb awoke with a start and wiped the sweat off his face. As far as he knew, Kyle had never hidden anything in Dan's room, but he wouldn't put it past him. Once Kyle got involved in the drug world he hadn't cared about anyone but himself.

He rolled over and said a prayer for Dan, and even though Kyle was long dead and gone, he said a prayer for him too.

~ * ~

Holly sprang from Tommy's car and almost ran toward her nana's door. Tommy hadn't picked up on anything wrong for which she gave thanks. Pauline's porch light automatically came on, and Holly rang the doorbell as if it were her admittance to paradise. When Nana was slow to come to the door, she hammeredd on it as hard as she could.

The door opened with a bang. "Holly! What are you doing here at two in the morning? What's wrong?"

Holly turned and waved to Tommy who drove away.

"Was that Dan?" Pauline demanded.

Holly didn't answer, but she stepped inside, and Pauline got a good look at her face. "Holly! Darling, what's wrong? You're scaring me!"

Holly tried to speak, but she couldn't make a sound; she threw herself into her grandmother's arms and cried as if her heart would break.

"Holly, stop this! Tell me at once why you are here and what the problem is."

"Tommy Price gave me a ride to your house. I told him I had heard from Loretta and needed to get back home. I didn't want him to guess the truth."

Nana reached for her hand. "What truth, darling?"

"Dan got arrested tonight."

"Arrested! What for?"

"Dealing drugs."

"No! It can't be!"

Tears streamed from Holly's eyes. "I saw it with my own eyes, Nana. We were in bed, and an FBI agent came to get Dan." Holly paused and drew a deep, shuddering breath. "He handcuffed Dan. He made Dan put his arms behind him, and the agent handcuffed him."

Pauline sank down onto the sofa and pulled Holly down beside her. "Darling, you saw an agent arrest Dan, but did you actually see him participating in a drug deal?"

"No, but I know he did." Holly sniffed and fumbled for a box of tissue sitting on the coffee table.

"Holly! What kind of rings are you wearing?" demanded Pauline. She snatched Holly's hand and studied the jewelry closely. "It's a wedding ring and a diamond. Where did you get this? No, wait a minute. Did you say you were in bed with Dan? Are you and he married?"

"Yes," cried Holly. She threw her hands over her face. "Nana, I'm married to a drug dealer! I don't think I can stand it."

"Holly, stop this crying at once! You're getting hysterical, and that won't help anything. Now you start at the beginning, and you tell me everything step by step."

Holly blew her nose and haltingly told her story.

"You were wrong to get married so hastily," Nana lectured, her voice stern. "Nevertheless, what's done is done. You consummated your marriage, and you're Dan's wife. If you loved him enough to marry him, you should have given him a chance to explain. He said he didn't do anything wrong. Were you afraid of him? Is that why you left?"

Holly shook her head as she mopped her face with her tissue. "I spent my whole life trying to avoid the mistakes my mother made, and I made one that's just as bad as anything she ever did. I left because I was a bad judge of character, and I let a…a…drug dealer use me for his pleasure. I feel dirty. I can still smell him on my skin."

She jumped to her feet. "I can't stand having his scent on me," she cried. "I'm going to take a hot shower."

Holly darted away to the bathroom where she used up all the hot water before finishing her shower. She stared at herself in the mirror. Her skin looked like it had been scrubbed with sandpaper it was so red.

"It's a good thing I keep a few clothes here," she said as she joined Pauline on the sofa. "Nana, can I stay here tonight? I don't think Dan would come to get me, but he might, and I don't want to see him."

"Yes, of course," Pauline said, "but you'll have to face him sometime." She twisted the rings on her hand. "Holly, I do wish you hadn't run away like you did. There may be a perfectly rational explanation for what happened."

"I can't think of one."

Nana wrung her hands. "How *could* you have been so impulsive? I don't want you to be married to a man who's unworthy of you, but I don't believe in divorce. I just wish you had given him a chance to explain."

"It's too late to worry about explanations now," Holly dully replied. "I know how you feel about divorce, but I can't be married to a drug dealer. As soon as possible, I intend to start divorce proceedings."

A look of pity spread across her grandmother's face. "You safeguarded your heart, my darling, but you got hurt anyway. Well, we'll worry about it in the morning. Come and let me tuck you in."

"I feel safe here, Nana. Thank you."

"I love you, darling. Try not to worry. Things usually work out for the best."

Tears filled Holly's eyes even though she thought she had cried herself out in the shower. "I hope so, but I don't see how."

Twenty-five

"What are you doing here?" Richard demanded when Dan walked into Hank Barnes' office.

"Why is he handcuffed?" asked Sheriff Kinkaid, who'd arrived to celebrate only minutes before.

"Thomas, you'd better have a good explanation for this," warned Barnes.

Thomas smirked. "I heard you say you wanted to bring him in, so I thought I'd save you a little time and go get him tonight."

"What kind of fool are you?" Richard said, the menacing tone of his voice flooding the office with tension. "In the first place, this is *my* operation, and you don't so much as breathe unless I give the okay. You *never* just decide to do something without my approval.

"In the second place, Dan Wakefield is an undercover agent working for the FBI. We wanted to bring him in to thank him for all he risked to help us nail Cam Simmons.

"I'll give you about five seconds to get those cuffs off him and get the hell out of my sight, or I'm going after your job." Richard's eyes blazed, and no one wanted to be in Agent Thomas' shoes at that particular moment. Lovinggood didn't look like a man to cross.

Without a word, Thomas removed the handcuffs from Dan's wrists and sprinted from the room.

"Dan, I'm so sorry," Richard apologized. "I'll see to it that he's reprimanded."

Dan skewered him with a look. "Frankly, a reprimand won't help me at this point. Holly saw him arrest me. I don't think she's ever had any dealings with the law, and I believe she assumes if you get arrested, you must have done something wrong. I think I'm in trouble there."

"If that's true, you'll have to tell her the truth. Do you think she can keep it quiet?"

"I don't know."

"I believe I'll tell her," Richard decided. "That way, she'll be in no doubt whatsoever of the truth, and I can explain how important it is that your role in this operation remains a secret. Let me take you back to the hotel. I'll walk up with you and explain right now."

Dan didn't move a foot. "I don't think so. You told me no operation was without danger, and I knew you were right, but you didn't tell me the FBI would be the one to screw me over. Cam Simmons was willing to do more for me than this. The FBI can leave me alone, and as far as Holly is concerned, if she won't believe me, that's her tough luck."

Dan's cold voice and hard, angry expression brought an alarmed look to Richard's face. "Listen, buddy, calm down a little. I know you're upset about what happened, but Holly's your wife. You have to smooth things over with her. Don't let that jerk cause you any trouble."

"I've taken enough advice from you. From now on, you can butt out of my business. What happens between my wife and me is none of your concern."

"Dan..."

"Your agent dragged me out of the room without my wallet. Is the FBI going to give me cab fare back to the hotel?"

"I'll run you back myself," Richard said.

"Then I'll walk."

"Dan, wait," Sheriff Kinkaid said. "I'm sorry about this mess. Let me take you back to the hotel."

Dan hesitated, but he was tired both mentally and physically, and it was a long way to the Ballentine. "Thank you. I'd appreciate it."

Dan stalked out of the room, and Richard and Sheriff Kinkaid exchanged a look that promised Barnes had trouble. "Stick around," Kinkaid ordered. "When I get back, maybe we can think of something interesting to do to Mr. Thomas."

Richard nodded, and Sheriff Kinkaid followed Dan outside.

~ * ~

"I'd be glad to talk to your wife and explain things," Sheriff Kinkaid offered, as his car halted in front of the Ballentine.

"I can handle this."

"Okay, it's your call. If you change your mind, let me know, and I hope you will. If you won't let me talk to Holly, think about letting Lovinggood do it. If he talks to your cousin Elizabeth, she may be real ticked off by his part in this mess. I doubt you want to make trouble for him there."

"No," Dan replied, and with no other goodbye, he left the car and entered the hotel. Sheriff Kinkaid sighed. They should be celebrating the downfall of a notorious criminal; instead they had to worry about the future of a new marriage. Like his grandson would say, this really sucked.

~ * ~

Dan knew Holly had left him the minute he entered the room. She wasn't in bed, and he heard no sound anywhere to indicate the presence of another person. He decided to check the bathroom anyway, and when he passed the bed, he saw the case with the diamond bracelet lying on top of the bedspread. How had the bracelet gotten on the bed?

When he got to the dressing room, he saw that all of Holly's clothes were gone, and two pairs of his pants lay crumpled on the luggage rack. His wallet hung out of one pocket. Obviously, Holly had found the money and the bracelet. After seeing him get arrested, she had no doubt she had married a drug dealer. Where else could he have gotten so much money and a bracelet like this? No wonder she'd left.

But wait a minute. What if she did find them? She was his wife, and he had asked her to trust him. How could she have married him if she didn't trust him? Didn't the intimacy they'd just shared mean anything to her?

He briefly considered returning to Fairfield, but he changed his mind. If Holly thought so little of him, they didn't have much of a marriage to begin with.

He had to stand there for a minute because it hurt too much to move. The pain eased off, and he removed his clothes and went to bed; but he didn't sleep in the bed he had shared with Holly.

~ * ~

Pauline slept poorly that night. How could she sleep after hearing Holly's story? If Dan really had followed in his father's footsteps, he might not give Holly her freedom without a struggle. He might try to force her to be his wife whether she liked it or not. It made Pauline's blood run cold to even think about it.

She had liked Dan when he and Jeb came to dinner at her house. His polite, respectful manner and the way he'd treated his grandfather had impressed her. Was it possible that he'd totally fooled her? Did Dan sell drugs to supplement his income?

Jeb impressed her as much as Dan had. If Dan sold drugs, Jeb would surely know, and she didn't think he would have encouraged Holly to go out with a drug dealer, not after losing Kyle, anyway. On the other hand, maybe Jeb thought if Holly and Dan fell in love, Holly would be able to keep him on the straight and narrow.

She got up for a drink of water and returned to her bed to toss and turn some more. Rita had to assume a large part of the blame for this fiasco. Her behavior after the death of Holly's father sickened Pauline, and she'd had enough of it. If Rita had taken care of Holly the way she should have, Holly wouldn't distrust men so much. She'd have dated the way a normal teenager should, and she would have married some nice young man and raised a family of her own. Her innocence and fear had made her vulnerable, and Dan had taken advantage of her when he got her alone.

Or had he? Dan didn't have to buy Holly a diamond ring, but he did, and it was very pretty. However, the ring undoubtedly didn't cost a fortune. If Dan had drug money for the taking, surely he would've bought something a little flashier.

Holly had told her Turnaround Farm was run down and on the verge of bankruptcy. Drug money would have taken care of those problems too.

For that matter, Dan didn't really have to marry Holly. Pauline had no doubt if he'd wanted her, he could have taken her without the benefit of clergy. Instead, he'd bought her a diamond and married her.

Dan had told Holly he could explain things, but Holly hadn't given him a chance. She had run away without even giving Dan the benefit of the doubt, and she had been wrong to do so.

I hate divorce. I think a lot of social problems could be solved if people would work out their problems and raise their children together. It hurts to think Holly will become a statistic, but she seems determined to divorce Dan.

Her thoughts kept going round and round in circles, and she couldn't make any sense of the jumble of facts that floated around in her mind. She needed to bring in the heavy artillery. Padding into the bathroom, she took an acetaminophen. She'd be asleep in no time.

~ * ~

Pauline might have slept poorly that night, but emotional tension and fatigue had drained Holly, so she slept deeply and didn't awaken until the middle of the morning. By that time Pauline had organized her thoughts and had come to several conclusions.

"Hello, darling," she greeted Holly, who staggered into the kitchen and dropped into a chair as if her legs would scarcely hold her up. "Do you feel any better after a good night's sleep?"

"No, I don't."

"You'll feel better after you get a little something in your stomach," Pauline said. "I didn't think you'd be able to eat much, but I do have fresh blueberry muffins and coffee."

Holly took the muffin and coffee and nibbled disinterestedly. "Dan didn't call, did he?"

"No, darling, he didn't." Her grandmother took a chair beside her. "I imagine he's too hurt and angry to call. Men have so much pride, and I'm sure you've hurt his ego. I'm afraid if you want this mess straightened out, you'll have to make the first move.

"It would be a good idea for you to get dressed, and let me take you to Turnaround to pick up your car. You did leave it there, didn't you? That way, when Dan gets home, you'll be there to talk to him."

Holly dropped her muffin and gave up on her attempt to eat. "I don't think so. I'll buy a new car before I'll go and get it."

"That's silly, Holly. Listen to yourself. You sound like a child."

"A child married to a drug dealer."

"I've been thinking about that," Pauline said as she reached for one of Holly's hands. "I'm a pretty good judge of character, and I don't think Dan sold drugs to anyone. I think there's something else going on that you don't know about, but I don't think he's a drug dealer. If I were you, I wouldn't be jumping to conclusions."

Holly bit her lip. "You weren't there. If you'd seen it happen the way I did, you might feel differently."

Nana ignored her and pressed on. "I also think you were wrong not to give him a chance to explain. You married him for better or for worse, and at the first sign of trouble, you ran away. That was wrong, Holly."

"It's too late to undo things now," Holly said. She scrubbed her face with the sleeve of her robe. "Even if you were right, and I don't think you are, he wouldn't want to stay married to a woman who didn't trust him. I'm seeing a lawyer as soon as I can."

"I urge you to reconsider, at least for a few weeks."

"No, Nana. It's only putting off the inevitable."

Pauline stared at the rings on Holly's finger. "Holly, do you love him?"

"Yes, I love him." Her voice wobbled. "I've been in love with him almost from the first time I saw him."

"But why? What is it that you love about him? He is terribly handsome, and he has a good body. Is that the reason?"

"I guess that's a part of it, but I always thought he was just so... sweet. I thought I saw sweetness, gentleness and strength in Dan, and I fell in love with my fantasy man."

"Frankly, I saw the same things in your husband. You'd do well to remember it before you see any lawyers." With this parting advice, her nana sailed from the kitchen to find Sadie and take her outside to bask in the sunshine.

Twenty-six

For what seemed like the millionth time, Jeb peered out the kitchen window to see if he could see Dan's truck coming up the drive. It was almost two o'clock, and he hadn't seen hide nor hair of Dan. "He should be here by now," Jeb muttered, "but on the other hand, Holly's with him, and they might be doing something before they come home."

Maybe he'd have a cup of tea and a cinnamon roll while he waited. Just as he stuck a cup of water into the microwave, he heard the unmistakable sound of Dan's vehicle in the drive. Abandoning his snack, he pulled on his coat and hurried outside. He'd been on pins and needles all weekend and couldn't wait to find out if the FBI plan had worked.

When Dan cut his motor off and jumped out of the truck, Jeb's heart sank. Without exchanging a word with Dan, he could tell something had gone terribly wrong. As he moved closer to the truck, he saw that Dan was alone. *Maybe he already took her home.* No, common sense told him Holly would have come to the farm to get her car. What had happened at the show?

"How'd it go?" he called.

"Fine. Help with this ramp, please."

They fixed the ramp, and Jeb watched as Dan backed the horse out of the trailer. "Hey, did he win?"

"Yes. We got a blue ribbon for Tommy. We also got one horse to board and one to train."

Jeb slapped Dan's shoulder. "Wow. You must have been impressive."

Dan just shrugged.

"How about that business with Cam Simmons?"

"It's over. He's in jail, and I'm off the hook. Richard's plan worked like a charm."

All excellent news, but it didn't explain Dan's mood or Holly's absence. Something told him he wouldn't like what Dan had to say, but he might as well get it over with. It could be that his imaginations had played tricks on him. "Okay, then, let's have it. Where's Holly, and why are you so upset?"

Dan shrugged again. "I don't know where Holly is, but I expect she's with her Nana or at home."

"Did you two have a quarrel?"

"No."

"Dan, you might as well tell me about it. My imagination's working overtime here, and I'm worried."

Dan reached for the barn door, and his wedding ring glinted in the sunshine, capturing Jeb's attention. "Dan, are you wearing a wedding ring?" he demanded.

"Yes."

"Did you and Holly get married in Greenville?"

"Yes."

Jeb followed as Dan led the horse into the barn. "You haven't said too many words of more than one syllable since you got here. Do you think you could start at the beginning and tell me what happened?"

Dan led Chief into his stall before answering. "What is there to say? We got married, and it was a mistake. I'm just sorry we slept together because now we can't get an annulment. It'll have to be a divorce."

"Dan..."

"All right." With no frills or embellishments, Dan told his story to his grandfather. It wasn't as bad as Jeb had expected; it was much, much worse.

"Well, it did look bad," he began, but Dan cut him off before he could make any excuses for Holly's behavior.

"I told her I didn't do anything wrong. I told her I would explain it to her. I told her to go to sleep and wait for me, but instead she went through my wallet and my coat and decided I was guilty of dealing drugs. She didn't trust me or love me enough to even give me a chance to explain. As far as I'm concerned, our marriage is over, but if she thinks I'll be the one to start divorce proceedings, she can think again. I don't date anyway, so it won't bother me to stay married. If she wants a divorce, let her get it."

Holly had done it now. Easy going and even-tempered most of the time, if Dan ever really got angry, he didn't easily get over it. Holly probably didn't know that about him, but she should have known her defection would devastate a new husband. Why hadn't she waited to let him explain?

"So what are you planning to do about this?" Jeb asked.

"Nothing whatsoever."

Jeb shook his head. "You can't ignore this. I think you should find out where Holly is and go to see her. I don't want you to throw your marriage away because your pride is hurt."

Dan glared at him as if he had suddenly become an enemy. "If Holly thinks I'd deal drugs, I guess I didn't have much of a marriage to begin with."

Jeb refused to back off in the face of Dan's anger. His grandson's future was a stake; he couldn't butt out until Dan solved this mess. "Come and have a cup of tea and a cinnamon roll, and then you can go and talk to Holly."

"I'm not hungry, and I'm not seeing Holly." With these final words, Dan shut the door to Chief's stall and refused to discuss the matter any further.

~ * ~

Dan had gone to bed, and Jeb sat alone in front of the dying fire in the keeping room. Jeb was of a generation to whom marriage was a serious commitment. In his day, if things went wrong in the marriage, you worked at it until you got it straightened out. *I don't understand how Holly and Dan can give up their marriage so easily. I bet Pauline will feel the same way I do.*

Pauline. She seemed like a fair person. Even if Holly convinced her Dan was selling drugs, she'd probably be willing to hear his side of the story. *If that's true, she might be able to convince Holly to hear him out.*

Pauline had called him over the weekend and talked to him about Holly's mother. He had intended to talk to Dan about it, but in light of what Dan had told him, he'd forgotten to say anything. Maybe they could talk tomorrow after Dan calmed down a little bit. Like Dan, Holly had had a traumatic childhood. He probably didn't realize that her mother's behavior partly explained her distrust of him.

Thinking of traumatic childhoods turned his thoughts to Kyle. He had tried to avoid thinking of Kyle all evening, but his memory betrayed him, and he thought of Kyle anyway. *Where did I go wrong? I raised him the best way I knew how, but I must have failed him. If he hadn't done the things he did, Holly and Dan would be sharing their lives right now instead of being separated.*

Holly had grown up in a small town that gossiped about Kyle's indiscretions, and whether she knew it or not, the Wakefield reputation had made her all too quick to place blame on Dan. Yes, Kyle had to assume a part of the blame.

But it was his fault too. He should have sold Turnaround after Kyle died and sent Dan to college. Dan wanted to keep the farm, but it looked as if keeping the farm had cost Dan his education and his wife. Nothing, not even Turnaround, was worth that loss.

Well, with a little courage, he could still make it right. He'd see Holly first thing Monday morning. She could tell those buyers of hers they had a deal. Dan could become an architect if he wanted, or he could move to California to be with Elizabeth. Moving to California was probably the better alternative. Out there he'd finally be free of his father's reputation.

Sorrow permeated Jeb's soul. He loved Turnaround so much he'd almost killed himself laboring to keep it, but Dan came first. If selling the farm would give Dan a better life, he'd do it in a heartbeat.

~ * ~

By the time Dan came downstairs the next morning, Jeb had breakfast on the table. He passed a cup of tea to Dan. "Why don't you eat before you go to the barn? You skipped lunch yesterday, and you hardly touched your dinner last night."

Dan really didn't have an appetite this morning either, but he still had work to do no matter how bad he felt, so he sat down to breakfast with Jeb. He had feared Gramps would try to make him talk, but thankfully his grandfather respected his privacy and let him eat in peace. He had just finished the last of his tea when Jeb cleared his throat.

"Dan, there's something I need to talk to you about," he said, his tone causing silent alarms to go off in Dan's head.

"If it's Holly you want to talk about, I don't want to discuss it."

His grandfather shook his head. "It isn't about Holly. Last night after you went to bed, I did some thinking, and I came to a decision. I don't know if you'll approve of what I decided or not, but after you've had a while to think it over, I believe you'll see that what I'm doing is the right thing."

"What are you talking about?"

"I'm going to see Holly on Monday morning and tell her I'm ready to sell Turnaround."

Dan's cup clattered onto the table. "What! Why would you do a thing like that? I've worked my butt off for the past ten years so we could keep the place, and now just when things are starting to improve you want to sell? Why? You told me you wouldn't sell Turnaround without my approval, and I damn well do not give my approval."

The implacable expression on Jeb's face made Dan's breathing quicken. His grandfather looked so resolute and hopeless!

"I should have sold the place ten years ago right after Kyle died. That way you could have gone to college and studied architecture. Instead, I let you sacrifice your future. I was too weak to take that step then, but I'm not too weak to take it now. You need a fresh start somewhere else. With the money I get from the sale, you can go to college or you can go to California and live near Elizabeth. Any way you look at it, you'll finally be free from your father's mistakes, and maybe the next woman you're interested in won't be scared off by your father's reputation."

Swift, hot anger came over Dan, and he clenched his fists under the table. "So, you decided all this without having the decency to consult me about it, and my wishes don't make any difference to you."

"It isn't a matter for discussion, Dan. I've made up my mind, and as soon as it can be done, I'm signing the papers. This is for the best. In time you'll see I did the right thing."

"I guess Holly gets what she was after all along," Dan said, with a sneer. He shoved his chair away from the table and stomped into the mudroom where he put on his coat and boots and left the house without another word.

Twenty-seven

On that awful Monday morning, a late winter storm made life miserable for the citizens of Fairfield. The sleet and freezing rain perfectly mirrored Holly's bleak emotional state. "Nana, I'm tempted to take the day off," she said, as she finished the last piece of a flaky, buttery croissant liberally drizzled with honey. "I'm not ready to face Loretta and the others and tell them about Dan."

"You have to do it sometime. If I were you, I'd get it over with."

"I guess so," Holly answered morosely.

Loretta had warned her to be careful. Too bad she hadn't listened because now her friends and employees would all know what a foolish mistake she had made.

"Nana? Dan'll need a lawyer, won't he?"

"If they charge him, he will."

"Do you think I should help him with his legal bills?" She pushed her hair over her shoulder and refused to think how Dan had run his hands through it. "He doesn't have much money."

"I thought you were divorcing him."

Holly winced. What a hateful word. "I have to do it. I can't be married to a man I don't trust, but I don't want to see him in prison either."

"He said he's innocent, Holly. They may not charge him with anything."

Holly doubted it, but she didn't bother to say so. If she intended to go to work, she had to get dressed. She had waited until the last minute as it was.

She borrowed Pauline's car with the promise she would send Loretta and Bonnie to Turnaround farm to bring her own car home, and with a knot the size of Texas sitting in the middle of her chest, Holly took herself to work.

~ * ~

"Well, good morning," Loretta greeted her with a huge smile. "You're usually the first one here on Monday. Were you late getting home yesterday? Did you have a good time at the horse show?"

"I...no, I wasn't late."

Loretta peered at Holly. "Let's go into your office for a minute. I need to talk to you."

Good idea. The quicker she got into her office, the quicker she could close the door behind her and shut out the curious, prying eyes of her agents. Obediently, she followed and Loretta closed the door behind them.

"Now, tell me what's wrong this morning. You look like you've lost your best friend. Did you and Dan have a quarrel?"

Holly flopped into her chair and covered her eyes with her hands. No one knew how she dreaded this! She drew a deep, shuddering breath, and when she looked up at Loretta, she knew her secret was out.

"That's a pretty ring. When did the two of you get married?"

"Saturday."

"Holly, what's wrong?" she cried. "What happened?"

"I can't talk about it, Loretta. I made a mistake, and now I have to fix it."

"You can't mean you're going to divorce him! You've only been married for three days! Don't you think you're being a little hasty? Unless he abused you, you shouldn't be thinking about a divorce. You should be thinking about what you can do to fix the problem."

Loretta's spirited defense caught Holly off guard. "I thought you didn't like Dan."

"It doesn't matter what I think. He's your husband, and if you cared enough about him to marry him, you ought to love him enough to work out your problems."

"This problem can't be worked out."

"Oh, please. What could be that bad?"

I'd rather die than tell her. "If you don't mind, I'd rather not talk about this, but if you will, you can do me a favor."

"What?"

"Tell the others for me."

Loretta hesitated. "I really think you should be the one to tell them, but since you're my friend, I'll do it. Are you sure you don't want to tell me what he did? Maybe I can help you."

She hung around for a few more minutes, but Holly refused to tell her anything. Nobody needed to know about Dan's fall from grace except her.

~ * ~

Jeb parked his car in front of Grant Realty and just sat there with the motor running. Guess he was weak after all. Going into that office was one of the hardest things he'd ever done, but he had to do it for Dan.

Holly's assistant Loretta greeted him as he opened the door. "Hi, Mr. Wakefield. Isn't the weather awful?"

"Yes, it is, Miss Patterson. Is Holly in the office this morning?"

"Yes, I'll tell her you're here."

"Thank you."

Loretta returned almost immediately. "Come right on back, Mr. Wakefield."

She led him back to Holly's office, and Holly rose from her desk to greet him. "Please, come in, Mr. Wakefield."

He suddenly realized he hadn't felt so angry with anyone in a long time. Holly had broken Dan's heart with her distrust and suspicion, and now thanks to her, they were losing the farm they both loved.

His conscience smote him. Holly didn't force him to sell Turnaround. He and he alone had made that decision, a decision he should have made years ago. It wasn't fair to make her the scapegoat for this mess, and he did distinctly remember telling Dan to marry her. He had to assume some of the blame for what had happened.

Actually, now that he took a moment to notice, Holly looked terrible. She knocked a folder off her desk and scattered papers everywhere when she sat back down, and when she tried to pick them up, he saw her hands shake. Her pretty blue eyes looked dull and shadowed with dark smudges underneath, as if she hadn't been sleeping well. Pity welled up inside him. She must love Dan! If she didn't, she wouldn't look so awful.

She cleared her throat. "Is Dan home yet, Mr. Wakefield?"

"Yes, he's home. He got back around two o'clock yesterday."

Holly sprang from her chair and paced around the office. "Oh, Mr. Wakefield, he needs help! I don't know why he…did what he did, but if he hasn't been involved with these men for too long, maybe he can cut his ties with them. Was he charged with anything? Will he have to go to court?"

"I would have thought that as his wife, you might help him if he needs it."

Holly blanched. "I'm sorry, but I can't be married to a drug dealer. My whole life has been a struggle to overcome somebody else's bad behavior. I can't, I won't go down that road again."

"So, without even talking to him, you assume he's guilty," Jeb marveled. "Why did you marry him anyway? To get Turnaround? Or did you just want to sleep with him and used the marriage to salve your conscience?

"No, sir, I married him because I love him." Her eyes filled with tears. "But I can't let him destroy my life. If I always had to worry about whether or not he was being honest with me and obeying the law, my life would be ruined. A marriage without trust and integrity isn't much of a marriage."

Jeb drew a deep breath and reined in his anger. "Do you want me to tell you what happened?"

Hope flared briefly in her eyes and died almost immediately. "No. I don't want to be rude, and I don't think you'd lie to me, but Dan may have fooled you too." She finally sat back down in her chair. "I...I understand why you'd want to believe him, really, I do, and I don't blame you, but ...because of Kyle, you may not be able to see Dan clearly."

Jeb sighed, his anger spent. "If you love him, you'd better talk to him. He's angry and hurt, and I don't think he'll make the first move. You'd be interested in what he has to say, Holly, and you'll never know the truth unless you take a leap of faith and talk to him."

Holly's eyes dropped, and so did Jeb's heart. She didn't buy anything he had to say.

"I'd like to think I was wrong about him," she said. "In fact, now that a few days have gone by, the whole thing sounds ridiculous. I can't imagine Dan being involved with a man like Cam Simmons, but oh, Mr. Wakefield, there's so much evidence to say he was."

What was wrong with the girl? Hadn't she learned anything at all about Dan? "Talk to him, Holly, and do it soon. He'll need you during the coming weeks."

"What's happening in the next few weeks?"

"I've decided to accept your client's offer. I'm selling Turnaround."

Holly's jaw dropped. "What does Dan say? I can't see him agreeing to the sale, and before I do anything, I want to know where he stands."

"He doesn't want me to sell, but I've made up my mind. With the money from the sale, Dan can go to school or do anything else he wants. He'll finally have a future, and if he wants to, he can move to California where nobody knows about his father."

"But he loves Turnaround," Holly cried, literally wringing her hands. "He's worked so hard for so long. It isn't fair to treat him this way. He isn't a child. He's a man, and he can decide what's right for him. I'm sorry, but I can't be the one to take away his home."

"Then I'll find someone else who will," said Jeb, as he pulled his overcoat back on. "Think about seeing him. He's in bad shape emotionally, and he sure won't accept comfort from me."

He made his way to the door, and at the last minute Holly cried, "Wait. If you're determined to do this thing, I'll handle it."

"Good. You won't drag your feet on it, will you?"

"Give me two weeks."

"You've got two weeks."

~ * ~

As Mr. Wakefield left her office, Holly's head dropped to her desk. She should have asked for three weeks. That would have given Dan an extra week to get his grandfather to change his mind. Well, she'd call Jeb at the end of two weeks and make an excuse about why she needed a third week. If she could help it, Dan would keep Turnaround.

~ * ~

Holly laid a stack of contracts on Loretta's desk. "Loretta..." She broke off when the office door opened and let in a huge blast of cold air and a tall, blond man who was every bit as physically imposing as Dan.

Loretta preened and spoke in her 'sweet' voice. "Can I help you?"

"Yes, ma'am. I'm Richard Lovinggood, and I'd like to see Mrs. Wakefield." He approached the desk and flashed a badge as he spoke.

Holly cringed. The FBI. She had wondered when they'd be along to speak with her. "If..."

"Let me see that again," Loretta interrupted. "We run a legal operation here. There's no use for the FBI to be butting into our business."

The agent threw up his hands. "Whoa, ma'am. I'm not here to snoop around in your business. I've got some property I want sold."

"Then why did you show me your identification?"

"Force of habit," the man replied. "Do you think I can see Mrs. Wakefield?"

Holly tried to jump in, but Loretta got there first.

"How did you know she got married? The sign on the door says Grant Realty."

"I'm related to her husband. Now that's enough questions, if you don't mind."

Holly grabbed Loretta's shoulder when her assistant drew a breath to speak. "I'm Holly Grant, Mr. Lovinggood. We'll talk in my office."

Holly took the precaution of shutting the door behind her. She wouldn't put it past Loretta to eavesdrop. "Sit down. Do you really have some property to sell?"

"Yes, but my wife is taking care of it. I came for another reason."

"I wondered when the FBI would show up," Holly said. "I'm afraid you've wasted a trip. I don't know anything about my husband's activities. I haven't known him that long, and we've only been married since last Saturday. I can't help you at all in your investigation."

Of course, if she could help him, she wouldn't. The idea of Dan behind bars was monstrous.

"There is no investigation. I'm here to clear up a misunderstanding. You're wrong about Dan, and even though he forbade my talking to you, I am anyway. Dan's a good guy, and he doesn't deserve to be treated the way you've treated him."

Holly's eyes narrowed. The FBI had no business butting into her personal life. "That's a personal matter. Unless you're here in an official capacity, I refuse to talk to you."

A smile flitted across the man's face. "Why don't you call me Richard? After all, we're related now."

"How are you related to Dan?"

"I'm married to Dan's cousin, Elizabeth."

"I see." Holly paused to collect her thoughts. Did he think identifying himself would cause her to spill her guts or something? "I'm afraid I still won't discuss the matter."

"If you don't want to talk, fine, just listen. Dan wasn't dealing drugs. He'd never do that. He agreed to be involved in an undercover sting operation to bring his father's old boss to justice. It worked too. Dan had completed his part of the operation and joined you when that fool arrested him. Agent Thomas overhead something he misunderstood and acted without authority. Don't worry. He's been punished for what he did."

At that particular moment, Holly didn't care a fig about what happened to Agent Thomas, and as usual when she got stressed, she found herself incapable of either movement or speech. *So, he was innocent. I threw away the best thing that ever happened to me all for nothing.*

"Can you tell me about it?" she whispered.

"Dan's safety might depend on your keeping this a secret. Can you do it?"

She nodded.

"All right, then, it was like this." Richard concluded his story with a warning. "Remember, this has to be kept a secret. If Simmons or any of the other drug bosses got wind of what we did, Dan's life wouldn't be worth a nickel."

"Whose hare-brained idea was that anyway?"

"Mine."

"Did Elizabeth know about it?"

"No."

Holly considered giving him the chewing out of his life, but it probably wouldn't help anything. FBI agents put their lives on the line every day. Richard must not have realized he'd asked anything out of the ordinary of Dan.

She fell silent, which must have alarmed Richard. "Do you need some water or something, Holly?"

Holly didn't answer; she dropped her head to her desk and started to cry.

"Hey, why are you crying? I thought you'd rush out to Turnaround Farm to kiss and make up with Dan." He jumped out of his chair and gingerly patted Holly on the shoulder.

Even through her tears, she heard the stress in his voice. "Please don't cry. I can't stand to see a woman cry. Elizabeth has me wrapped around her little finger and plays me like a violin, but I hate to see a woman cry."

"I didn't believe him," Holly choked. "You did a good job with your operation. I believed it was all true."

"Now you know better. Dry your eyes, and go make up with him. It'll be okay."

Holly swiped her eyes with the back of her hand. "Huh! That's a joke. I don't see how he can ever forgive me. How could I have been so blind?" She hugged herself tightly and rocked to and fro in her chair.

Richard knelt beside her and pulled her into his arms "It's okay, don't cry," he soothed.

Holly didn't like him to touch her; he had put Dan in danger, but she felt so miserable she hugged him back and cried on his shoulder.

As he gently patted her back, the office door opened, and a woman's amused voice was heard across the room. "It's been a while since you snuggled with a blonde, Richard."

Holly raised her head from Richard's shoulder and immediately recognized the woman who stood there. "You're Dan's cousin, aren't you?"

"Yes," Elizabeth answered with a smile.

Holly gave Richard a push, and off-balance as he was, he had to grab the desk to keep from falling. "We weren't snuggling," she said, her heart sinking at the prospect of dealing with an irate wife and Loretta too. Loretta had escorted Elizabeth to her office and showed no signs of leaving.

"I was only teasing Richard," Elizabeth said. "I know you weren't doing anything wrong."

"You shouldn't let him hug you," Loretta lectured. "That's how rumors get started. My grandma always said not to do anything people could misinterpret. Remember, you're a married woman even if you are planning to divorce Dan."

Both Richard and Elizabeth gasped. "Why, Holly?" Elizabeth demanded with a scowl. "Why are you doing this to Dan? Don't you think you owe it to him to at least let him explain? You don't know the truth about what happened, and I'm here to tell it to you."

"I already told her," Richard said. "Holly, you've got to give up this crazy idea. Dan didn't do anything wrong. Why are you punishing him?"

Holly appealed to Loretta. "Loretta, could you go out front and watch the desk, please?"

Obviously Loretta would have preferred to stay, but in the face of Holly's request, she returned to her office, slamming the door behind her to indicate her displeasure.

"I appreciate both of you coming here," Holly quavered. "It's a comfort to know that Dan has people who care about him, and I hope you'll try to support him now. Jeb Wakefield told me this morning he intends to sell Turnaround."

"No," Elizabeth cried. "That's going to break Dan's heart."

"I know," Holly agreed, as her eyes filled with tears again. *It's all my fault. If I hadn't pestered Mr. Wakefield to sell Turnaround, none of this would have happened, and Dan would get to keep the place he loves.*

"Dan needs his wife, not his cousin," Richard said. "You can comfort him in ways Elizabeth can't, and he needs you right now. Why break his heart twice? He'll forgive you if you only ask."

Holly shook her head "No, I don't think so. How could he forgive me? I don't deserve to have someone like Dan. I should have known he'd never do anything so terrible, but I didn't believe him. I let him down the first time anything went wrong. I'll never forgive myself for it, and I can't expect him to either."

"Isn't that his choice to make?" Richard asked. "He's a grown man and can decide for himself if he wants to forgive you or not. I think he will because it seemed to me like he's in love with you."

Holly wiped her eyes. "Yeah, he was, but if I were Dan, I wouldn't want to see me."

~ * ~

Sheriff Kinkaid arrived right after lunch, determined to tell Holly the truth, and so did Agent Thomas, who, to do him credit, did feel bad about his mistake, but Holly stumbled through the rest of her day in a fog. She even missed an appointment to show a large home for which she'd receive a big commission. The prospective buyer called to ream her out about standing him up, but she didn't care. She hung up and refused to speak with him.

How could she have doubted Dan? What was wrong with her that she'd let idle gossip and circumstantial evidence break her faith in the best man she'd ever known? She had given him her heart because he was worthy. Why had she forgotten that? Because of idle gossip about his father, of course. She clenched her computer mouse so tightly that her knuckles turned white.

By five when the office closed, she had worked up a major case of nerves. Her fingers shook as she tried to lock the office, and she thought she'd never get into her car. Had it always been so hard to unlock?

She turned her car toward home, but when she came to Maple Street, she gunned her motor and drove on past. She didn't deserve Dan, that much was evident, but she couldn't rest without seeing him. If nothing else, she owed him an apology. She drew a deep breath. If things went well, maybe she wouldn't be spending her evening alone after all.

~ * ~

Jeb's jaw dropped when he saw her standing on his door. "Holly! I...what..."

"I'd like to see Dan, please," Holly quavered. Jeb had always been so welcoming, but tonight he didn't even invite her in.

"He's at the barn tending to a sick colt. I'll get him for you."

"No, don't do that. I'll run over to the barn." She gave thanks for this unexpected development. She'd be able to talk to Dan without worrying about his grandfather overhearing them. She pulled her coat around her to ward off the wind and dashed for the barn.

She saw Dan the minute she opened the door. He was fondling the ears of a small, gray foal who looked as miserable as she felt, if such a thing were possible. When he saw her, his face went as hard and cold as granite.

Holly drew a deep breath and gathered her courage. His face told her he wasn't glad to see her. "Hello, Dan," she called.

Dan came to meet her, his shoulders tense and set. "What do you want now?"

Holly gulped, but she'd come too far to let his anger scare her. "I want to talk to you about..."

"Well, I don't have anything to say to you."

"Oh, but I wanted to..."

Dan thrust out his hand as if to stay her words. "Did you come to get Gramps' signature for your buyer?"

"No, I told…"

"Just…go away, and leave me alone. Haven't you done enough?"

Holly grabbed his arm. "No! You don't under…"

He jerked his arm away as if it would soil him to touch her. "Don't come back, Holly, not unless you're coming to see Gramps. I don't want to see you again."

He turned his back on Holly and strode back to the foal. Holly stared at his back for several moments and left without a word.

With flagging steps and spirits, she made her way through the cold and gloom to her beautiful home. She usually felt a sense of welcome and homecoming when she first entered her house, but tonight it only seemed dark and quiet.

She didn't bother to turn on any lights or hang up her coat. With a long sigh, she lay down on the sofa in front of the fire and drifted off to sleep, grateful for a respite to her misery.

She awoke around eleven, excitement dancing along every nerve in her body. *Why didn't I think of this before? It's the only thing I can do for him, and if it does work out, maybe he can find it in his heart to forgive me.*

Holly leaped off the sofa and moved into her home office with purpose in her step, her heart lighter than it had been since Dan's arrest.

Twenty-eight

Jeb set a plate of bacon, eggs, and toast in front of Dan and poured him a cup of steaming hot tea. "Thanks," Dan mumbled. He attacked his breakfast as if his wellbeing depended on getting the food into his stomach as quickly as possible. He had done this ever since he found out Turnaround would be sold. Jeb knew Dan gobbled his food so he could get away from the house as soon as he could.

At first he had assumed Dan would see reason and get over his anger, but so far his grandson hadn't forgiven him. Almost a week had gone by since he told Dan about his decision, but if anything, Dan's anger had deepened. Jeb prayed daily that selling Turnaround wouldn't ruin his relationship with his grandson, but in spite of his fears, he hadn't changed his mind about the sale. Dan needed a new start, and selling Turnaround would give him one.

Jeb cleared his throat. "Are you going into town today?"

"Yes."

"Could you stop by the feed and seed store and make a payment for me?"

"Yes."

Dan jumped up and left most of his breakfast on the table. "Where's the money?"

Jeb nodded toward the other end of the table, and Dan grabbed it and hurried to get his boots on.

Jeb watched as Dan got into his truck. *If he'd make up with Holly, he'd feel a lot better. Maybe she could give him a little perspective on things.*

Sighing, he turned away from the window and sat in front of the fire. Seemed like he had no energy at all today.

~ * ~

Dan couldn't wait for the tea to cool enough for him to drink it, so he left it on the table. He loved tea, and his grandfather knew how to make it, but he couldn't bear Jeb's company. Being in the same room with his grandfather gave him a knot in his stomach and the urge to hit something.

He stopped at a convenience store for a cup of coffee and a newspaper. The pretty clerk behind the counter was one of Nikki's cousins.

"Hi, Dan. How're you doing?" she asked.

"Just fine. How about you?"

"I'm good. Nikki told me you got married."

His toes almost curled in his boots. "Yeah, I did."

"Well, congratulations."

"Thanks."

He got out of there as soon as possible, but his spirits sank even lower. He had grown adept at pushing all thoughts of Holly out of his mind, and he wanted it to stay that way. Why did everyone always bring it up? It seemed like everywhere he went people had heard about his marriage and wanted to congratulate him. Why hadn't they heard about his separation from Holly as well? Maybe, they had and were congratulating him just to see what he'd say about his marriage. They probably wanted to hear all the juicy details of the latest Wakefield scandal.

He got to the feed and seed store pretty early. There were only two trucks in the parking lot. Good. If he were lucky he wouldn't have to make polite chitchat to anyone. Talking to Nikki's cousin had left a sour taste in his mouth, and he hated to repeat the experience.

Terry Hawk, the proprietor of the feed and seed, greeted Dan with a big smile. "Morning, Dan. What can I do for you?"

"I want to make a payment on our account."

Terry laughed. "Didn't your wife tell you? She settled your account day before yesterday. You don't owe me a thing."

Dan's stiffened. "How did my wife know I owed you money? I didn't tell her."

"Ah, I saw her having lunch at Marie's, and I mentioned it to her." Terry looked faintly shamefaced as well he might.

"My grandfather and I have been doing business with you for years, and we've always paid you every cent we owe. You've got a hell of a nerve dunning Holly."

"Dan, I'm sorry, but I heard you'd sold Turnaround and…"

"You thought I wouldn't pay you. So long."

He spun around and strode away, ignoring Terry who called weakly, "Dan, wait a minute."

He slammed the door of his truck and took deep breaths to calm himself. Too bad his grandfather had decided to sell Turnaround. He'd like to have had the satisfaction of telling Terry he planned to take his business to Chad Franks who operated the other feed and seed in the area.

He started to go home, but half way down River Road, he abruptly, made a U turn and headed back toward Fairfield. He and his wife had some business to talk about.

~ * ~

Loretta barged into Holly's office without bothering to knock. "Dan's here, and he wants to see you."

Holly jumped and spilled coffee all over the Bannister contract. Dan had come to talk to her. Maybe, he wanted to work things out after all! She hurried to the front to greet him, but hope vanished when she saw Dan's face. He hadn't come to make up.

"I'd like to talk to you," he said.

"Sure. Come on back."

Holly led the way to her office and shut the door behind them. She took a deep breath. "I've…I've been hoping to…to see you. I wanted… want to…"

Dan laid a check on her desk. "Here's the money you paid to Terry Hawk."

"I don't want any repayment for that."

He treated her to a cool stare. "You're not paying my bills, Holly. Terry had no right to even mention it to you."

"But…"

His jaw tightened. "I won't take any favors from you. If anyone else asks you for money, refer them to my grandfather. I'd appreciate it if you'd hold the check until the sale goes through. If you don't, it'll probably bounce."

"But…"

Dan left the office without even waiting to hear what she had to say. A moment later she heard the front door slam. She dropped into her chair and stared at the check. Why wouldn't he let her help him? She could afford to pay the feed bill, and he couldn't. Didn't he know she had used the bill as a way to reach out to him? Why wouldn't he let her apologize? Didn't he love her? Wasn't this distance between them killing him too?

Holly lay her head down on her desk and blinked the tears away. Even when she tried to help him, she messed up. Dan would have been better off if he'd never met her.

~ * ~

Nikki's old car sat in the driveway when Dan got home. He thought about hiding in the barn, but curiosity won out, and he went inside to see what she wanted.

He didn't see Nikki, but Michael and Teddy greeted him with cries of joy. They'd never had a real father, and they loved Dan who had always helped their mother take care of them. Unhappily, Richard Lovinggood also sat in the kitchen with them.

After Dan kissed both children, they went back to their play. "I thought you went home to California."

"I did, but Elizabeth and I came back this morning."

"Where are Elizabeth and Nikki?"

"They went shopping." Richard cleared his throat. "I stuck around to talk to you."

He didn't have anything to say to Richard, nothing Richard would enjoy hearing anyway. "We don't have anything to talk about. I've got work to do."

"This is important."

"I'm not interested in anything you have to say."

"You might be." Richard drew a deep breath. "I've asked Mr. Wakefield to sell Turnaround Farm to Elizabeth."

"What would Elizabeth do with a farm?" Dan scoffed.

"Sell it to you."

Why did everyone want to hurt him? What had he done to deserve so many humiliations? "We barely make ends meet as it is," he said. "There's no way I could make payments to Elizabeth."

"She wouldn't charge you any interest, and she'd be flexible about repayment."

Dan gave a short, bitter bark that might have passed for laughter. "In other words you want to give it to me. Well, thanks, but no thanks."

Richard leaned forward. "Dan, you aren't thinking straight. Elizabeth can well afford to buy the farm, and..."

"Excuse me," Dan interrupted. "I've got work to do."

He slammed the door on the way to the barn, and Richard sat back with a sigh. "I should have let Elizabeth talk to him."

Jeb shook his head. "It wouldn't have made any difference. He's too proud to accept a favor like that, and I don't blame him."

Richard sighed again. "I don't either. I wouldn't do it myself."

~ * ~

"I look awful," Nikki moaned, as she and Elizabeth left the beauty salon. "Everyone says Jon is the best stylist in Fairfield, but look at me. I look dead."

"Oh, hush, you do not,"

"I liked my hair blonde. Why'd you make me dye it my natural color?"

Elizabeth snorted. "Because you looked like a floozy with brassy, blonde hair."

"I did not!"

"You did too!"

Nikki subsided because Elizabeth's success made it hard to argue with her.

"You need some decent clothes as well," Elizabeth said. "Where can we go shopping?"

"I like Super Mart. I got my blouse there, and I just love it."

Elizabeth stared at the blouse. "It's too tight, and your skirt is too short. You'll attract the wrong kind of man wearing a get-up like that."

"What's wrong with flaunting the assets?" Nikki asked.

Elizabeth giggled so hard she had to hold onto Nikki's arm. "Why did I wait so long to get together with you?"

"What did I say?" Nikki begged.

"Nothing. Let's finish your shopping, so we can get a snack. Being pregnant makes me hungry."

Nikki cheered up when she thought of shopping. "If you don't want to go to Super Mart, we could go to Pace's. They have nice stuff."

"I remember Pace's. For a small department store, they do carry some good stuff. I bet we can find something there."

"What are you naming the baby?" Nikki asked as they strolled into Pace's.

"Richard Henry Lovinggood III."

"That's a mouthful. I named Michael and Teddy after characters in a book."

"Well, I'm naming my baby after his daddy."

They wrapped up their shopping at Pace's and decided to have a bite at Marie's. Everybody in the diner recognized Elizabeth, so she signed autographs before she and Nikki ordered.

Over tea and chicken salad sandwiches, Elizabeth said, "The two of us have to help Dan. He's so angry he won't even see Holly, but I can tell he loves her. Think of something we can do."

Nikki took a bite of her sandwich and washed it down with tea. "It'll need to be something that throws them together. They avoid each other like crazy, but what?"

"We could give a party," Elizabeth said.

"Why?"

"Well, you could say you're giving the party for me, and you could get Dan to come that way. I could persuade Holly to come by telling her I want her to help me find a house."

"If they see each other, they'll run away," Nikki objected.

"Can you think of anything better to do?"

"Yes! Let Richard handcuff them together, and don't let them go until they work it out."

"Nikki, he'd get into trouble for doing something like that."

Nikki rolled her eyes. "Oh, I doubt it, but if he did, his daddy would bail him out."

"You'd better not say a thing like that to Richard. He'll be angry if you do."

"So what? He's not the boss of me."

They argued amiably until they finished their lunch. "How about Saturday night for the party?" Elizabeth asked, as she tossed a tip onto the table.

"Yeah, that's good for me."

They paused a moment to share a conspiratorial smile. They'd help Dan in spite of himself.

Twenty-nine

The party blossomed into a major production. The Lane family was big enough, but all of Elizabeth's relatives on her mother's side of the family wanted to see her too, and the Bailey family had almost as many members as the Lane family.

Dan hadn't wanted to go, but Elizabeth had insisted. "If you and Mr. Wakefield don't come, it'll hurt my feelings," she said. "I love you and Nikki more than you know, and it hurts me that you won't come to my party. Don't I mean as much to you as you mean to me?"

"You know you do, but you also know I don't like parties."

Elizabeth used her acting talent and cried a little bit, and as she had expected, Dan agreed to come.

She had to work a little harder getting Holly to come because Holly didn't want to go anywhere near the Lane family. She knew everyone blamed her for breaking Dan's heart.

"I hope you'll come, Holly," Elizabeth said. "I have to go back to California first thing Sunday morning, and I never did get to talk to you about selling Mother's property. Besides that, Richard and I are thinking of buying a home in Fairfield, so I can visit Dan and Nikki without worrying about where I'll be sleeping. I was hoping you could recommend something."

"You'd really need to see the properties," Holly protested. "Can't you stay another day at least?"

"No, I have to be back at work, but you bring me some pictures, and we'll talk business at the party."

Holly agreed to go because she knew Elizabeth would buy an expensive home, and she might as well buy it from Grant Realty.

She gave a bitter little chuckle. Her business had taken off like a rocket. Even without the sale of Turnaround Farm, Grant Realty had had an excellent year so far. What a shame Dan wouldn't have let her pay his feed bill.

~ * ~

"Are you ready to go?" Jeb asked. "We don't want to be late to the party."

Dan bent over to tie his shoes. "I'd rather take separate cars. I might take Elizabeth and Nikki out when the party ends."

"But the party won't be over until really late," Jeb protested.

"You go on. I'll be along."

Dan watched as Jeb put on his coat and went outside. He had lied to his grandfather, but the less time they spent together the better.

When he arrived at Nikki's house, he saw his grandfather talking with Nikki's mother, but he turned his back and pretended not to see Jeb.

Elizabeth saw him come in and bustled over to greet him. She kissed Dan and slid an affectionate arm around his waist. "Thanks for coming, honey."

She acted so glad to see him that Dan felt guilty. Elizabeth had wanted to give him Turnaround Farm, and he had growled because she asked him to come to her party. He needed a major attitude adjustment. "You know I wouldn't miss your party. I've...had a lot to think about, but I shouldn't have taken it out on you. Are you mad at me?"

Elizabeth stood on tiptoe and kissed him. "No."

Richard materialized from somewhere in the crowd. "Hi, Dan. How's it going?" He stuck out his hand for Dan to shake, but Dan didn't want to. If not for Richard, he and Holly wouldn't have had trouble. Well, Richard treated Elizabeth like a queen, so he'd be nice to him. Anyway, if Holly had really loved him, it wouldn't have mattered whether Agent Thomas arrested him or not. He couldn't blame Richard because his wife had used him to get his grandfather's land. He took Richard's hand and saw Richard's shoulders relax.

"Let's find Nikki and go hide somewhere so the three of us can talk," Elizabeth said as she linked her arm through his.

Dan smiled. He remembered so many fun times when the three of them had hidden away to talk. It used to drive the other cousins crazy and probably still would. "Let's do that," he agreed.

"I'll find Nikki," Richard promised, so Dan and Elizabeth sneaked away and hid themselves in Mrs. Lane's small sewing room.

Richard sent Nikki to join them and stationed himself to watch for Holly. Elizabeth had ordered him to take her to Dan when she arrived. He hoped this plan worked, so he could feel better. His conscience had hurt him something awful about his part in Dan and Holly's separation.

~ * ~

It surprised Holly to see all the cars parked in Nikki's yard. How did all these people fit inside such a small house?

Not all of them did. Holly saw a large metal container that roared with a huge bonfire. Men wrapped in coats and hats clustered around the bonfire and passed a bottle around.

She parked on the grass and followed several people to a small, screened porch with jalousie windows. A kerosene heater sat in the center of the room, and the porch stank of cigarette smoke. Obviously, the Lanes hadn't heard that cigarette smoking was harmful to their health. Where was Elizabeth? She wanted out of there as soon as possible.

Richard Lovinggood approached her before she even had to ask for Elizabeth. "Hi, Holly. Are you looking for Elizabeth?"

"Yes, I am."

"She's waiting for you in her aunt's sewing room. Let me show you where it is."

A small boy raced from the kitchen and barreled into Holly who took a step back. "Hey, Holly," he cried.

Oh, this was Nikki's son. Was it Michael or Teddy? Oh, never mind. She didn't have to mention names at all. "Hi there," she answered. The less said the better. She wanted to get out of there fast, not stand around having conversations with children.

The child tugged on her hand for attention. "Holly, now that you and Dan are married, why don't you live in the same house? Aren't married people supposed to live together?"

Holly swallowed hard. "Most of the time they do, but not always."

"I guess you should live in the same house with Dan. Mama told Elizabeth he's acting like an old sore-tailed bear these days. Maybe you could cheer him up."

Happily, Richard brought this awkward conversation to a close. "You can talk to her later, Michael," he said. He took Holly's arm and propelled her through the crowd, but David Lane blocked their path. He looked sober, which would have pleased Dan if he had known.

"So, you remembered that you're married," David said, his voice cold and cutting. "Nice of you to join the family get-together. Where's your husband?"

Holly's face burned. Why had she ever come here? No commission could make up for this humiliation.

David took her arm from Richard. "Excuse us for a minute," he said, and he maneuvered Holly into the bathroom and shut the door behind him before either Richard or Holly could protest.

David glared at her with no sign of friendliness on his face. "I apologize for the meeting place, but every other room in the house is full. I want to know why you're not living with Dan. You're his wife, and he has a right to expect the comfort of your presence, such as it is. What's wrong? Isn't selling his home out from under him bad enough? Do you have to be too prissy to act like a wife as well?"

"You..."

"Come on," David reproached. "The whole family knows how you've treated him. How can you look at yourself in the mirror every morning? You stood in Dan's barn and promised me you weren't seeing him because you wanted his land. Now that you've got what you wanted, you don't have any use for him, right? What kind of woman are you?"

Richard hammered on the door, and with a snort of disgust, David dropped Holly's arm and wrenched the door open. "Talk to her if you want to. I don't have the stomach for it." He pushed his way through the crowd, leaving Holly on the verge of tears.

"I shouldn't have come here," she cried. "I knew everyone would be mad at me."

Richard didn't try to deny the truth of it. "David loves Dan. Of course he's angry with you."

"Just let me talk to Elizabeth, so I can get out of here," Holly begged.

Richard led her down the hallway and tapped softly on the last door. "Come in," Elizabeth called.

No! Through the door Richard just opened, she saw Nikki and Dan sitting there with Elizabeth. Blood roared in his ears as Richard shoved her into the room and slammed the door behind him. Neither Holly nor Dan said a word.

"I'm tired of the way you two are acting," Elizabeth said. "Both of you need to settle down and talk your problems out."

She and Nikki joined Richard at the door. "Dan, you'd better stay in this room and talk to your wife," she said, as she shut the door behind them.

"I didn't know they planned this," Dan said. "I'm sorry to inconvenience you."

His set and angry face caused Holly's heart to sink into her shoes. The Lanes were mad at her for not living with Dan, but she'd love to apologize to him and beg him to take her back. She had made a mistake, but Dan acted like he couldn't forgive her. He had reamed her out about the feed and seed bill, and now he didn't like being forced to spend a few moments with her.

I really have ruined everything. Dan doesn't want anything to do with me. Okay, if that's the way he wanted to act, let him. Anybody would have believed he sold drugs for Cam Simmons. The FBI had devised a flawless plan, so why blame her for her doubts?

"I didn't know about their plan either," she said. "I'll leave now, so you can enjoy your party."

She tried to open the door, but it was locked. "Who has doors that lock on the outside?" she cried.

Dan shot her a cold look. "Sit down. They'll open the door soon, and if they don't, I'll break it down for you. I'd hate to force my company on you."

"I'm sure you feel the same way."

Dan skewered her with a black and fiery glare. "That's right, I do. I told you I didn't do anything wrong, but you thought I was a drug dealer and a liar to boot. No, I don't want to spend time with you. In fact, I don't care if I ever see you again. Thanks to your meddling in my life, I've lost Turnaround and my grandfather, and you've shamed me in front of my family and the entire town. Do you know what Tommy Price asked me?"

Holly mutely shook her head.

"He asked me if you'd be trying to claim a part of the money from the sale."

"I'd never do a thing like that!" She took a step forward, her hands held out in eager appeal. "How can you say such things?"

"You figure it out, but just in case you thought about it, let me remind you that the farm belongs to my grandfather. I don't get one penny from the sale, but you're welcome to half of what I've got, Holly, and that's half of nothing. You can't even file a claim based on my future earning potential. I don't have any potential."

"Stop it," Holly cried. "Just stop it!"

"Why? Does the truth hurt? What's wrong, Holly? Are you ashamed of using me to get Gramps property?"

Holly gave a strangled cry and ran across the room to beat on the door that Richard immediately opened. Since he worked for the FBI, he probably worried she'd charge him with kidnapping or something.

Shoving past him, she ran through the living room and caught a glimpse of Elizabeth and Nikki in the kitchen, but she didn't stop to say goodbye. She clattered down the porch steps and ran across the yard, ignoring the men around the fire who cheered and catcalled when they saw her run by.

She jumped in her car and didn't slow down until she'd left the Lane house far behind.

She offered to drive to the Chicken Shack, which thankfully wasn't far from her office. The less time she spent with her mother the better.

As usual, the Shack buzzed with lunchtime customers. Most people thought this place had the best fried chicken in the state. Their French fries weren't bad either. If she had to spend an hour with her mother, she could think of worse places to do it.

"There's a table near the door," Rita said.

Holly shivered when a gust of cold air struck her. They were too near the door for comfort, but this was the only empty table she saw. March had sure come in like a lion this year. She idly looked up to see who'd come in. No! Oh, no! Dan stood in the door, and he'd seen her. Defiantly, she raised her chin. She refused to grovel in front of him!

~ * ~

Dan wanted to speak to Holly. He hadn't gotten much sleep the night before because he was ashamed of how he'd treated her. Letting his anger get the better of him was bad enough, but Richard said everyone had been cold to her. It probably scared her when he started fussing at her too.

He had actually taken two steps toward her when pride stayed his feet, and he took a stool at the counter instead. Holly didn't care about him; if she did, she'd be living with him as his wife. Instead, she ran away from him, and even though she knew the truth about what happened at the horse show, she had made no effort to apologize to him.

It didn't take a genius to figure out she had married him only because she wanted the Wakefield land. He knew one thing, though; she had given an Oscar winning performance. She could give Elizabeth a run for her money any day.

Thinking of Elizabeth calmed him somewhat. She and Nikki had done everything they could to fix things between him and Holly. It warmed his heart to think that no matter what happened to him, he'd always have their love and loyalty. He ordered his lunch and tried not to think of his wife sitting so close and yet so far away.

~ * ~

Holly stared at Dan's back and gulped her chicken as if she feared that someone would take it away from her. How dare he sit there and ignore her! Whether he liked it or not, they were still married. It was super rude of him to pretend he didn't see her.

Dan finished his meal and got up in record time to pay his bill.

"Excuse me, Holly," her mother said. "I'm going to the restroom. Be right back."

Adrenalin flooded Holly. She'd be alone if Dan came to her table. Her heart lurched. Surely he would!

He didn't. As Holly watched, he got into his truck and drove out of sight.

Rita returned to the table just as Holly dabbed at her eyes. "Holly! What's wrong?"

"Nothing. Are you ready to go?"

Rita sat back down instead of answering. "What's got you so upset?"

"All right, if you must know, I just saw my husband. We didn't talk, so there's nothing else to say."

"I can think of one thing the two of you have to talk about."

Holly resisted the impulse to roll her eyes. "And what's that?"

"Like whether you want to stay married or not. Mother told me the two of you are in love, and if that's the case, you need to iron things out with him."

"It's my affair, Mother. It doesn't concern you, so let's drop the subject."

"You're my daughter. Of course your happiness concerns me."

Holly laughed as if her crazy mother had said something hysterical. "Really? You have a funny way of showing it. Ever since my father died, you've neglected me so that you could sleep around with every loser who'd give you a second glance. You gave up the right to advise me years ago."

"I lost the man I love," Rita said. "I don't want you to have your heart broken like I did."

"Which man are you talking about, Mother? Kevin?"

Rita glared at Holly. "Don't talk to me that way, Holly. You know I meant your father."

"You aren't fit to talk about my father. You're a disgrace to his memory, and you've cheapened his name by your behavior. Tell you what. You leave me alone, and I'll leave you alone. I don't need you now. I did when I was a child, but you weren't there for me. Don't try to pretend that you care."

Holly strode toward the cashier where she paid for their lunch, and in ten minutes, she turned her car onto Cherry Street and parked in front of her grandmother's house. "Goodbye, Mother."

"Can't you come in to say hello to your grandmother?"

"I could, but I don't want to."

~ * ~

Rita got out of the car and stood by the road watching as Holly drove away. First Pauline and now Holly had turned against her. Had she really acted so horribly? Had she really ruined Holly's life and worried her mother half to death? She had some thinking to do.

~ * ~

Holly felt terrible. For years she'd bit her tongue and said nothing, but today the angry words had poured from her mouth, and she couldn't seem to stop them. She had always wanted to tell her mother off, but she didn't have the feeling of satisfaction she had expected to have. It just made her feel worse.

Thirty-one

Jeb stood in the doorway of Kyle's room. He never went into the room other than when he vacuumed and dusted four times a year. Like the rest of the upstairs, the room had no heat, but he'd worn a heavy coat, so the cold didn't bother him much.

The room looked pretty much like it had on the day Kyle and Millie died. Their clothes still neatly hung in the closet, and Kyle's good riding boots stood in the corner. Jeb had always meant to move those boots, but he couldn't bear to touch them even though they did bother him. They made it look as if Kyle would return momentarily to put them on, and he could never forget that Kyle didn't need those boots anymore.

Several weeks after the accident, he had come up to pack everything away, but he had started to cry and had to hurry out of the room. So everything remained as it had been on that fateful morning ten years in the past.

Dan didn't like to go in here either. Jeb had seen him hesitate in front of the door and then hurry away, but they didn't have that luxury now. Once they sold Turnaround, they'd have to move their things, and he didn't want to wait until the last minute to go through this room.

Jeb's hands tightened around the bedpost. "You'll have plenty of money. You can do anything you want. Personally, I'd like to see you leave Fairfield."

"No, you'll have plenty of money," Dan corrected. "I'm not taking a penny from you."

Fear roughened Jeb's voice. "Don't talk like a jackass. Everything I have is yours."

Dan shook his head. "Your name's on the deed to Turnaround, not mine."

I should have expected this, Jeb silently agonized. To Dan he said, "If you don't want to go to California, I'll ask Holly to find us a house. I bet she could find one near the college, so you won't have a long commute."

"Aren't you listening to me?" Dan's voice vibrated with anger. "I'm not going back to school. The time for school is past. If you insist on selling the farm, there's only one thing you can do for me."

"What's that?"

"Let me buy Lady from you."

"Lady was your mother's horse. She belongs to you now. I wouldn't ever sell her. I hope you don't think selling Turnaround means you have to give up riding. I thought we'd board Lady in a nice stable, so you could go riding whenever you like."

"Uncle David already offered to let me keep her at his place."

Jeb pictured the rundown, drafty barn and the barbed wire fences that David Lane had put up. "Dan, don't do that. Board her in a nice place."

"I can't afford it."

"Of course you can. We'll have plenty of money after the sale goes through."

"I told you I won't take money from you."

Jeb's jaw tightened. "Then just what do you intend to do with your life?"

"I'll have to get a job."

"Doing what?"

Dan shrugged. "All I know is horses, so I'm applying at some of the big stables. I have my first appointment on Monday."

"Good grief! You can't make a decent living cleaning stalls and grooming horses."

"I planned on helping them train, but if that doesn't work out, I'll find something else, maybe construction, and don't worry about buying a house big enough for two of us. I intend to rent an apartment. Nikki might like to share one with me."

Jeb skewered Dan with a fiery glare. "That's a great future you've got there, Dan. Mucking out stables and living with your cousin. What you need to do is enroll in school and make up with your wife."

"Whatever."

His words hit Jeb like an insulting slap in the face, and for a moment, he feared he might strike Dan. "Do you think I'll enjoy losing my home at my age?" he shouted. "I'm doing it for you, and I don't deserve your sarcasm and disrespect."

Dan said nothing for a moment. "I'm sorry I was disrespectful, but it doesn't change my plans. Do whatever you want, Gramps, but let me manage my own life."

He picked up his parents' things and went to his room. Jeb went downstairs.

Thirty-two

"Loretta, I appreciate the invitation, but I don't feel like going to a movie. You and Michael go on and have a good time."

"That's just it," Loretta moaned. "Michael's friend, Oscar, drives me crazy. Michael and I can't have a good time with him tagging along. I want you to go with us to keep him occupied."

Holly chewed her lip for a minute. "I don't know if that's a good idea. I'm still married, after all."

"I know that, but this isn't a date. Oscar knows you're married. He is too, and he misses his wife something terrible."

"Where is his wife?"

"She's on a church mission trip to Eastern Europe. He's visiting Michael until she gets back, but he's so lonesome he's driving us crazy. Please go and take his mind off his troubles."

Holly wavered. Being alone in the evenings had become almost intolerable, and this would get her out of her house for a few hours. "Well, if you're sure he understands why I'm going..."

"Thank you, Holly. You're a lifesaver. You can talk to Oscar, and Michael and I can get a break from his everlasting whining."

~ * ~

Holly didn't think Oscar Reeves whined at all. He looked around forty, and while he did talk about his family, he didn't run it into the ground as Loretta had said. Loretta probably resented having to share Michael with his friend. Since she and Michael got engaged, she'd been super possessive about him.

After the movie they decided to go to the Dairy Queen to get some dessert. Most of the booths and tables were taken, but Holly and Oscar found a booth just vacated by a group of teenagers and sat down together while Michael and Loretta waited for their order.

Holly had tried not to think of Dan this evening, but ordering a chocolate fudge brownie with ice cream had made her think of him whether she wanted to or not. Dan had told her he loved the gooey, rich confection. Her heart burned when she remembered the chocolate rose he had bought for them.

"A penny for your thoughts," Oscar offered with a smile.

"I'm sorry. What were you saying?"

"You're thinking about your husband, aren't you?"

"Well..."

"Loretta told me the two of you are separated, but she didn't say why."

She didn't intend to tell Oscar either; she remembered Richard's warning all too well. "My husband did something I can't forgive him for," she said. Silently, she begged Dan's pardon for the lie.

"Holding a grudge takes a lot of time and energy. It would be a lot easier to make up. Of course if you don't love him..."

"I do love him, but not everything can be worked out." She could have told him it was Dan who didn't want to work it out, but why bother. Nothing she told Oscar could change a thing.

From behind her, a familiar voice interrupted. "Hello, Holly. Are you having a good time?"

Holly whirled around and bumped Oscar's knee. "Dan! What are you doing here?"

"Having something to eat."

"Oh." Of course he came here to eat. How stupid could you get? "Let me introduce ..."

"How civilized of you," Dan mocked. "Why would you think I'd be interested in meeting your new boyfriend?"

"What's your problem?" Oscar demanded as his face reddened. "Why don't you go on about your business? We aren't bothering you, and we don't want any trouble."

"Oh, you're bothering me all right. My wife and I may be separated, but I still object to her dating other men."

Alarm flashed across Oscar's face. "Look, this isn't what you think it is. Holly and I aren't..."

"Don't bother. I'm not interested in your excuses." He turned to Holly. "Come with me, Holly. I'm taking you home."

Oscar refused to stand so Holly could slide out of the booth. "No, don't try to get up. I'll take you home."

"Oscar, it'll be okay," she assured him. "Thank you for a lovely evening."

Oscar let her leave the booth, and she meekly followed Dan outside and got into his truck. Dan didn't have a thing to say. He just sat there with a ferocious scowl on his face. She'd have to say something, or the silence would kill her. "This is the second time we've met in a restaurant," she said. "You must eat out a lot."

Dan grunted.

Holly tried to think of something else to say, but for the life of her, she couldn't. What could she say now anyway? She had said it all when she ran out on Dan.

They reached her house where Dan parked his truck in her driveway. "Would you like to come in for a while?" she asked. She had never seen him so angry, but if they didn't talk, they had no chance of patching up their marriage.

He surprised her by wordlessly getting out of the truck and following her to the front porch. She fumbled for her key and finally got the door open. Shrugging out of her coat, she hung it in the closet. "Let me take your coat."

"That isn't necessary. I won't be staying but a minute."

"How about some tea?"

"No, nothing."

"At least have a seat for a minute."

She took a step toward the living room to see if he'd follow, but he didn't.

He acted as if he hadn't heard her. "I don't enjoy being publicly humiliated. Everyone in Fairfield knows we aren't living together, and most of them are waiting for us to formally announce a divorce. I don't think it's asking too much for you to wait until we're divorced to start dating other men."

"I wasn't trying to humiliate you!"

"How did you think it would make me feel to see my wife out on a date with another man? I know our marriage is over, but I haven't done anything to deserve what you did tonight. So how about knocking it off?"

It hadn't occurred to her that Dan would misunderstand why she went out with Oscar. "You don't understand," she cried. "It wasn't…"

"I understand plenty. For once, Holly, try to think of someone besides yourself."

He turned his back on her and stalked toward the door, but Holly chased after him. "Dan, wait. You have to listen to me."

Dan spun around. "I don't have to do anything," he taunted.

Holly's anger boiled over; she grabbed Dan's arm and shook it. "Why are you so stubborn? Why won't you…"

She never finished what she'd started to say because Dan grabbed her and jerked her against him. He held her firmly by the back of her neck when she started to struggle and shoved her against the wall.

He had a nerve! Nobody manhandled her, especially Dan Wakefield. Holly struggled to free herself and felt a mean sense of satisfaction as he grunted when she kicked his shin. She squirmed around in hopes of gaining her freedom, and then he kissed her.

That kiss changed everything. Holly melted against him and hugged him with all of her strength. She could only breathe in gulps, which made her feel slightly dizzy. She pressed against Dan, trying to get even closer to him, but he made a sound low in his throat and thrust her away.

"What's wrong?" she cried. "Kiss me, Dan."

Dan backed away from her. "No. I don't want to kiss you."

"Yes, you do! What's wrong? You know you want to."

Dan laughed even though he sounded anything but amused. "Giving me a roll in the hay won't change anything."

Cut to the quick, Holly dropped her head. "That's not what it was."

~ * ~

Dan's conscience flared up and accused him of hurting her, but he ignored it. Holly had thought she married a drug dealer and a liar, and she had never even apologized for it. She didn't deserve his compassion. She had stolen his home and alienated him from his grandfather, and she'd hurt him so bad he couldn't even look at himself in the mirror without cringing. How could he? If Holly thought so little of him, he must be pretty worthless.

"I have to go," he thickly mumbled.

"No, wait! Don't go, Dan. You're my husband. Stay with me tonight."

For a moment the issue was very much in doubt, but he remembered with the force of a blow that he had caught Holly with another man. "I guess I messed up your evening," he said. "I don't believe I caught your boyfriend's name, but tell you what. You call him and see if he'll accommodate you. I sure won't."

Holly blanched and of course he knew it was because of her mother. Shame seared him, but he couldn't take it back now. With an exclamation of regret, he vanished into the dark.

~ * ~

Rita got lucky. She found a job at Chef's Pantry, Fairfield's largest grocery store, and two days after she began her job search, she started checking out groceries and making money. She had never thought about working at a grocery store, but she had to admit you could meet a lot of nice people there. Naturally, some of the customers weren't too pleasant; even hateful people had to eat, but most of the folks who came through her line were friendly.

One man acted especially friendly. She knew his name was Stanley because he wore a blue shirt with his name written in a little oval on his shirt pocket. He told her he worked as a mechanic at a local Ford dealership.

Rita didn't know why, but mechanics always liked her. She never encouraged mechanics any more than other men, but they seemed to naturally gravitate to her. It didn't surprise her when Stanley came to Chef's Pantry three days in a row.

"Good morning, Rita. Raining like cats and dogs out there."

"I got soaking wet when I came to work."

"I'm off today."

"That's nice, but if I were you, I'd have waited until the rain stopped to go grocery shopping."

He smiled at her. "Well, now I could have waited, but I wanted to talk to you."

"What about?"

Eagerness spread across his face. "There's a nice little club over in Fort Timothy, and I decided I'd run over there tonight. I thought I'd ask you to go with me."

Words of acceptance bubbled up, but for once Rita remembered Holly and Pauline and their scorn for her. "Tell me about the club, Stanley."

"Oh, it's a fun place. Lots of good music, plenty to drink, and some wild dancing. The last time I went there, they had a wet tee shirt contest." He leered at her. "The girl who won couldn't hold a candle to you."

She had gone to a club like that with Kevin right before they split up. It hadn't been too bad, and at her age...At her age she ought to know better. Stanley was another Kevin. Holly had said she shouldn't even speak her dead husband's name because she had dishonored his memory. If she went to that club with Stanley, Holly would find out and be hurt, but worse yet, in that dim, far off heaven where Charles resided, he might find out about it too.

"Stanley, that's not my kind of club," she said. "Thank you for the invitation, but no thanks. You owe me fifty four dollars and twelve cents."

Thirty-three

Jeb had waited for Holly all morning. He'd been on pins and needles ever since she called and said to expect her right after lunch. His life would never be the same after he signed her contract, and neither would Dan's.

It didn't matter about him; he had lived his life and made his mistakes, but Dan was different. He had almost his entire life still in front of him.

Jeb shifted restlessly in his chair. If Dan would make up with Holly, he might use the money from the sale to go back to school. Then he could finally become an architect.

I wish Dan could understand why I have to sell the farm. I've tried to explain that I did it for him, but he won't listen to anything I say. His palpable, bitter anger scared Jeb to death. He could lose Dan so easily if in fact he hadn't already lost him. Dan had spent a lot of time away from the farm the past couple of weeks. He had no idea where Dan had been or what he had been doing, but his grandson had volunteered nothing, and this time he couldn't ask.

He heard a car in the driveway, which sent his heart thudding against his ribs. He swallowed hard. Probably Holly and he had never wanted to see anyone less than he wanted to see her. A brisk knock on the door sent him shambling to meet his dim and uncertain future.

"Come in, Holly."

She looked so bad he felt sorry for her in spite of everything. She had lost weight, and she still had those dark, heavy circles under her eyes. Dan might be suffering, but Holly lived in misery too.

She followed Jeb into the house. "Have a seat on the sofa," Jeb invited. "I've got a ham in the oven, and I need to baste it. It won't take but a minute."

~ * ~

Holly sat down and looked around. *I guess I'd have spent a lot of time in this room if things had worked out for Dan and me. He wanted this to be our home.*

She gave free rein to her imagination and pictured small children playing on the floor and jumping up to greet Dan as he came in from the barn. *He'd give them a hug and a kiss, and then he'd put his arms around me and kiss me. He'd probably ask me what we were having for dinner, and after we ate, we'd all sit together around the fire.*

Unconsciously, Holly sighed. She hoped the day would finally come when she wouldn't think of what she had lost with every breath she drew. She'd never have a life with Dan now. He had told her to trust him, but she had refused to even give him the benefit of the doubt. Well, she was paying for her stupidity. Sure she deserved it, but why did it have to hurt so much?

Jeb finished basting his ham, wiped his hands, and joined Holly. "I was afraid you'd try to stall, Holly, but you didn't. It's been two weeks to the day since we talked. Do you have papers ready for me to sign?"

"Yes, sir, I do, but I wanted to ask you once more to reconsider. Unless Dan's had a change of heart, I don't want to do this."

"I don't want to do it either, but it's for the best. If I sell the farm, Dan's financial troubles are over, and eventually he might decide he wants to go to school or maybe to California. I know you feel bad about it, but in the long run, it's good for him."

She twisted a piece of her hair between two fingers. "Is he angry with you?"

"He's not happy with me," Jeb admitted, "but I think he'll get over it. I pray he will, because I'm not doing this to be mean to him. I'm doing it to help him."

Holly opened her briefcase, and passed a set of papers to Jeb. "Read that, and see what you think."

As Jeb read the papers, a look of surprise filled his face. "What is this?"

"A compromise. I spent the entire two weeks negotiating with my client, who finally agreed to buy only forty percent of Turnaround and build an upscale housing development instead of a golf course. The forty percent is the property across the highway. Dan said you don't use it a lot anyway, and even though you won't get as much money, it'll still be a considerable amount, and more importantly, Dan gets to keep most of Turnaround."

Jeb looked almost shell-shocked. "I never thought about doing it this way. I can give Dan a chance and still keep the farm." He looked around the room as if he had been away for a long time and wanted to savor his homecoming for a bit.

"Do you understand why I agreed to sell, Holly? It's because Dan didn't have any choices in his life. I know he said he wanted to stay on the farm, but what did he know about it? He never had the chance to do anything but work with the horses. With the money, he can either go to school or to California, and if he wants to stay on the farm, we can use the money to get out of debt and do repairs to the house."

"He'll still be tied to his past," she reminded Mr. Wakefield.

"It doesn't matter. As long as Dan has some choices, it doesn't matter what he decides to do. "Do you have a pen?"

"Yes, sir."

Holly passed Jeb a pen and watched as he signed the papers. "Are you sure, Mr. Wakefield? You're losing almost half of your land."

"But I'm keeping over half. Thank you, Holly."

"You're welcome."

She fumbled around with her papers before she brought herself to ask about Dan. "Do you mind if I tell Dan about the change in plans?"

"No, I don't mind. You're his wife, and you made it possible for him to keep Turnaround. He's in the office in the barn."

She picked up the contract. "Thank you. I'll go talk to him now."

~ * ~

Jeb watched from the window as Holly made her way toward the barn. "You are his wife," he muttered. "Start acting like it."

~ * ~

Dan didn't hear Holly come in, so she paused just outside the office door to gather her courage. Lord, but she loved him! He sat behind the desk reading a newspaper, and she noticed at once that he still wore his wedding band. Judging by the look on his face, whatever he was reading was pretty engrossing.

He fumbled for a pen on the desk and circled something. As he laid it down and reached for his coffee cup, he saw her standing there.

"Hi, Dan," she called, praying he'd let her share the news with him before he went ballistic.

~ * ~

"Hi, Holly. Come in." Dan's heart leaped and skittered like a new spring colt, but he had made up his mind that when he saw her again, he'd act like a decent human being. He had treated her brutally the last couple of times they'd met. Heat flooded his face. He was ashamed of how he'd acted toward her.

It was his shame that had finally dissolved his deep anger. Being angry all the time made him feel hard, bitter, and cold. His marriage had ended, but he wanted this last part to be filled with dignity if nothing else. It took a lot of willpower, but he indicated the chair in front of the desk with a wave of his hand. "Have a seat."

Holly sat down and cleared her throat. "What are you reading?"

"Classifieds."

"Are you looking for something in particular?"

"Yes, I'm looking for a job."

"A job! Why do you want a job?"

Dan shrugged. "I have a fondness for a roof over my head and something to eat every day."

Holly gasped. "Surely you know your grandfather didn't plan to throw you out on the street! The only reason he'd ever sell Turnaround would be to get money for you."

"I'm a grown man, Holly, and I won't live off my grandfather. It's one thing to help him run Turnaround, but I'm not moving into some little tract house with him and sit around all day doing nothing. I still have a little too much pride to do that."

"He thought you'd want to go back to school," Holly cried. "He wants you to have the life you always wanted."

He looked her straight in the eye. "If he wanted me to have the life I want, he should have listened to me. I don't want to go to school. There is such a thing as timing, and in this case, the time for college is past. I did find several things that interested me, though."

"What things? I can't picture you anywhere except on a horse."

He sighed. "Neither can I. I applied for a job with Sunny Dale Stables. They're a huge outfit about fifty miles north of Chamberlain, but they didn't want me."

"Why not?" Holly cried, her eyes flashing. "Nobody's better with a horse than you are."

"Yeah, that's what they said."

"Then why didn't they hire you?"

"The Wakefield reputation."

Holly bit her lip and said nothing, but he saw the look of shame and guilt on her face.

"I found a job in the paper that looks okay," he continued. "It's working for a residential construction company, and the pay isn't bad either. Assuming I get the job, where's the cheapest, decent place to live in Fairfield?"

"Botany Arms apartments, I think, but don't be too hasty about this, Dan."

He shrugged. "There's no need to wait until the last minute to get things done. I imagine your buyer will want Turnaround vacated as soon as possible, so I want to have my ducks in a row. What's that you have in your hand? Something to do with our divorce?"

Her fingers tightened on the folder in her hand. "No."

She passed the papers to him. A sales contract. Did he really want to look at it? It already hurt like hell to lose the place he loved; seeing his grandfather's signature that confirmed the deal might just kill him.

No, he had to see it for himself. Until he did, leaving Turnaround wouldn't seem real. He unfolded the papers and read for several minutes before looking up with a frown. "I must be reading this wrong. It looks like he only sold the part across the road."

"You're reading it right. I spent the last two weeks pulling together some facts and figures, and I finally convinced the buyer that he could make a tidy profit without buying the whole farm. I presented your grandfather with the idea, and as you see, he signed the papers."

The papers slipped through Dan's frozen fingers and fluttered to the desk. "I don't know what to say. How can I thank you for saving something that means so much to me? I know it won't be as big as it was before, but it's still plenty big enough for me. I'll never forget that you did this for us, Holly."

Color flooded Holly's face. "I didn't do it for your grandfather. I did it all for you. In fact, I was in such a hurry to see you I forgot to give this to your grandfather." She slid an envelope across the desk. "Would you take it to him, please?"

"What is it?"

"My commission for selling Turnaround. I won't take it."

"You deserve it. Take it."

Holly shook her head. "No, I can't do that."

The conversation flagged. "Was there anything else?" Dan finally asked.

"I guess not." Holly rose from her chair and turned away, but she stopped before she'd taken two steps. "You're still wearing your wedding band."

"I am married. You may not want to be my wife, but until you get your divorce, we're still married." He shot a glance at Holly's hand.

"I'm surprised you're still wearing your rings. I figured you'd toss them in a jewelry box or sell them."

Her head tilted, reminding him of a curious kitten. "Who told you I plan to get a divorce? You're the one who wants a divorce. You told me you never wanted to see me again, remember?"

Oh, yeah he remembered all too well. He remembered the look in her eyes too. "I'm sorry I said that. I didn't really mean it. I mouthed off because you'd hurt my feelings."

He saw the sheen of tears in Holly's eyes as she stumbled toward the door, but she didn't make it out of the office this time either. "If I could do it all over again, I'd be in the bed waiting for you when you got back. I'd trust my own instincts, which told me you couldn't possibly have done anything so bad, and more importantly, I'd trust you. I don't expect you to forgive me. I can't forgive myself, but I regret it with all my heart.

"I don't deserve to have a man like you. You deserve a woman who won't let you down at the first sign of trouble, a woman who loves you and believes in you with her whole heart. I know it's too little too late, but I'm sorry, Dan. I never meant to hurt you."

Dan watched her walk away; he watched his hopes and dreams for the future walk away with her. In a way being angry felt better than this. He didn't feel much of anything right now, and it scared him. Being empty inside was far worse than anger or pain.

He leaned back in his chair, and a funny thing happened. He had used that chair for years, but without warning the darn thing went over backwards and threw him into the floor. Thank goodness Holly hadn't seen him go over and fall out of a chair like a two year old.

He picked the chair up, and his mother cried, "Stop her! Don't let her get away!"

He dropped the chair on his foot and hurt his toe. The strain must be too much for him. He remembered his mother's voice very well, but he didn't believe in ghosts, and she had died ten years ago.

A huge surge of emotion almost choked him. He kicked the chair aside and chased after Holly who had just reached the barn door. "Holly, wait!" he yelled.

Holly whirled around Her eyes had gone wide. She probably thought he wanted to tell her off again. She did deserve it, but he hadn't stopped her to beat her up with her mistake. "I'll forgive you if I damn well want to," he shouted, "and I don't want to hear any more talk about who deserves what."

Holly stared at him, and with a strangled cry, she hurled herself into his arms. "You forgive me? Are you saying you'll give me another chance?"

"If you're sure. Don't come back unless you're sure. I can't go through another two weeks of hell."

Holly didn't answer, but she scared him anyway. Why was she crying like her heart was broken? "Please don't cry," he begged. "You'll make yourself sick."

"How can you take me back?" Holly sobbed. She hugged him and pressed her face against his neck. "I treated you like dirt. I don't deserve you. How can you take me back?"

"Because I love you," he whispered. "I've loved you from the first moment I saw you. Even if I keep Turnaround, life without you would be pretty grim."

He kissed her again, and they clung to each other with hearts full of joy. Neither of them had expected this moment to come.

He ran his hands through that beautiful mass of blonde hair. "I love you, Holly. Don't get a divorce. Let's stay married."

"No divorce. I don't want one either. I love you too much to divorce you." Holly pulled his head down, and his eyes closed as his lips met hers. The kiss deepened, and Dan pulled her tighter against him.

"Make love to me, sweetheart."

She pulled out of his arms with a frown. "Right now? Remember the time your grandfather surprised us while we were kissing?"

Dan laughed. It felt good to laugh. "Yes, right now, but not here. You're my wife, so there's nothing to stop us from spending the afternoon in our bedroom."

"Our bedroom," she muttered. "I thought you'd want to divorce me, and now you're sharing your room with me." Her face fell. "Your grandfather is home. We can't."

"Why not? We're married, right? We'll be living here, so Gramps will expect us to need some privacy every now and then."

"Won't it be embarrassing to just say hello and then go up to your, I mean our, bedroom?"

"Maybe the first time," he admitted, "but I need you so much I don't care."

"Then I don't either."

Hmm. Holly had just told him a story. She did care. She cared very much, but after they'd lived together for a while, she'd get over her shyness. He grabbed his jacket and took Holly's hand, and they hurried toward the farmhouse.

The smell of cooking ham met them as they opened the door. The fire on the hearth crackled merrily, but they didn't see Jeb anywhere. Dan peeked out the window. "His car's gone. I didn't notice it coming in."

"Good. Let's hurry upstairs before he gets back."

"Fine by me." Dan took his bride by the hand and led the way up the stairs. "Do you remember which room it is?" he teased.

"Oh yes, I remember." Holly laughed. "Dan Wakefield, you'd better never tell a soul what happened that night."

Dan pulled Holly inside his room and firmly shut the door. "If you like we can use some of the money to upgrade the heating system. You may not like sleeping in this frigid room."

"Why don't you warm me up?"

"Okay." His eyes locked with hers as he slowly unbuttoned her blouse. As the second button parted, he burst into laughter. Holly was wearing her red Valentine bra.

"I didn't expect anything," she explained, "but I did hope."

They laughed together, and downstairs Jeb set his groceries on the table and smiled at the sounds of mirth.

Thirty-four

When Holly opened her eyes, the light in the room had faded considerably while the lengthening shadows across the floor told her it was late. *We've been up here the entire afternoon. I told Loretta I'd be back in no time. I hope she isn't worried.*

She turned over to look at Dan who still slept and kissed his shoulder. The lines had smoothed out of his face, and he looked peaceful, relaxed, and oh, so wonderful. She didn't deserve him, but she'd spend the rest of her life trying to make him happy.

The freezing air made snuggling absolutely wonderful, but she should get up and call Loretta. Her stomach growled. In spite of her fear of meeting Mr. Wakefield, she was desperate for something to eat. If he didn't have an apple or something, she had some crackers in her car that should hold her until Dan got up. She wished she could sneak downstairs and drive home without meeting Jeb, but she couldn't leave without saying goodbye to Dan.

She dressed as fast as she could in the icy room and hurried down the steps into the warm keeping room. Nobody knew how she dreaded seeing Mr. Wakefield. He'd know exactly what she and Dan had been up to.

Jeb sat in his chair beside the fire reading. He looked up when he heard the door opening, but he acted as if she spent every afternoon upstairs with Dan. "Hello, Holly. Is Dan still asleep?"

Holly gulped. She wouldn't mind if the floor swallowed her whole. "Yes, sir, he is."

"Good. He probably needs the rest. I don't think he's been sleeping too well."

"Mr. Wakefield, I'm sorry about that."

"Why don't you call me Jeb? I am your grandfather-in-law, aren't I, and I wasn't trying to make you feel bad. I'm not going to throw it in your face every time you turn around. Everything's fine now, right?"

"Yes, sir, it is. He forgave me. I still don't know how he could do it, but I'm more grateful than I've ever been about anything in my life."

"He loves you, Holly. That's why he forgave you."

Holly smiled and hoped he was right; Dan had a lot to forgive. "Mr. Wakefield, I mean Jeb, do you have a problem with Dan and me living here together? If you do, we can always live in my house." And wouldn't that be lovely?

Jeb answered the way she had anticipated. "Don't be silly, Holly. This is Dan's home, and we're both well aware of how he feels about the farm. Both of you are welcome."

"I just wanted to be sure. I didn't know if you'd want me in your house after the way I treated Dan."

"All of that's in the past. I don't want you to worry any more about it. As Dan's wife, you're the mistress of this house now."

Just what she had thought.

Jeb turned to other things. "Guess who's coming to dinner?"

"Who?"

"Pauline. I called her and told her I thought we had something to celebrate. She's bringing dessert too. You and Dan don't have any plans, do you?"

"No, we don't. Can I do something to help you get ready?"

"Actually, there is something you can do. I went to the grocery store earlier today, but I forgot to buy any tea, and we're totally out.

Could you run down to the little store at the foot of the hill and pick up a box for us?"

"Sure," Holly said, glad of the opportunity to do so. She'd have a cracker in the car, and maybe when she got back, Dan would be awake. Jeb had treated her as a valued family member, but she still felt uncomfortable around him. She had spent too many years fearing intimacy to feel comfortable around a man who knew how she'd spent her afternoon.

She found her coat lying where she had thrown it across the sofa and pulled it on. "I'll be right back."

~ * ~

Her car had just turned onto the main road when Dan hurried downstairs and saw Jeb standing beside the table. For the first time in two weeks, he willingly spoke to his grandfather. "Hey, Gramps."

"Hi, yourself. Are you feeling better?"

"Yes, I guess so."

"Are you pleased about the sale? Will it help you get over being mad at me?"

Dan stiffened. "You betrayed me, Gramps. You promised me you wouldn't sell Turnaround without my permission, but you did. You shouldn't have done it without my approval. I put in a lot of work around here for my opinion to count for nothing."

His grandfather held out a hand as if pleading his case. "Don't look at it that way. You had to have some choices in your life. You had to have the chance to get away from Fairfield or follow your heart to become an architect. You and Holly only had trouble because of your father's reputation. I wanted you to have the chance to leave it behind if you wanted to."

"Why didn't you listen to me? I told you what I wanted, but you wouldn't listen to me."

Jeb nodded. "That's right, I didn't. I didn't listen because you didn't know what you were talking about. You've never had the chances you should have had. I wanted the money, so you could find out what you've been missing."

Dan shook his head. "I haven't missed out on anything. I love Turnaround, and I love working with the horses. It's my life, Gramps. I don't want to give it up."

"Thanks to Holly you won't have to."

"Are you sure?"

His grandfather frowned. "What are you talking about?"

"Will you pull this trick again a few years from now? Can I really be certain you won't try to sell Turnaround ever again?"

"You have my word on it."

"How much does that mean?" Dan shrugged. "You promised before, remember?"

"Maybe I made a mistake, but I did it for you," Jeb said. "Can you forgive me? You have my word of honor I'll never sell Turnaround."

Dan didn't know if he could believe his grandfather or not, but he couldn't live in the same house with Jeb and be angry with him. He had to let the anger and bitterness go. "I love you, Gramps. I don't have much choice about whether I'll forgive you or not."

Jeb sighed, and Dan saw the tension in his shoulders relax. "Thanks, Dan. I've prayed for two weeks that you'd forgive me. Maybe tonight I'll finally be able to sleep. If I'd lost you..."

"Let's just forget it," Dan said, as he went to the sink for a drink of water.

"If you're pleased about the sale and you've forgiven me, why are you moping around like you are? Are you too proud to ask where Holly is? That's the trouble, isn't it?"

Dan drank an entire glass of water before he turned around to face his grandfather. "I thought everything was okay with us, but I guess I was wrong again. I'm an idiot to think she might want to stay married, but you know what? She won't get a third chance to run out on me."

"Dan, calm down," Jeb pleaded. "She didn't run out on you. I sent her to the grocery store."

"Oh."

"She's coming up the drive now."

~ * ~

In the parking area, Holly bounced out of her car and hurried to get out of the cold, but she paused when she reached the door. She had never just walked into this house. In spite of her afternoon with Dan, she felt like a guest here, and guests didn't walk in unannounced.

Before she could make up her mind, Dan flung the door open and put an end to her hesitation. He swept her into his arms and kissed her, uncaring of his grandfather's sensibilities.

"I thought you'd left me again," he whispered.

"No, never. I'll never leave you again."

Pauline arrived in time to see them kiss. "Darlings, this is wonderful," she cried. "I've prayed this day would come, and I know God heard my prayers because here you are."

She hugged and kissed both of them. Then she and Holly had to wipe their eyes. And Jeb and Dan hoped they wouldn't have to.

Holly took the chocolate cake Pauline had brought and put it on the table. "Nana, my mother isn't coming, is she?"

"No, she isn't. She was home when Jeb called and asked me to come to dinner, but she didn't want to spoil the evening for you, so she stayed at home."

Holly felt vaguely guilty, but mostly she felt relieved. She didn't want Rita to mess everything up by flirting with Jeb or Dan.

As usual Nana read her mind. "Your mother's changing. You wait and see. She'll turn her life around yet."

Everyone enjoyed the celebration dinner. They made plans for a party for Dan and Holly, which thrilled Holly. Even Dan didn't seem too upset at the thought of a party. Her heart sang at the expression of happiness on his face.

They ate their dessert in front of the fire, but their time together drew all too quickly to an end. "I hate for the evening to be over," mourned Holly. She put her arm through Dan's and leaned her head against his shoulder. "Leaving you tonight is pure torture."

As luck would have it, a silence had fallen on the room, so both Jeb and Pauline heard Holly's lament. Both of them listened unashamedly to Dan's reply too.

"Honey, where are you going? Why aren't you staying with me tonight?"

Dan's question confused Holly. She knew he wanted to live at Turnaround, but living there seemed like something that would happen in the future, not tonight. Tonight she expected to go home, so she could get up and go to work tomorrow. She really didn't have an answer for Dan. Heck, she didn't understand why herself. "I...I don't know why I can't stay. I didn't think about it."

"You're my wife, and I want you to live with me. Don't go. I don't want to spend another night without you."

"I don't have any clothes or makeup with me, and I can't go to work without clean clothes and fresh makeup."

"You can go home tomorrow morning to get dressed for work," Pauline chimed in. "If you and Dan intend to live here, you may as well start now."

As usual Pauline had given good advice. She didn't want to live at Turnaround, and subconsciously she had tried to put it off as long as possible. Still, husbands and wives belonged together; she saw no reason in the world not to share his bed tonight.

"Do you have a clock, Dan?"

"Yes, but why do you ask?"

"I have to be at work at nine. What time do you get up?"

"Whenever you do," he answered, causing Holly's eyes to fill with tears of love and tenderness. How had she ever gotten so lucky? She didn't deserve him, but by nothing short of a miracle he belonged to her, and God willing, he'd never regret marrying her.

"Well, that's settled," Jeb said with a smile.

Pauline glanced at her watch. "Where has the time gone? Rita will be worried about me." She made her goodbyes and kissed Holly. "I'll call you tomorrow, and we'll go to lunch."

"I'd like that, Nana."

"Walk me to the car?"

"Yes."

The two women strolled toward Pauline's car, both reluctant to part. "He'll be good to you, darling," Pauline said. "I know you don't want to live here, but he does. You can gradually make changes in the house, and then you'll feel at home."

"I know. It's just tough at first, but you know what? I love him so much I really don't care where I live as long as he's there."

Pauline hugged Holly as her eyes misted with happiness. "In spite of everything, you've found happiness that I think will last a lifetime." Gesturing toward the door, she indicated Dan who waited in the doorway, the light shining behind him throwing his body into sharp relief. "Hurry, darling. He's waiting."

With one final hug, Holly ran back to Dan who threw his arm across her shoulders and kissed her forehead before shutting the door. With a sigh of pure happiness, Pauline turned her car around and started back to Cherry Street to tell Rita about Holly and Dan.

Thirty-five

It was the first really warm day of spring. The chilly wind that sucked the warmth from the air had totally died down, and the earth thankfully soaked up the sunshine.

Dan hadn't come here in ten years, but he still vividly remembered where they lay. He parked his truck, took his flowers, and walked to his parents' graves. His vision blurred when he saw their names.

He knelt and laid the bouquet of daffodils on the grave. His mother had loved daffodils; she'd appreciate these that looked so fresh, sunny, and full of joy. He gently traced the letters of their names on the stone, first his mother, then his father.

"I thought I'd come to tell you how it all turned out," he said aloud. "The most important thing is that Holly and I made up. We're living at Turnaround with Gramps, and Holly's made the biggest difference in the place. She redecorated what she calls the keeping room first. Everything is really bright and cheerful now. She had a picture of the two of you enlarged and hung it over the fireplace. It's the first thing you see when you come in.

"She put in a lot of new appliances too, so Gramps says the kitchen's a lot better to work in now. He and Holly both like to cook, so they each take a turn in the kitchen.

"We've replaced the roof and the heating system, and as soon as the weather's warm enough, we'll paint the outside of the house.

"Turnaround belongs to me now. Gramps deeded the place over to me. He said he never wanted me to waste a minute worrying that he might sell my home. I can't deny I was relieved. I don't think he'd ever try a stunt like that again, but...well, anyway, it's mine now. Mine and Holly's, and Holly wants to fill the place with children. Before we got married, I agreed to have two, but something tells me there'll be a lot more.

"The business is picking up too. So much so that before too long, I'll have to hire some help. Dad, you should have seen the Price horse last week. I took him to the show in Greenville, and when they called for the rack, I don't think his hooves ever touched the ground. We won first, and the horse took the judge's trophy."

Dan wiped his sleeve across his eyes. Kyle had done some bad things, but he knew and appreciated good horseflesh. He would have dearly loved to see that horse in action. "I used your saddle, Dad. Maybe it brought me luck.

"Cam Simmons is in prison," he continued. "I worked with the FBI in a sting operation, and we got him. He won't be destroying any more lives."

From nowhere, a warm hearty little breeze blew around Dan's shoulders. He didn't know why, but the little breeze comforted him.

He placed his hand on his mother's name and whispered, "Thank you, Mother. I couldn't get out of that chair to save my life. Thank you for Holly." He wiped his eyes again, and that warm little breeze caressed his face and rumpled his hair.

"I thought I might find you here."

Dan stood up and took Holly's hand. "How'd you know where I was?"

"Jeb said you had a bouquet of daffodils with you. It wasn't hard to guess where you were going."

Holly carried some flowers herself. "I thought I'd bring them some flowers too," she said. She laid her tulips beside Dan's daffodils and slipped her arm around his waist. "They'd be so proud of you, Dan."

"Do you really think so?"

Holly laughed, a joyous, free sound that warmed his heart. "I don't think so, Dan Wakefield. I *know* so."

Dan smiled too and hugged Holly so he could wipe his eyes without her seeing. "What time are we meeting your mother?"

"In an hour."

"Then we'd better go. I need to shower and shave first."

That warm little breeze enveloped Dan who commented. "The wind's picking up."

"What are you talking about? There's no breeze at all today."

"Nothing. I must have been mistaken."

Hand in hand they left the cemetery to get ready for their dinner with Rita.

Meet Elaine Cantrell

Elaine Cantrell was born and raised in South Carolina. She holds a master's degree in personnel services from Clemson University and is a member of Alpha Delta Kappa, an international honorary sorority for women educators. She is also a member of Romance Writers of America. Her first novel, *A New Leaf*, was the 2003 winner of the Timeless Love Contest. She's retired and spends her spare time collecting vintage Christmas ornaments, reading, and playing with her grandchildren.

Works From The Pen Of Elaine Cantrell

The Captain and the Cheerleader - (*https://wingsepress. com/the-captain-and-the-cheerleader-207128186/*) Susan English can't stand Robin Lanford! She's so full of herself she irritates everyone on the faculty of Fairfield High. When Robin bets Susan fifty dollars that she can't get a date with Kurt Deveraux, the head football coach, Susan jumps at the chance to put the little heifer in her place. She had no idea that teaching Robin a lesson would irrevocably change her life, strain treasured friendships, and throw two families into chaos.

The Welcome Inn - (*https://wingsepress.com/the-welcome-inn-1125116469/*) Julianna can't stand Buck Abercrombie! He's rude, chauvinistic, and exasperating, and he's her new boss. Why wouldn't the bank loan her the money to buy The Welcome Inn? As manager she has proved her worth.
Worse yet, Buck's criminal brother Travis works for him, and her friend Melanie likes him!

Flood - (*https://wingsepress.com/flood-1361092100/ 0)* Drawn together by their love of animals, Aria De Luca and Caleb Hawkins burn for each other. They never suspected that malignant forces around them were successfully plotting Caleb's ruin from the moment he entered her life. When the flood of a century strikes Aria's hometown, an alienated Caleb is all that stands between her and catastrophic loss

Letter to Our Readers

Enjoy this book?

You can make a difference

As an independent publisher, Wings ePress, Inc. does not have the financial clout of the large New York Publishers. We can't afford large magazine spreads or subway posters to tell people about our quality books.

But, we do have something much more effective and powerful than ads. We have a large base of loyal readers.

Honest Reviews help bring the attention of new readers to our books.

If you enjoyed this book, we would appreciate it if you would spend a few minutes posting a review on the site where you purchased this book or on the Wings ePress, Inc. webpages at: https://wingsepress.com/

Visit Our Website

For The Full Inventory
Of Quality Books:

Wings ePress.Inc
https://wingsepress.com/

Quality trade paperbacks and downloads
in multiple formats,
in genres ranging from light romantic comedy
to general fiction and horror.
Wings has something for every reader's taste.
Visit the website, then bookmark it.
We add new titles each month!

Wings ePress Inc.

3000 N. Rock Road

Newton, KS 67114